Life seemed to be going smoothly, I had a boyfriend, an awesome gig working with kids...what could possibly go wrong?

She snapped her head up, eyes blazing at me. It was at that point that I realized that the stakes had gone up. Everything changed. She straightened, ready and eager to go again.

We faced each other, with the score tied, both hungry to win. The tension was thick in the air. She came at me with a low kick, which I blocked, and then she tried to strike once more but aimed too high. It went wild and hit my head, hard on my left cheek, the force whipping my face to the side.

I could've sworn I heard a bell ring somewhere, an echoing sound in my ears. White, pinpoint stars swam in my vision.

The room spun around. I staggered for a moment, dazed.

Voices began to fade. I struggled to hold onto my sanity. Confusion began to set in, and I felt lost and out of control...

Being a teenager is hard enough. To be hard of hearing on top of that is like being stuck in the middle of a never ending soap opera.

In Compass, the sequel to Sway, Jessie's life begins to change its course, sending her toward a new reality. When her world is suddenly ripped apart by an angry rival, the one person she trusted to stand by her side simply walks away. With her composure shattered, Jessie questions everything she believed about herself, and as her life takes her on a new path, it becomes a perilous journey full of surprising twists and turns.

Kudos

I found the book a powerful look into the complex world of a hearing-impaired adolescent, written from the heartfelt perspective of someone who has been there. A real eye-opener to the challenges of everyday life with the added anxieties and social stresses that come with being seen as an outsider. An enjoyable and insightful read. – *S. Kloosterman*

I can relate to Jessie because I've had hearing issues all my life...so I was very excited when I read about your books Sway and Compass. It shows readers that even with an impairment, she is still able to have a life outside of school with a job, a hobby, a boyfriend and she even teaches other kids at camp. I was easily able to jump into the story and get lost in it almost as if I was there in Jessie's place and it was great to be able to read about Jessie's life dealing with a hearing loss and how she handles it. This is one of those stories you cannot put down and you never want them to end. – *T. Nichol*

Compass by Jennifer Gibson is a very good book. – *Taylor, reviewer*

Gibson's books open a window into the world of the disabled that is blunt, honest, and touching. Perhaps if her books had been available when she was a teenager, those idiots I want to beat senseless might have had a little more compassion. – *Regan, reviewer*

Compass

With bonus story Awake

by

Jennifer Gibson

A BLACK OPAL BOOKS PUBLICATION

GENRE: YA/PARANORMAL ROMANCE

This is a work of fiction. Names, places, characters and incidents are either the product of the author's imagination or are used fictitiously, and any resemblance to any actual persons, living or dead, businesses, organizations, events or locales is entirely coincidental. All trademarks, service marks, registered trademarks, and registered service marks are the property of their respective owners and are used herein for identification purposes only. The publisher does not have any control over or assume any responsibility for author or third-party websites or their contents.

COMPASS (with bonus short story AWAKE)
Copyright © 2013 by Jennifer Gibson
Cover Design by Jennifer Gibson
All cover art copyright © 2013
All Rights Reserved
Print ISBN: 978-1-937329-90-7

First Publication: FEBRUARY 2013

Published by Black Opal Books **http://www.blackopalbooks.com**

Acknowledgements

I would like to express my gratitude to all of my fans and readers who have graciously cheered me on every step of the way. As promised, this one is for you!

To my family, thank you so much for your never ending support and inspiration. A special note of thanks goes out to my mother who has graciously provided her extensive editing skills and assistance in producing this book. I couldn't have done it without you.

I would also like to acknowledge the team at Black Opal Books for helping me produce this book - you made a dream come true.

As soon as I arrived at the Bucky Mucky Swamp, I knew that someday I would write a story about it. I was surrounded by amazing people and children who provided incredible insights to what makes us so special. Over the course of a long and hot summer, we became family. I've never forgotten you.

Most of all, as you reach for the stars, find a place in your heart to believe that your dreams can come true. The best advice I've received is from the immortal words of William Shakespeare: "To thine own self be true." Hamlet

CHAPTER 1

Portent

Random thoughts swirled around in my mind and our shoes squeaked and squealed loudly on the gymnasium floor as we started our light jog, warming up for practice. I kept thinking about how it seemed as if I was stuck between two worlds. I wasn't considered to be a fully-hearing person nor completely deaf. I didn't really fit in either group. I felt as if I was twisting in the wind as I pondered about where I belonged in school and life in general. It seemed as if I was stuck in the middle of a never-ending soap opera.

Ahead of me, Donna, Amber, and Jackie, were chatting back and forth as they ran. I had stopped trusting them last year after they'd played a cruel trick on me for my birthday. Unfortunately, we all played on the same basketball team, and I was stuck with them for the time being. I was sure that the feeling was mutual.

We had a new coach this season, Mr. Collins, a delightful character if you're interested in tortuous drills. He strutted across the floor like an arrogant peacock with his back ramrod straight, a perfect image of a drill sergeant. His hair was cropped short, sticking straight up, as white as snow. He scowled darkly at us, whistle in his mouth, ready to blast it on a moment's whim.

His gaze caught the animated discussion in front of me, which I'm sure was highly intellectual and engrossing—not. I stared at them, dumbfounded that they would be so reckless. He froze and an eager, malevolent smile spread across his features.

Crap. I saw what was coming and mentally cursed them for being so careless. Who knows? Maybe it was deliberate.

He blew sharply on his whistle, a high shrill sound that momentarily caused my hearing aids to stop functioning. Pointing at the group in front of me, he bellowed, "If you have enough energy to talk, then you're not working hard enough. Five extra laps!" He blew the whistle again. "Move! Pick up your pace!"

I groaned inwardly. My legs were already starting to burn.

The drills became much harder as we darted back and forth across the floor, doing sprints.

Sweat was beading across my forehead, making my hair slick. I was utterly exhausted and panting hard. My lungs felt as if they were going to explode.

Coach Collins bellowed at us again, his booming bass voice echoing off the ceiling. "All right, ladies, form two lines." He gestured at the line in front of me. "This line gets the ball." Then he pointed in my direction. "And this line is the receiving end."

"The objective is to bounce the ball to your respective partner. The other person then shoots it straight across, hard and fast."

He stared at us with steely eyes, his broad chin jutting out as he spoke. "Keep your heads up and your hands in front of you. We will start slowly, and then quickly pick up the pace. It will get harder and faster." He nodded at us, whistle in his hand. "Ready? Go!"

I looked across the floor and did a double-take—Jackie was my partner. Beside me was Donna. Her partner was Amber. Buffy was on my other side. Great, I thought, *I'm flanked by the evil Addams family*.

Jackie quickly shot out the ball, bouncing it hard on the slick, glossy floor, catching me off guard. I nearly fumbled the ball and caught it in the nick of time as Coach Collins glanced in my direction. I blew out a sharp breath, relieved that I didn't look like an idiot at that point.

I looked at Jackie and saw her standing there, smirking.

I tossed the ball toward her. It veered off slightly to the right. Her sneer grew as she realized that I was slightly shaken by her aggressive move.

She threw harder this time and I had to take a step back to avoid being hit in the face. My nerves were getting more rattled by the minute.

I gulped back the fear that was rising in my chest, took a deep breath, and blew it out again, feeling my frustration mount. I rolled my shoulders to ease the building tension, no thanks to her, and shot the ball back at her.

She quickly responded, ramming it to the floor with ferocious intensity. It collided with Amber's ball and they spun wildly out of control, slamming into Donna's face.

She screamed as I frantically caught one of the balls as it zoomed toward me.

She held her hands over her nose, blood streaming through her fingers, sobbing incoherently.

Coach Collins came running over with a box of tissues in his hands. "Give her space, ladies." He gave her a handful of tissues and instructed her to squeeze her nose tight to stem the bleeding.

He turned around to face us with a dark glare. "Would someone kindly tell me how the hell this happened?"

Donna looked at me through her teary eyes and pointed her bloody fingers at me. "It was her fault!"

I stood there, still holding the ball, stunned. I sucked in a sharp intake of breath, shocked that she would try to place the blame on me.

I reached out to put my hand on her shoulder to reassure her, she shrugged it off vehemently. "Go away!" she mumbled through the thick layers of bloody tissues.

"I swear it wasn't me! I was standing right beside you!"

Jackie chimed in, "Yeah, right. Liar," she said sneering at me as she steered Donna toward a nearby bench. She crooned over her, carrying the box of tissues, looking over her shoulder to stare at me scornfully.

Coach Collins sighed deeply and ran his fingers through his hair, clearly exasperated. "I warned all of you to be cautious! That's six laps for you, Jessie, get going!"

His voice echoed in my head as I made my way around the gym, jogging slowly. My feet felt like lead, completely drained of energy. I quickly wiped a tear away from my left cheek, trying to hide it from the stares of the rest of the team.

My chest tightened painfully, not only from the running, but also from feeling so betrayed. I swallowed back my sobs as I ran past my teammates.

They all completely ignored me. I stared down at the floor, watching my feet as I ran, hearing the rhythm as it slapped down on each step.

Gasping with each breath, I was determined to be strong.

Gradually, the team broke apart as they finished their drills and strolled toward the locker rooms. I still had one more lap to go when I noticed that the gym was empty. It was at that moment I realized how utterly alone I felt.

Coach Collins barked at me from one corner as he picked up an errant ball. "Jessie! I would like to speak with you." He pointed his finger downward at the floor where he stood.

I stopped in front of him, gasping and bending over slightly, hands on my hips.

He waited for a moment, then brusquely said, "Jessie, look at me when I speak to you."

I straightened up, trying hard not to puke at his feet, my mouth completely dry. "Yes sir." My words came in a harsh whisper. I barely had enough strength to speak.

"What you did today was inexcusable. I'm appalled at the lack of respect that you showed for your teammate's safety."

Flustered, I threw up my hands, palms facing upward, in a futile gesture. "But...I had nothing to do with that! I was..."

He put his hand up in my face like a stop sign. "Uh-uh! I will not discuss this with you. I will not tolerate any more reckless behavior on my team. Is that understood?"

"But..." I tried feebly to tell him that it wasn't my fault but he refused to let me speak another word. He pivoted and walked away from me, carrying the basketballs into the storage room.

I took a step toward him, and then changed my mind.

Instead, I spun around and stomped angrily back to the locker room, whipped off my wet T-shirt and shorts, and threw my shoes on the floor. I looked around and saw that the room was empty.

I sighed and muttered, "No surprise there."

Sitting on the bench, I leaned my elbows on my knees, my hands in my hair, trying to control my emotions, which were spiraling out of control.

After a few minutes, I grabbed my watch from the pocket of my blue hoodie and glanced at it. "Aw Crap. I'll be late if I don't get a move on. Ethan is supposed to meet me at home soon." I blew out a sigh of frustration. "Could this day get any worse?"

I pulled on my hoodie, zipped up my jeans, and tucked my wet gym clothes into my backpack.

By the time I got home, the sun had dipped behind the clouds, turning the sky a brilliant glowing orange, a perfect complement to the vibrant trees along the lane. They appeared to have exploded into a splendid display of rich hues of crimson and gold. I kicked the fallen leaves as I strolled along the well-worn path to the house.

I looked up to find Ethan, sitting on the porch swing, waiting for me and smiling broadly. The sun cast a golden halo around him, making him appear angelic.

I dumped my backpack on the porch as I leaped up the stairs and strode toward him.

His smile vanished as soon as he saw me, concern etched onto his handsome features.

He reached out to embrace the sides of my face, stroking gently as if to soothe away the despair. "Jessie, what's wrong?"

I muttered to him, "Coach Collins..." My voice broke. I grabbed the front of his shirt and pulled him in, resting my cheek on his chest, feeling his warmth. I felt safe and loved in his arms.

His chest rumbled as he spoke. "What did he do?" Alarm was evident in his voice.

I closed my eyes. I didn't want to move, didn't want to say anything. I wanted to banish every thought and feeling that had happened today. All I wanted to do was hold on to him.

"Jessie?" His hands gripped my shoulders and pushed me away. "Look at me please." He gently lifted my chin up with his hand. "I swear to God, if he did anything out of line—"

I quickly stopped him with a touch of my fingers on his lips. "No. It wasn't like that." A fresh tear slid down my face.

He brushed it away with his thumb. "Okay, come here," he said as grabbed my hand and tugged me onto the porch swing.

He held on to my hand as I spoke. "Coach Collins went berserk today, more than usual, and dumped the blame on me. It was uncalled for since I had nothing to do with it. It was my partner, Jackie, who hit Donna in the face with the basketball. I was standing beside her when it happened."

My voice started to waver. "Everyone automatically assumed that it was my fault and blamed me for it," I said sniffling. "He made me do extra laps!"

"At least it was good exercise. It'll make you stronger." His eyes twinkled mischievously.

I smacked him on the arm. "Ethan! That's so not the point! He was mean and cruel. The whole team hates me."

"I'm sorry to hear that. Would you like me to beat them up for you?" he replied as his grin grew bigger, and his eyebrows climbed high into his forehead.

I snorted. "Heh. Cute. Yes, could you please? That would make me feel so much better," I replied sarcastically.

Smiling, he pulled me into his arms.

I drew up my knees beside him, savoring the warmth of his body. I leaned into his chest as he rocked the swing back and forth in a gentle motion.

We stayed together on the swing as the air became increasingly cooler. I started to shiver.

"Getting cold?" he asked as he rubbed his hands vigorously on my arms to warm them up. He brought the swing to an abrupt stop, jarring my thoughts. "Want to go inside and get something to eat? You must be famished."

I blinked and looked up at him. He bent down and gave me a passionate kiss, his lips tasting mine, sending a rush of emotions through me.

My hands were still gripping his shirt when we finally broke apart, gasping. "Mm, I suppose so. Or...we could continue this." I brought him closer to me, kissing his soft, tender lips.

Until my stomach growled angrily. I sighed, feeling a bit embarrassed.

"I think your stomach just vetoed that thought. Time to eat!" He slapped my thigh as he stood up. "You'll need your strength for the tournament."

He pulled me up with his strong hands. The breeze sent a batch of leaves swirling around us as we strolled toward the kitchen. I bent down and snatched up my backpack on the way in.

I was way too exhausted to think of anything creative and grabbed a box of mac and cheese from the pantry drawer. As I stirred the pasta in the simmering pot, Ethan stood behind me and slipped his arms around my waist, his chin resting on my shoulder.

He snickered as he watched me cook the macaroni.

I glanced up at him. "What's so funny?"

He shook his head, the corners of his mouth curling up seductively.

I playfully elbowed him in the ribs. "Come on, out with it."

Finally, he conceded, "I find it hugely ironic that you are making macaroni and cheese, when your mom is a chef."

"Actually, she's a caterer," I corrected him, feeling like a dimwit, my face flushing beet red. "So, sue me. I obviously didn't get the cooking gene," I added snarkily.

He spluttered, barely holding back his laughter, giving me a quick kiss on the forehead. "I'm just teasing you. Tell you what. While you make supper..." he said with a mischievous smile. "How about I make a fire in the living room and we can eat out there?"

I nodded as I added the butter and milk. "Sure. That's sounds great."

As I carried the plates of steaming pasta toward the couch in front of the fireplace, Ethan stood up like a perfect gentleman and grabbed both of the plates. "Oops, let me help you with that."

"Thanks. Wow, that's a great fire," I said as we sat down. "I can never get it going like that."

I looked at him as we ate, admiring the effect of the flickering light and shadows as they danced across his chiseled features. It was at that moment that I realized just how lucky I was to have him in my life.

Afterward, I leaned into him at we gazed at the flames. As he draped his arm across my shoulders, he said, "Don't worry...you'll do fine at the tournament this weekend. I know that in my heart."

He reached up with his hand and rubbed my back as he leaned in with a tender kiss.

"God, I hope so. I could use some good news for a change."

His eyes crinkled at the corners as he chuckled. He stroked the back of my neck with gentle fingers, sending delicious shivers down my spine, the heat of his hand soothing me.

I sighed and snuggled in closer to him, feeling utterly content.

CHAPTER 2

Eclipse

I was bent over, packing my bag, when the doorbell rang. Feeling a little anxious, I strode over to the broad window overlooking the front yard and peeked out.

"Oh crap! He's already here!" I frantically slung one bag over my shoulder and carried the other one in my free hand.

Mom's voice floated up the stairs. "Jessie! Ethan's here!"

"All right, I'm coming!" I said as I ran down the stairs, trying not to trip and break my neck. At this rate, my unlucky streak could go from bad to worse pretty quickly.

I prayed that my luck would change soon since it usually ran in threes, whether it be good or bad.

As I clomped down to the last step, my pink sneakers looking a bit worn out, I blew out a short breath, relieved. Then my heart stopped as I looked at Ethan.

The door was open and he was standing in the middle of the doorway, waiting for me. The sunlight streamed in from behind him. A bit of cool morning breeze kicked up a swirl of dust around him, and for a moment there, I could've sworn that he had on a pair of shimmering wings.

I blinked at him, holding onto the post for support. *God, he's striking*, I thought. His green eyes seemed to pierce my soul, turning my legs into jelly.

"Hey, Jessie." His features glowed in the sun as he grinned. His smile widened upon seeing me. Any brighter and I would need sunglasses.

He wore black jeans that outlined his long, lean legs, topped off with a black zippered sweater, which enhanced his muscular arms.

"Morning, Ethan." I smiled back at him, my heart skipping a beat.

He leaned in and gave me a quick peck on the lips as he grabbed one of my bags. "Ready to go?" he asked and tucked an errant strand of hair behind my ear.

I gulped, suddenly feeling nervous about today. "Yeah, I think so. Bye Mom!" I said as I turned around to give her a hug.

"Good luck honey! Have a good time!" She strode over to the door and waved as we stepped down off the porch toward Ethan's car.

"Call me if you have any problems!" She brought her hand to her ear, mimicking a phone and waved at Ethan's dad who was putting away the bags in the trunk.

As slid into the seat beside Ethan, I said hello to his father. "Hi, Sensei Jonas. Thanks for giving me a ride."

"No problem, Jessie, and please call me Jonas," he said as he turned around in the driver's seat to look at me. He knew how much I relied on lip-reading and body language.

"I'll try but it's a habit. It's so natural for me to call you Sensei."

He turned back to the front and started the car, tires crunching on the gravel. I could still see Mom standing in the doorway waving at us as we rolled down the lane, past the long line of trees.

My gaze met Ethan's. I rolled my eyes in exasperation and he laughed.

He reached over and gripped my hand, giving it a squeeze.

I looked out the window, watching the scenery blur into streaks of glorious fall colors. "How long will it take to reach the train station?"

Ethan looked toward his dad. "Fifteen or twenty minutes maybe?" He saw his father nod in agreement.

"Cool. I've never been on a train," I said nodding.

We held hands for the duration of the ride. Once in a while he would reach out with his other hand and stroke my arm, in soft massaging motions.

"Here we are folks!" said Jonas as he maneuvered the car into the parking lot.

We unlatched our seat belts and stepped out of the car, grabbing our bags.

"Oh! Before I forget...I just wanted to say thanks for letting me borrow your sparring equipment." I lifted the bag of sparring gear as I spoke.

Both Ethan and his father beamed at me. "Not a problem, Jessie. We are more than happy to help out," Jonas said.

Ethan briefly looked at the ground, appearing a little bit sheepish at the moment.

We moved briskly through the station and stood outside as we waited for the train to arrive. Ethan's father had already purchased our tickets in advance.

"All righty then...just in time, here it is," said Jonas as he strolled onto the platform.

The train came to a screeching halt, whipping up the wind all around us, blowing my hair into my face. It was a massive silver train and resembled a formidable speeding bullet with its sleek metal jacket.

Several porters stepped out of the cars, placing small stepstools at each of the stairways. As the passengers filed out, I strode toward the nearest one, getting ready to board.

Ethan placed a hand on my shoulder and urged me toward the first car. "Um, this way, Jessie," he said as he winked at me.

As we approached the stairway, the porter took a small step toward me, "May I take that off your hands for you, ma'am?"

I blinked. *Wow. What service*, I thought, momentarily dumbfounded. "Yeah, sure. I guess." I looked at Ethan for confirmation. He nodded, indicating it was okay.

Ethan led me to a pair of large plump seats by the window as his father sat in the row in front of us.

"Holy schamoley. Is this what I think it is?" I said as I gestured around me.

Ethan nodded, smiling rather complacently. "If you mean by first class, then yes."

I tried to speak but didn't know what to say except, "This. Is. Cool."

Out of the corner of my eye, I saw his dad smile. He appeared to be equally delighted with my reaction.

The train had barely started moving when an attendant, in a crisp blue suit, stood beside us and offered rolled towels on a platter. He transferred the towels to our trays, in a professional and precise manner, using silver tongs.

I looked at Ethan and pointed at it.

"To clean your hands," he said.

"Ah." I grabbed it, feeling like an idiot. It felt warm and smelled like fresh lemons.

Within minutes, the attendant was back. "Refreshments, sir? Ma'am?"

"What do you have?" I asked curiously.

He eyed me and decided which age range I fell in regarding the drinking menu. "For you, we have a lovely sparkling Perrier, juice, coffee, or tea."

"Do you have any jasmine tea?"

He smiled kindly and nodded at us politely. "Certainly, Ma'am."

I poked Ethan in the ribs. "He didn't even ask your dad what he wanted."

"Dad's a frequent traveler. They know him well."

No sooner had Ethan spoken, when the attendant presented Jonas with a sparkling glass of wine.

I sat there with my head spinning. This was simply too much. God, I felt like royalty. I wondered if this was what it must like for the Queen. "Wow. All I can say is wow!" I looked at Ethan. "I'm honored. Thank you," I said to him rather shyly.

He leaned in and kissed my forehead tenderly, as soft as a sigh. "You're welcome, Jessie."

The train picked up speed and began to sway from side to side, accompanied by rhythmic clacking sounds as it rushed along the tracks.

"Oh! I have something for you." Ethan snapped his fingers as if he'd just recalled his stray thoughts. He reached into his pocket and presented me with a small box, neatly wrapped up in pink ribbon.

My eyes widened as he handed it to me. "For me?"

"I thought you could use a little pick me up. A sort of good luck charm." He smiled seductively.

I narrowed my eyes suspiciously at him. "You didn't have to do this Ethan." My breath caught in a gasp as I opened the rich-brown, chocolate-colored box, "Oh! It's beautiful!"

Inside the folds of the pink tissue paper was a silver bracelet with the engraving *Believe* in an elegant cursive font. It looked expensive. I was stunned.

My hand flew to my mouth. Suddenly bashful and overwhelmed, I glanced out the window, willing myself not to cry.

"Jessie, you okay?" Ethan asked as he reached out and touched my face, brushing the hair out of my eyes.

I took a deep breath and closed my eyes for a moment, suddenly feeling out of place.

He placed his hand under my chin, prompting me to look at him.

On seeing his face, I nearly fell to pieces. He became blurry as tears trickled onto my cheeks. He swiped them away with his thumb in a caressing motion.

Alarmed, he grabbed my hand and pulled it into his chest. "Jessie, what's wrong?"

Comforted by his warm hand, I summoned up the courage to speak. Almost breathlessly, I asked, "What did I do to deserve this?"

His brow furrowed quizzically. "What do you mean? The tournament?"

I was afraid of the answer. "No, never mind." I glanced down at the glittering bracelet, my eyes watering over again.

He leaned over and gently touched our foreheads together, a gesture of the intimate bond we shared. I could feel his eyes on mine.

"Jessie, please look at me." His voice was tinged with concern. "Did I do something or say something to hurt you?" As he spoke, he gripped my hand tighter, keeping it close to his chest. I could feel his heart beating wildly.

"Oh, Ethan. This is too much. I don't deserve this."

He pulled away and looked in to my face, searching imploringly. "What are you talking about?"

I looked up at him and felt a sudden pain in my heart. "It's not you. It's everything that's happened lately. It's as if the weight of the world is on my shoulders. I guess yesterday was the tipping point with the coach." As I spoke, I glanced down at his hand. He intertwined his fingers with mine. I paused for a moment then said, "And I woke up this morning with this feeling of darkness, a sense of dread." I looked back at him. "I haven't been able to shake this feeling that something bad will happen, like an omen. I guess in a way, I feel like a freak. Like no one wants me."

Ethan scoffed. "That's not true and you know it."

I took another breath to calm my shaky voice. "Believe me, it feels true."

Feeling very self-conscious and unbelievably insecure, I searched his eyes. "I look at you and I wonder what you see in me."

He brought my hand to his lips and gave it a tender kiss while his other hand stroked my forehead, as gentle as a feather.

"I see passion, warmth, and love. You're someone who lights up my soul. My heart sings every time I see you."

"Really?"

"And this," he said as he reached down and placed the bracelet on my wrist, "is a token of my never-ending love." He smiled as he finished clasping the bracelet together. "Whenever you feel alone or lost, this will help remind you of my love for you. My faith will be your strength."

My heart began to glow, spreading a loving and gentle warmth throughout my body. I felt loved and safe at that very moment.

"You'll be fine, Jessie," he said as toyed with the bracelet on my wrist. "It looks great on you."

"It does, doesn't it? Thank you, Ethan. It's beautiful."

He looked over his shoulder and waved for the attendant, who came over and presented us with elaborate menus.

"Holy cow. Everything seems so fancy here...I don't know where to start."

I chose the smoked salmon on toasted ciabatta bread, slathered with cream cheese, and a delicate salad topped with sweet figs.

It was amazing and what surprised me the most were the utensils. They were authentic silverware, not the cheap plastic kind. "This is insane, Ethan! I feel like royalty!"

Afterward, we were treated to a silver platter of elegantly arranged, scrumptious, chocolate truffles.

"Mmm, this is good," I said as I bit into the chocolate.

Ethan had a smudge of chocolate on his lower lip. I reached over and traced my fingers over his mouth. "Um. You have chocolate right here..."

His eyes twinkled with delight as he watched me gently wipe it off. He licked his lips seductively. I had to restrain myself from kissing him passionately right then and there. I felt too self-conscious to act on my feelings on the train.

We spent the next few hours watching the scenery as he pointed out the various cities we passed. The countryside was mostly flat, dotted with farms. Lake Ontario was on our right side, an impressive vista stretching out as far as the eye could see, its dark blue surface shimmering in the sunlight.

Occasionally, we would pass through a city, abruptly changing the elegant view from calm rural to hectic urban sprawl. The buildings climbed higher the closer we got to the city.

The train gradually slowed down, the sway becoming more pronounced as we switched tracks.

"All right, here we are, our final designation...Ottawa," Ethan said as he glanced out the window.

The rest of the passengers began to gather up their newspapers and briefcases as we came to a stop.

We grabbed our bags from the luggage rack and made our way down the steep steps.

The porter greeted us as we stepped onto the platform. "Have a nice day folks."

"Thanks."

"What do we do now?" I asked Ethan, wondering which way to go.

"We go down those stairs which will take us to the main lobby." He pointed off to the right where a thick line of people slowly marched down the long tunnel.

We emerged into a majestic spacious lobby, the ceiling arched high overhead with gleaming windows, exposing the bright blue sky and soft wispy clouds.

The sound of hundreds of shoes clattered all around me, echoing everywhere. There was the occasional bark of announcements on the PA system, the noisy surroundings making it too difficult for me to make out the words clearly.

I looked around in awe. It was impressive, a central hub of activity.

"Are we taking a taxi?" I asked, not knowing what to do next.

"Hmm? No, Dad has a rental car waiting for us."

"Oh, okay." We strolled toward the large wall of glass doors where a long line of yellow taxis sat, bumper to bumper.

The traffic wasn't too bad, a bit congested in the more populated areas. We finally reached our hotel after 20 minutes of driving. A valet was already standing at the front doors, ready to whisk the car away as we went inside to check in.

It was an opulent scene everywhere I looked. I was astounded at how richly decorated the hotel was. The floor shone brilliantly and looked very much like real marble. There were glittering chandeliers hanging from the ceiling and the main lobby was filled with luxurious furniture.

I looked down at myself and felt completely out of place. I was dressed rather shabbily in comparison to everyone else around me.

"Ethan, I'm not appropriately dressed for this place." I glanced at him worriedly as I spoke.

"What? Jessie, you look fine, don't worry about it."

We passed a conference room on the way to the elevators. It was as lavish as a ballroom, with elegant floor to ceiling mirrors and a coffered ceiling that seemed to be made out of gold. My jaw nearly dropped upon seeing such a posh meeting room.

I pointed wordlessly at the room in awe. Ethan saw me glance in that direction and caught my reaction. His lips curled up in a delicious smile, clearly amused.

A quick ride on the elevator led us to an equally lavish floor. Our room was just a few steps down the hall.

We entered a large and spacious suite, complete with a separate bedroom furnished with french doors. There was a small kitchen off to the left, a microwave and coffee pot sat on the polished counter top. A large bed and a couch were on the right side of the room.

Ethan strolled over to the couch and dumped his bags on top. I placed my bags on the floor next to the coffee table and sat on the bed, looking around.

"Um, where's the other bed?" I asked.

Ethan looked up as he rifled through his bags. "There is a pull out bed in this couch."

"Ah, I see. I'll sleep there, then."

"What? No, you get the bed," replied Ethan. "I'll sleep on the couch. Dad will sleep in the other room."

"Uh, no, I don't think so. I'm a guest here, I should use the couch. Ethan, please, I'll feel more comfortable that way."

He sighed and ruffled his hair with his hand as he thought about it. "Are you sure?"

"Yes! Now move or I'll throw my stuff on top of you."

He grinned. "I'd like to see you try that."

I stuck my tongue out at him as I picked up my bags and moved them closer to the couch.

I walked around the room, marveling at its enormous size and splendor.

"Sweet! Would ya look at this?" I said as I came out of a walk-in closet. It was huge, nearly the size of my bathroom at home.

Ethan's dad came out of his room. "Okay, guys. Did you want to go out for a walk and get something to eat?"

We both said yes at the same time, prompting all of us to laugh.

It was a beautiful day as we strolled down the sidewalks, hand-in-hand, visiting various stores. We stood in awe in front of the Parliament Building and walked around famous landmarks, absorbing the rich history.

CHAPTER 3

Impact

The next morning we took a quick ten-minute ride to the arena. We strode through the doors and went straight to the registration table to sign in for the tournament and pick up our schedules. Afterward, we found the changing rooms and swiftly changed into our uniforms.

As the three of us stepped into the arena, the noise all around me was deafening. It was a loud fusion of sounds as bursts of *"Kiais"* broke through with the odd shout of, "Point!" from a nearby referee. It all blurred into a hive of activity.

My eyes darted everywhere. There were so many competitors on the floor, all organized into groups according to their age and rank. Off to my right were younger children wearing white and yellow belts. A little further down were the orange and green belts, the rank going higher as you progressed down the row. On my left were the adults, also organized in a similar manner.

Something pinged at the back of my mind. Then I figured out what was missing. The black belts, where were they?

"Um, Ethan, not to sound like a twit...but where is the division for the black belts?"

Ethan turned away from his father momentarily to look at me. "Hmm? Oh, they compete last. That way, there will be enough judges and referees to help out with the tournament."

"So you won't be competing this morning?"

"No, it will likely be later in the afternoon. Much later."

"When do I compete?" I asked as I shifted the bag of sparring gear from one hand to the other.

He turned back to his dad who was currently perusing the schedule. Ethan leaned over his father's shoulder. Using his finger, he traced a path down the page and stopped almost halfway.

"Here it is...it looks like 10:30 a.m. And it will be over there." He looked up and gestured toward the far end of the arena, just past the younger kids.

"Dad and I will be at various stations throughout the day. He'll be the referee for the sparring matches, and I will be judging the Katas."

I nodded as he spoke, suddenly nervous. I blew out a shaky breath, trying in vain to calm my nerves.

He put one hand on my shoulder and reassured me. "Tell you what, I'll take you to your station while Dad gets set up."

As he spoke, another black belt marched up to his father, an older gentleman with a gray beard and red uniform, and clapped him on the back, his booming voice greeting him heartily. The two of them bantered like old friends and strolled off toward the adult divisions on the floor.

Ethan slid his hand down my arm and locked his fingers with mine as we made our way down the arena.

The floor had a glossy gray sheen. Sections were taped off into large neat squares for the competitors. At the back of each section was a row of chairs for the judges, all black belts. They each held a placard filled with numbers. In the center was a lone student performing a Kata, a series of crisp and elegant moves, filled with punches and kicks aimed at an imaginary opponent. All around the square, on the outside of the tape, were the rest of the competitors, kneeling and waiting for their name to be called.

The closer we got to my designated area, the more nervous I became. My mouth seemed to be getting drier and my palms were starting to sweat.

Ethan glanced down at me, sensing my sudden tension. "Don't worry Jessie, you'll do fine. Just think of it as a practice for your blue belt grading next month."

"Oh sure...practice." I sarcastically drew out the last word. "In front of hundreds of people," I said as my eyes roamed around the arena.

The stands were filled with friends and family of the spectators, the main floor restricted to competitors only.

His eyes crinkled at the corners as he smiled. "Remember, I have faith in you. All you have to do is believe in yourself."

I sighed, not quite sure that I could live up to his expectations. "Okay, could you get any more cryptic than that?"

He chuckled. "Well, I gotta go. Don't worry, you'll do fine. I'll be right over there with the kids."

He gave me a quick kiss on the forehead and briskly marched away.

Okay, I thought, I can do this. I walked over to the wall behind the judges and sat down, placing my bag beside me, the floor a bit cool beneath me.

I closed my eyes and concentrated on the Kata in my mind, visualizing the moves in perfect form.

Feeling a bit calmer and more confident, I opened my eyes to watch the scene in front of me.

After what seemed like an eternity, my name was finally called and I promptly strode over to the judges. There were six of us in our group, fairly close in age and rank. I joined the line-up and stood in front of the black belts. I bowed as the central judge barked out the commands. We all knelt on the outside of the taped off area. As our names were called, we stood up, bowed at the edge of tape, stepped into the center, and bowed to the judges, stating our name and the title of our Kata.

One by one, we performed in front of the black belts. At the end of our Katas, we stood anxiously awaiting our scores as they brought up the numbers on the placards.

As soon as it was my turn, my entire body shook. I was that nervous. I went through the motions, starting off with a block on my left side and following it up with a punch and sharp kick. I continued to move around, much like a dancer, delivering strong strikes. I fumbled once and tried to recover myself as smoothly as possible.

I stood in front of the judges, my nerves jangling. I was sure that they would give me a low score because of my mistake. When they lifted the numbers, I was relieved. I ranked higher than several of the other competitors.

Once it was over and everyone performed their Katas, we lined up again in front of the judges. As they called our names, we stepped forward, bowed, and accepted our trophies. I was awarded third place and given a heavy trophy made out of carved marble. It was beautiful. I was elated that I had won and slightly disappointed that I didn't get first place.

I looked around for Ethan and saw him look my way. He pointed two thumbs up as I showed him the trophy.

My name was called out again, this time for the *Kumite*. I quickly put on my sparring gear and knelt down to wait for my turn. The matches went by quickly. I was sweating in my equipment, anxious to get it over with.

Then it was my turn. I bowed at the edge of the tape, stepped in, and bowed to the referee and to my opponent. I stepped back into a fighting stance and raised my fists, ready to go. I went through this match fairly easily against an inexperienced fighter. All it took was a few well-placed punches and loud "*Kiais*" to convince the referee that I had the winning strike. We bowed out and went back to kneeling on the floor once again, waiting for our next match.

After several more rounds and a process of elimination, I was called up once again for the final match. This was the big one to decide who would be awarded first place.

I bowed to the referee again, turned to face my opponent, and bowed. We both took a step backward and raised our fists into a fighting stance. I narrowed my eyes at her, completely focused and feeling confident. Her brown hair was sticking straight up through her helmet in a ponytail, like a mohawk. Her nose and cheeks were dotted with freckles. She chewed nervously on her mouth guard.

The referee placed his hand between us and asked us if we were ready. We both nodded. He quickly removed his hand and yelled, "*Hajime!*"

I delivered a swift kick to her right side. She managed to slap it away. I followed up with a punch to the ribs. At that precise moment, she moved inward, toward me, coming in contact with my fist. She cringed and took a step back, bent at the waist, clearly stunned.

I muttered, "Sorry!" It hadn't been my intention to physically strike her hard, just to go through the motions. She snapped her head up, eyes blazing at me. It was at that point that I realized that the stakes had gone up. Everything changed. She straightened, ready and eager to go again.

We bowed and resumed our fighting positions. This time she lunged at me with a wild kick, which I blocked with my upper arm. I delivered two kicks, one after another in quick succession, thus earning me another point.

We faced each other once again, with the score tied, both hungry to win. The tension was thick in the air. She came at me with a low kick, which I blocked, and then she tried to strike once more but aimed too high. It went wild and hit my head, hard on my left cheek, the force whipping my face to the side.

I could've sworn I heard a bell ring somewhere, an echoing sound in my ears. White pinpoint stars swam in my vision.

The room spun around. I staggered for a moment, dazed. My hearing aid squealed and I yanked off my helmet, shoving my hearing aid back into my ear, frustrated and embarrassed.

The referee stepped in between us, stopping the fight. He asked me if I was all right. I blinked and looked at him, taking a few deep breaths to gather my wits. I nodded, not realizing that I should've stopped at that point. He turned around and gave her a stern warning.

I slipped my helmet back on, my cheek a little tender. We faced off again. I was determined to win this round. I wanted to win so badly that I could literally taste it. I squared my shoulders, snapped up my hands, and curled my fingers into a tight fist. I grounded my feet and narrowed my focus, feeling strong and ready to fight.

She immediately darted at me, throwing a punch toward my solar plexus. I quickly blocked it and snapped my fist up to deliver a back fist strike near her head, stopping an inch away from her face. Her eyes grew wide as she realized what just happened.

"Break!" The referee stepped between us, his hand stopping the match. "Judges call?" He looked at the judges in each corner of the ring and nodded as he counted the points. He gestured in my direction. "Point! And winner!"

I was relieved. A hard battle was finally over. We all lined up in front of the black belts and stepped forward to accept our trophies. I stared at mine, amazed that I won first place. We bowed out and it was at that moment everything started to go nuts. I felt a strange rushing sensation, then my vision swam, and the room started to tilt.

Voices began to fade. I struggled to hold onto my sanity. Confusion began to set in, and I felt lost and out of control. I started shaking. The room grew dim. I lost track of time. Nothing seemed to make any sense. I turned around, searching for a familiar face, the people in front of me blurring. I felt like a tiny child, lost in a large crowd.

Terrified, I grabbed my bag and ran out of the arena, searching for a room away from everyone. I was dimly aware of a voice calling out my name behind me. The women's changing room loomed in front of me and I dashed into it. Thankfully, it was empty. I slid down along the wall to the floor, ripping off my shin pads, helmet, gloves, and footgear.

My mind began to play tricks on me. Was I dreaming? I couldn't even remember how I got here. Everything that happened this morning was disappearing, like sand falling rapidly through an hourglass. I wanted to scream. I hugged my legs, whimpering like a lost child.

Ethan burst through the door, running toward me, his face filled with worry. Behind him was another black belt. Ethan turned to him. "Go fetch my father!" He skidded to a stop in front of me and knelt down, running his hands all over me, searching for injuries. He touched the side of my face where it was sore. "Jessie? Are you all right? You have a bruise on your cheek." When I didn't answer, he looked up into my eyes and froze. "Jessie? Please tell me what's wrong?"

I tried to say something. Stammering and at a loss for words, I muttered, over and over, "Am I dreaming? How did I get here?"

His hand flew to his mouth in shock. With trembling fingers, he pulled me into an embrace, stroking my hair. "Oh my God. What happened to you Jessie?"

I couldn't stop shaking. My teeth chattered loudly. Everything seemed dull and hazy. My mind felt heavy as if it was wrapped in a thick fog.

His father came rushing in and was immediately by our side.

I listened numbly to his words, my mind too far away to fully comprehend the situation, their words fading in and out.

"Ethan, I talked to the other judges and they said that she took a hard hit to the head. She may have a concussion."

"We need to take her to the hospital. Now." As he spoke, Ethan quickly gathered up my gear and placed it in my bag.

I felt his hands slide beneath my legs. He picked me up and carried me out to the car.

A few minutes later, the fog in my brain began to lift. I blinked and looked down at my hands, startled to realize that he was holding on to them, gripping them fiercely as if he didn't want to let go.

"Ethan, I'm okay."

He blinked back tears as he looked at me. He reached out and gently touched the side of my face. "Are you sure, Jessie? A few minutes ago you didn't even know where you were. You had this faraway look in your eyes. They were glazed over."

"I felt far away...lost even. It was weird. I can't explain it...it felt like a dream. Nothing felt real. It was as if I was separated from my body." I squeezed his hands as I spoke. "It was terrifying."

"Do you know where you are now?"

"Um, sort of. The tournament, right?"

"Okay, what else do you remember?"

"I won first place in sparring. It was a back fist strike that cinched it."

He raised his eyebrows inquiringly. "Uh-huh. Anything else?"

I looked up and saw his father watching me through the rear mirror, concern etched on his face.

My mind went blank. I could recall vague snatches, bit and pieces, but they didn't make any sense. Fear suddenly infused my body. I started to panic.

"I'm sorry. I can't remember anything else. It's too vague..."

As I searched through my mind for answers, it felt as if someone was using an Etch-A-Sketch and wiping the slate clean. It was fading into smoke, vanishing into thin air. I tried to grasp at the last remnants of clear thoughts from that morning, but they slipped through my fingers, forever.

Ethan exchanged a worried glance with his father. I could feel him press on the accelerator, trying to get to the hospital faster.

CHAPTER 4

Recall

I was admitted within minutes of arriving at the emergency room. One of the nurses, tsking at me in a motherly fashion, handed me an ice pack as soon she saw the bruise on my face.

Ethan walked over to the side of the bed and held onto my hand. His father stood at the foot of the bed, watching for the doctor.

My face was growing cold and numb from the ice. I shivered and grabbed my arms. Ethan glanced at me. His eyes, a hazel color under the fluorescent lights, were full of unease. "Jessie, do you remember anything from yesterday?" he asked as he rubbed his hand along the bracelet he gave me.

At least I remembered that. Thank God.

"Yes, the train ride...and the bracelet." I looked down and touched the bracelet as I spoke.

"Anything else?"

"Yeah, the fancy hotel. The huge suite..." A smile spread across his face while I recalled how posh it was.

"What about the other trophy? Do remember that?"

I frowned in concentration. "What other trophy?"

Just then, a tall, older gentleman breezed in. He was impressive, with broad shoulders, gray hair and a strong chin, reminiscent of B-movie stars. He wore a white lab coat, his pink shirt and gray tie peeking out from under the stethoscope wrapped around his neck.

"Hello. I'm Dr. Hobart. Am I correct to believe that you are Jessie McIntyre?" He spoke in a courteous voice, his words clipped in what sounded almost like a British accent. He reminded me of my grandfather, a kind and dear soul. I got the impression that he came from a noble background. His mannerism were graceful and precise.

"Yes." I whispered, feeling a bit shy.

"Ah! Good to meet you." He gestured toward Ethan's dad. "Is this your father?"

Jonas stepped forward and gave the doctor a hearty hand shake. "No, sir. I'm Jonas Appleby. This is my son Ethan. Jessie is one of the students at my martial arts school."

"Aha. Excellent." Dr. Hobart moved to the side of the bed and took a look at the side of my face. "And what happened here?"

He held a pen above the clipboard, ready to jot down the details

"We were at a tournament and she took a hit to the side of her head during a sparring match," said Jonas as he looked my way.

"Ouch. I'm a boxer myself. So, Jessie, how are you feeling now?"

"My head feels a bit fuzzy...you know, kinda heavy. Little bit dizzy."

"Any nausea or headache?" he asked.

"Mm, don't think so..."

Ethan spoke up. "She can't remember anything from this morning. When we found her, her eyes were glazed over. She seemed out of it."

I suddenly felt very fragile, like a small child. Scared and alone.

"Well, let's take a look here, shall we?" He placed his fingers along my jaw, pressing lightly here and there, feeling his way around my face. When he touched the cheek, I winced and sucked in my breath.

"Ooh. A wee bit sore there, eh? You do have some bruising along here." He glanced down and spotted the ice pack. "Continue to keep the ice pack on it. It will help with the pain and swelling. Okay. Now, Jessie, I'm going to shine a light in your eyes and take a look at them."

I blinked as it shone brightly in my pupils, feeling self-conscious.

"Good, now I want you to follow my fingers without moving your head."

As I watched his fingers move back and forth, up and down, I started to feel a little woozy.

"All right, Jessie, I'm going to order a CT scan as a precaution. One of the nurses will be along shortly to take you to the radiology department okay?" he said as he looked down at the chart and jotted down a few more notes before pivoting around and strolling out the door.

I nodded feebly, feeling a bit anxious.

After what seemed like hours, a tall, male nurse, wearing a crisp white uniform, came in with a wheelchair. He had short tousled dark hair and a white ID tag neatly clipped to his breast pocket. "Hi! You must be Jessie. My name is Ben and I will be taking you to the CT room."

I rose on shaky legs and sank into the wheelchair, holding the ice pack on my cheekbone. He wheeled me through a series of hallways, into a spacious and brightly lit room. He parked me beside the bed and briskly walked out.

In the center of the room was a large cylindrical tube with a bed inside it, the end sticking out. The rest of the room was fairly sparse and polished. On the far side of the wall was a two way window that looked into a dark room.

Another nurse marched in wearing purple scrubs covered in cheerful whimsical cartoons. She had a rather neat streak of purple hair in her bangs. Her blond hair was done up in a large clip at the back, a few tendrils falling around her eyes.

"Hello, dear, are you Jessie?"

I nodded at her shyly.

"I'll be guiding you through this procedure okay?" She spoke in a cheerful voice.

"Um. Just to let you know, I'm hard of hearing. Is it safe to wear my hearing aids in here?"

"Well, it might be a bit loud for you. You would be better off removing them. Is that all right with you?"

"Sure." I raised my hands toward my ears.

She put her hand out to stop me. "Before you take them off, I wanted to let you know that you may feel some vibrations. That's normal. And you'll need to remain as still as possible until I come back to let you out."

"Okay." The room fell silent as I turned my hearing aids off and handed them over to her.

She gestured toward the bed that was connected to the CT scanner. I climbed on top of the bed and stretched out, resting my head on the pillow. The nurse pushed a button on the side and the bed began to slowly move into the tube.

I saw her walk outside and reappear in the darkened room, her face lit up by the computer console in front of her.

There was not much space around me, and I started to feel a little bit claustrophobic. Within a few minutes, part of the machine began to rotate around me, sending a deep rumbling sensation through me. I didn't hear much, just a muffled sound as it spun around.

I stared at the smooth surface, thought of white fluffy clouds, and tried to imagine myself floating high in the sky, soaring through the heavens.

After a few minutes, the spinning slowed down and came to a stop. The bed slid out slowly. The nurse was already standing beside it, smiling down at me. She gave me back my hearing aids.

As soon as I turned them back on, sounds rushed in once again.

She said, "See? Now that wasn't so bad was it?"

She helped me step down from the bed and into the wheelchair.

After a minute or so, Ben came back in and whisked me through the never-ending corridors.

Ethan and his father were still waiting in the room when we arrived.

Ben parked the wheelchair beside the bed and I slid back onto the crinkling sheets.

Ethan walked over to stand by my side. He held onto my hand while we waited for Dr. Hobart to come back.

After what seemed like forever, the doctor finally showed up with a new sheet of information clipped to the chart. He scanned through it and looked up at me. "Well, the CT scan results were normal and there doesn't appear to be anything broken, just some bruising on your cheek."

"You may experience some dizziness or headache for the next day or so. I want you to take it easy for the next couple of weeks, no sparring until you are completely free of any symptoms. Okay?"

"What about my memory?" I asked, feeling alarmed.

He sighed, thought about it, and replied, "It may or may not return. Give it time to heal."

I nodded numbly.

"Good girl. Please contact me if anything changes or gets worse, all right?" He reached out and gave me a strong hand shake. "It was nice to meet you, Jessie."

He turned toward Ethan's father and gestured for him to step out of the room. I watched the two of them converse for several minutes then shake hands, which left me wondering what they talked about.

Jonas strode back in, hands clasped together. "All right, Jessie, he said that we can go now. Ethan can you help her?"

I sat back in the wheelchair as Ethan gripped the handles and wheeled me out of the emergency room and out to the parking lot. He helped me get into the car then rolled the wheelchair back into the hospital.

I leaned my head against Ethan's shoulder on the way back to the hotel. He cradled his arm around me protectively.

Once we made our way back into the room, I sat down on the couch and drew my knees up, hugging them with my arms, feeling dazed and tired after a long day.

I looked up at both of them. "Why don't you guys go back to the tournament and see if you can still participate? I feel kinda bad that you didn't get a chance to compete."

Ethan sat down beside me, rubbing his hands on my legs. "Oh, Jessie, don't worry about it. I have competed in this tournament many times. It's not a big deal. I would rather stay with you."

"Ethan's right. Someone needs to be with you for the next few hours...just in case." Ethan and his father locked gazes, as if sending a silent signal.

I wondered what that was all about.

"Tell you what," Jonas said. "I'll go back and see if they need any help with anything. Ethan can stay here with you okay?"

I nodded. "Sure."

He turned around and went out the door, keys jingling in his hand.

Ethan sighed miserably, his face filled with concern as he looked in my direction.

"Ethan, what's wrong? You're starting to scare me," I said as I reached out and touched the side of his face.

He grabbed my hand and held on to it. "I'm scaring you? Holy smokes, Jessie, you scared the crap out of me today."

I could see tears starting to well up in his eyes. He turned to look out the window, swallowing loudly as if trying to control his emotions, gulping back the rising fear. I thought he was going to cry.

I was growing more concerned by the minute. "Ethan? What is it?"

He turned his face toward me, his hazel-green eyes filled with grief. A wash of sorrow ran through me as I looked at him.

"Jessie, I almost lost you today." He stopped for a moment, swallowed again as if it was painful to breathe. "I thought you were gone when you couldn't remember where you were." He took another breath, his voice shaking. "My God, when I looked into your eyes, you didn't seem to know me." He gripped my hands tighter. "It's hard to explain...it was as if you looked right through me. You were so far away." Looking down at my hands, he gave them a gentle kiss. "You broke my heart."

I leaned in and touched my forehead to his, a silent moment of affection. "Oh, Ethan, I'm sorry."

He looked up and laughed. "You're sorry?" His eyes lit up once again. "That's funny, ya know? At least your sense humor is still intact." He paused for a kiss. "It's not your fault, Jessie. The referee told Dad that your opponent's kick went wild. She was out of control. She shouldn't have aimed for your head like that, certainly not with a kick."

Curious, I asked, "Why do I need someone to keep an eye on me? I feel fine, mostly. Not that I'm complaining about the company."

He smiled briefly at that last comment. "I've seen my share of students that took a hit to the head. Some of them ended up with a headache, others experienced dizziness. Your reaction was the worst I've seen." He paused for a moment. "Head injuries are serious, Jessie—you can die from them." His voice cracked as he spoke the last few words.

"Oh, I didn't know that," I said in a quiet voice.

He pulled me into an embrace and I leaned into him, feeling comforted by the warmth of his body.

Apparently, I fell asleep. When I woke up it was already dark outside. I was momentarily disoriented, wondering where I was, and then I recalled I was in the hotel.

Ethan and his father were sitting at the table eating and chatting quietly.

"Hi," I said, looking at them through bleary eyes.

"Right back at ya, kiddo," replied Jonas, smiling at me. "How are you feeling?"

Ethan set down the glass of juice he was drinking and strode over to me. He knelt on the floor beside me, and placed his hands on my top of mine.

I sighed. "Um. A little tired and foggy."

Ethan looked at his father then back again at me. Again, there was that silent signal.

"Did you want anything to eat?" Ethan asked. "We have some food here." The table was covered with plates, half-empty glasses, and food.

"No, thanks, I'm not really hungry."

Concern passed over Ethan's face as I spoke.

"How about some crackers?" he said as he walked over to the table and picked up a small package of saltines.

"Sure, I guess."

He ripped open the package and placed them gently in my hand.

His father spoke up. "Do you want to try some tea Jessie?"

Tea sounded good right now. "Yes, that would be nice."

He got up, went over to the kitchenette, and turned on the kettle. As he waited for it to boil, he rummaged through the cupboards for a mug and a spoon. He placed a tea bag in the slim white mug as he spoke. "Did you want any sugar or milk?"

"A little bit of sugar, please." I gestured with my fingers just how much I wanted.

I munched on the crackers as he stirred the water in the cup and removed the tea bag. He carried it over to me, "Here you go."

"Thanks," I said as I accepted it, feeling the warmth seep through the mug. I blew on it, sending tendrils of steam swirling into the air.

I sat on the couch cross legged, resting my elbows on top of my legs as I held onto the mug. Ethan sat down beside me and placed his arm across my shoulders, stroking the back of my neck.

There was a bit of awkward silence for a moment, and then Jonas began cleaning up the table, putting away the food, and washing the dishes.

"Dad, did you want some help with that?" Ethan asked as he watched Jonas move around the kitchen.

"Heavens, no, Ethan, it's fine. Besides I'm almost done." He swirled a wet cloth on a plate he held in his hands, glanced over his shoulder, and tipped his head toward the TV. "Why don't you guys watch a video? I'm sure there are plenty of choices. I'll go in the other room, there's a TV in there, too," he added with a smile as he sauntered off.

Ethan picked up the remote, sitting nearby on the coffee table, and clicked it on.

"Can you turn on the Closed Captioning on the TV?" I asked. "I can't watch it without the subtitles. It's usually marked on the button on the remote by the letters CC," I added, since Ethan was scrutinizing the remote, his thumb roaming the buttons, until he found it. "Much better, thanks," I said as the captions came on. I smiled as a memory flashed into my mind. "You know what? This is how I learned to spell certain words when I was younger."

He glanced at me, raising his eyebrows and smiling mischievously. "By certain words, you mean...uh...slang?"

"Yeah, you could say that."

He chuckled. "Ooh, how about this show?" he said as he stopped flicking through the channels.

Typically, it was an action movie. "Sure, why not? My attention span is way too short at the moment for anything else."

He snorted at my response.

We snuggled together comfortably on the couch. I fell asleep again. When I woke up, I was still leaning against Ethan. He glanced at me as I stirred.

"Hey there, sleepy head," he said as he brushed the hair out of my eyes.

I looked at the TV. The movie was over and the credits were scrolling across the screen. "It's over already?"

A bit stiff, I stood up and stretched. I felt a little funny. Everything seemed to move in slow motion.

Ethan's hand gripped mine. "Jessie, you okay?"

"Hmm? Yeah, it's just that my vision seems a bit sluggish."

He stood up beside me and placed his hands on either of my face, looking into my eyes.

I held onto his arms for a moment, not wanting to let go. "It's okay, it'll pass."

We broke apart and I headed toward the bathroom, picking up my pjs on the way in.

When I came back out, he already had the couch bed pulled out, with the sheets neatly folded back for me. "Oh wow, the all-star treatment. Shall I tip you, sir?"

"Cute." He held out his hand and guided me to the couch.

I intertwined my fingers with his, pulling him closer to me, and gave him a lingering kiss, enjoying the sensual feeling of his lips against mine.

I wasn't sure if the woozy sensation was from the kiss or my head injury. "Hang on, the room's spinning again," I said as I leaned back on the pillow.

He grinned. "Should I accept that as a compliment?"

"Heh." I managed to utter a little laugh before my eyes began to feel heavy.

"Night, Jessie."

"G'night, Ethan," I said in a whisper as I took out my hearing aids and placed them on the coffee table beside the couch.

I felt him touch my forehead with his warm hand then a feather light kiss, as soft as a sigh.

I slept fitfully throughout the night, my dreams filled with random images from my past that didn't make any sense. The sheets kept getting twisted around me as I tossed and turned, trying to escape the frightening visions. I felt like I was being sucked into a dark vortex, falling endlessly.

There was screaming in my left ear and it wouldn't stop. It sounded like children, a high pitch, terrified shriek. I tried to clamp my hand over my ear to quell the screams. It was futile gesture.

"Stop it—stop the screaming."

Ethan was beside me, one hand on my shoulder, the other on my forehead.

I blinked my eyes open. My face was slick with sweat, damp hair plastered along the sides.

Ethan turned on the lamp sitting on the table beside us, sending a sudden glow of light into the room.

I was panting and shaking uncontrollably. Ethan stroked my face softly, tucking the wet strands of hair behind my ear.

"Jessie, you okay?"

Since I didn't have my hearing aids on, I had to lip-read him, which took a lot of effort. I was still a bit a disoriented. He signed the word okay with his fingers, forming the letters "O" and "K."

"Nightmare," I mumbled through chattering teeth. I drew up my knees, hugging my legs.

He rubbed his chest with a closed fist in a circular motion, the sign for sorry. "I'm sorry."

"Stay with me please?" I asked him.

He nodded and pulled me into his arms, resting his chin on top my head. I fell into a warm and gentle slumber in his arms. When I woke up, I was still reclining against him. The sun streamed in through the window. As I tried to sit up, the room spun crazily in a swift and violent motion.

I clapped my hand onto my mouth and ran into the bathroom, barely making it in time to throw up.

Ethan appeared by my side, rubbing my back.

"I'm sorry," I mumbled as he handed me a glass of water. I gingerly took a sip, grateful to be able to refresh my mouth.

"It's not your fault Jessie. Can you stand up?"

I nodded. "I think so."

We slowly moved back to the couch. I sagged onto the pillows, waiting for the room to stop spinning. After a few minutes of sitting still, I reached out and grabbed my hearing aids and put them on. I was suddenly infused with a rush of sounds that seemed far too loud.

"Tell you what," he said. "I'll make some tea, maybe that will help." He strode off to the kitchen, rummaging through the cupboards.

His father joined him, the two of them speaking in low whispers, exchanging worried glances. I couldn't hear what they were saying and did not feel like lip reading them at all since it would've taken too much of an effort.

Ethan brought over the cup of tea and placed it in my hands. I watched the steam curl up in a lazy motion.

"Ethan? What's going on?" I asked as I bobbed my head in the direction of where they had talked to each other a few minutes ago.

"Dad's going to call the doctor and ask him a few questions. Don't panic. He is just being cautious which is good. Okay?"

I felt my face blush warmly, feeling really embarrassed about it. "Ah, you mean because of this morning?"

"Please don't worry about it." His hand gently touched my cheek. "You know—last night you were saying something about screams or screaming. What did you mean by that?" His eyebrows creased together as he looked at me, searching for answers.

"Hmm?" I could remember being absolutely frightened at one point, but it was a faint memory, slipping away from me the more I tried to recall it. "I don't remember much. The only thing I can recall is the sound of children screaming. They sounded absolutely terrified."

"You did have your hand over your ear at one point. Were you in pain?" he asked as concern grew on his features.

"Pain? No, I don't think so. You know what? It may have been the ringing in my ears."

"What do you mean?"

"Well, ever since I was very young, I've always had ringing in my ears. It sounds like a Cicada."

"Cicada? What's that?"

"Um, it's basically a giant bug that can fit in the palm of your hand. It vaguely resembles a fly. You can hear them on a hot summer day. They produce a sound like a high pitch buzz."

He laughed as the answer dawned on him. "Is that what makes all that noise?"

"How did you know what they look like?" he asked curiously.

"Easy, my cat Parker caught one. You should have seen him. He was carrying it carefully in his mouth while it made this huge racket, vibrating like crazy. I managed to rescue it and put it in a safer spot. Although it was kinda creepy holding it in my hand. Ew." I shuddered at that thought then laughed as an old memory crossed my mind.

Ethan smiled and touched my nose briefly. His eyes twinkled merrily as his face relaxed and softened. "What's so funny?"

"It's just that when I was really young, I used to think that someone was trying to contact me, you know from out there, through the radio towers. Sending me secret messages. I had no idea that the sound was just plain old ringing in the ears at that time."

"Out there? You mean, not of this earth?" He pointed skyward as he said this, evidently holding back a laugh.

"Heh, yeah. I told you I was imaginative."

"Ha! It's cute!" His smile grew as he spoke, enjoying this moment.

I stared into the cup, taking a small sip. "Something must've changed the pitch."

"No kidding." He sighed. "It doesn't sound at all pleasant or even something that you could get used to." He glanced out the window for a moment and then looked back at me. "You know, I can't even begin to imagine living with the drone of the Cicada in my ears. I would go nuts."

"I can handle it. All I have to do is simply subdue the sound with my mind. It really is mind over matter—well, almost always. The hearing aids override it most of the time."

"Interesting. That's impressive that you can do that."

"I just hope that the screaming is not a new addition. It scared the hell out of me."

"Yes, I noticed that. You reacted really strongly to it last night."

"Thanks, Ethan. For being there for me. It helped," I said softly, feeling a bit sheepish.

He smiled as placed his hand on my shoulder. "No problem, Jessie."

Just then his father came back in. "Jessie, I talked to Dr. Hobart and told him about your symptoms. He said to bring you in if it gets any worse. For now, he said for you to take it easy and I agree." He glanced toward the entertainment center. "Why don't you guys relax and spend the day watching movies, browsing on the internet. There might even be a gaming console in the cabinet."

Ethan perked right up as soon as he heard that. "Ooh, yeah! Great idea. What do you think, Jessie?"

"Sure, that sounds fine. But weren't we supposed to go back home today?"

"We can always go later in the evening or even tomorrow," Jonas said. "It's not a problem." He smiled. "In the meantime..." He clapped his hands together eagerly. "Is there anything you need?"

"Food, snacks, ya know, everything a growing teenager needs."

I rolled my eyes skyward at Ethan's comment.

His father snorted back a laugh and smiled mischievously. "How about you, Jessie?"

I thought about it for a moment. "Can I have some dark chocolate and if possible, those cute little goldfish crackers?"

"Is that all? Ethan is getting the whole nine yards worth of food. I don't mind getting these things for you, Jessie, after all, it's your day off."

I hesitated, very shy with all of this attention. "Are you sure?"

He nodded and mimed writing on a notepad. "Let's hear some more requests."

"Um, I feel really silly saying this, but I would love to read a teen or fashion magazine."

"Perfect! I'll go get them right now!" He turned around, pulled on a dark jacket, and grabbed his keys.

When he came back, we spent the day pigging out, spending some quality time together, laughing and joking around. I loved it. We had a great time despite the fact I was pretty much bedridden.

CHAPTER 5

Compass

I gingerly opened one eye, peeking out from beneath the warm covers, then the other eye. The sun streamed through the window, turning the dust motes into a glittering beam of light.

Parker lifted his head in response to my movement and promptly sat up, stretching his spine, then stood up to look at me. He was a handsome tabby with stunning chocolate colored fur and bold green eyes. He walked toward me, his paws sinking into the soft covers, and sat upon my chest.

He blinked, tilted his head to the side, parted his jaws, and meowed. I didn't have my hearing aids on and as a result, I heard nothing when Parker said, "Hello." However, it was obvious by his body language, and I could literally lip-read him even though he was a cat.

He leaned in to me and gave me whisker kisses, his cool wet nose touching mine. It was a sweet gesture, a little personality trait that I loved about him. He was full of spunk and deeply protective of me. On our outdoor walks, he always stayed by my side. I guess you could say that he was my official hearing-ear cat.

"Aw, thank you, Parker. You're adorable!"

He squeezed his eyes shut for a quick moment as if he smiled, and I swear that he nodded his head in response. Parker raised his paw and gently touched my cheek, trying to tell me that was it time for school. Or to feed him.

I stretched and reached out to give him a scratch on his furry head as I talked to him. I had always considered him to be smarter than most cats.

"Sigh. You know, it's days like this that I wish I didn't have to go to school."

I flung back the covers and got up, shivering from the sudden blast of cold air, picked up my shamrock green hoodie and navy blue sweatpants, and padded into the bathroom.

I was momentarily stunned from the sight I saw in the mirror. The bruise from the karate tournament this past weekend had left a large path of destruction across my face. The dark purple tint spread along my cheekbone, leaving ugly, angry red marks around my eye. I sucked in a gasp as I realized the true extent of the injury.

The concussion left a huge, gaping hole in my memory. My mind was like a sieve as bits and pieces of my life fell through. I couldn't recall anything that had happened that morning prior to the hit.

At least I don't have to worry about wearing makeup today, I mused.

I dapped a little bit of concealer here and there to hide a couple of blemishes and swiped on some pink glittering lip gloss. My curly blond hair was an unruly mess. So I grabbed the thick strands and bundled them up into a ponytail.

Cute, I thought and walked back into my room.

I sat down at the table near the window, searching for my earrings. "Aha!" I found the long chain of tiny silver stars that Mom had given me for my birthday last year.

I turned to the side, reached over, and grabbed my hearing aids, the large body a translucent green, showing off the electronic inner workings attached to vibrant green-and-white marbled earmolds. The earmold was soft beneath my fingers as I pushed it in and tucked the shell behind my ear. I repeated the same motion for the other side.

As I turned them on, I waited for a moment to get used to the rush of sounds coming from all around me. The house gave off a soft rumbling hum from the furnace. I could hear Parker muttering from somewhere in the room, along with a skittering sound as if he was swatting at a toy.

Looking in the mirror, I picked up an earring and placed it through my ear lobe. I reached down again and came up empty. I looked all over the top of the table, fingers searching for it, then at the floor all around me. "Strange, where did it go? It was right here a minute ago, I know I had it my hands."

I heard Parker chirruping from the other side of the bed. Curious as to what he was doing, I leaned across the bed and peered down. "Parker! That's mine!" He was carrying my dangling earring in his teeth, looking as proud as a royal king.

"Gimme me that! Ya little thief," I muttered as I bent down and snatched up the earring, nearly falling off the bed in the process. I put the earring in my other ear lobe then pulled on my socks.

Parker was sitting beside me, watching every move I made, hoping that I'd drop something interesting for him to play with. I gave him a quick kiss on his furry head and murmured, "I'll see you later, munchkin."

My feet made a racket on the creaky wooden steps on the way down toward the kitchen. Backpack slung across my shoulder, I grabbed my lunch from the refrigerator, tucked it into the backpack, and snatched up a couple of muffins on the way out.

Reaching into the closet, I grabbed a thick navy blue vest and pulled it on, feeling warmer already.

I bounded down the gravel lane, past a row of trees on either side, resplendent in bursts of crimson red and gold leaves. I yanked my fingerless gloves out of my pocket and slipped them on as my feet crunched loudly on the fallen leaves that littered every available surface.

I got to the end of the lane and stood beside the red mailbox featuring the name "McIntyre" as I waited for the bus.

It came to a screeching halt several minutes later. I grudgingly climbed up the dingy steps, sighing miserably, and sat down on a worn seat, its cracks biting into my legs. As I expected, it was a long and torturous ride. I endured the jeers of fellow students from behind me. They'd tried everything in the book to drive me up the wall. They were unbelievably rude, taunting me relentlessly. It didn't matter what I said or did, they always found a way to twist it around and turn it into a vulgar joke, making me feel small and dimwitted.

The bus came to a rumbling stop in front of the old concrete sidewalk, a worn out pathway that led to the main entrance. All around the school was thick lush grass, with a natural wall of tall, majestic Maple and Pine trees.

I blew out a sigh of relief as I quickly burst through the doors of the bus and briskly strode toward the red brick building, past tall pillars on both sides of the double doors, and marched into Beaverdale Middle School/High School.

On my way to the locker, I picked up my FM system, a small blue box that fit in the palm of my hand, outfitted with a tiny microphone and long plastic loop for the teachers to wear in class. I wore the receiver, which was a wireless set of clear "boots" that clipped on to the ends of my hearing aids. It helped me hear the teacher's voices, sometimes as clear as a bell, although there were times when I wished I didn't. Especially when they forgot that they were wearing it. I mean, *ew*, talk about gross.

I glanced at my schedule and snatched up several books. Then I slammed the locker shut with the palm of my hand, making a loud and satisfying metallic clang.

Everyone stared at me openly as I walked down the polished floors toward the gymnasium. I stopped by the Phys-Ed teacher's office and gave her the doctor's note excusing me from gym for the rest of the week.

Her jaw dropped visibly as she accepted the note, her hand frozen midair. "Oh my, Jessie. Are you sure you want to be here today?"

Her face devoid of any makeup, Mrs. Stewart stared at me in shock. Her flat, dark brown hair was turning gray at the sides. It was cut bluntly short. As usual, she wore a shapeless track suit that was an unflattering shade of powder blue.

I sighed. "I can't do any physical activity for a couple of weeks, depending on my symptoms. But I can still attend classes." I muttered, "Unfortunately," under my breath.

Her eyes were tinged with concern, a rare sight from her, I might add. "All right, you can sit in the bleachers and watch the class or do your homework if you wish."

I nodded. "Okay."

I strolled through the large double doors to the entrance of the gym and turned left, toward the stands. I plunked down my heavy books and sat on the uncomfortable bench.

Several of my classmates were already in the gym, gathered in a group, chatting amongst themselves, hands flying in animated gestures, punctuating their remarks.

One of them was Donna, who was mean to the bone. She saw my bruised cheekbone and did a double-take. A slow and fiendish smile spread across her face.

She stopped the conversation and jabbed a finger in my direction. The group sauntered over to me, mischief clearly etched on their faces.

"Holy...looks like you finally got what you deserved, eh, Macky?" Donna said, her voice tinged with malice, emphasizing a nickname that was not at all flattering.

I groaned inwardly. This was the last thing I needed today. A headache began to form, thanks to them.

The rest of the group chimed in, "Yeah, guess someone finally found a way to shut you up, Macky." They drawled out the last word like a petulant, whiny child.

I clenched my fists, anger rising like a hot flame through me. "It was just an accident, okay? If it makes you feel any better, I can't remember what happened."

Hands shaking, I opened my notebook and rifled through my pencil case for a pen.

They were stunned into silence. Their mouths gaped open for a second and then clamped shut, clearly at loss for a witty comeback.

I crouched over the open pages and began scribbling, hoping to dispel any further arguments.

More students piled in, along with Mrs. Stewart who pushed a cart full of basketballs in front of her. She blew her whistle sharply, yelled at the group to form a circle around her, and began to discuss the drills for this morning. Then she ordered them to begin their warm ups.

Their shoes squeaked madly as they dashed back and forth, practicing a three on three on the right side of the court.

Once in a while, I glanced up to watch the action, wishing that I could participate.

The left side of the court was empty, except for a lone student struggling to dribble the ball toward the hoop. She lifted it up and delivered a feeble shot. She moved awkwardly in a somewhat clumsy manner, obviously not familiar with handling a basketball.

I had never seen her in the gym before, and I suspected it was because she was with the Special Education group. Her features held the distinctive earmarks of someone with Down's Syndrome.

Her straight, chestnut-colored hair swayed from side to side as she bounced the ball. She glanced up at the net, tried to shoot the ball, and faltered, then stood forlornly as the ball rolled away from her.

I got up off the bench and picked up the ball, striding toward her.

"Hi! I'm Jessie. May I show you a trick?"

She looked up at me, sniffling. Her eyes were brimming with tears. She blinked and nodded.

"Hold your right hand at the bottom of the ball. Let it sit in your palm like this." I demonstrated the position. With my fingers splayed up, I raised the ball near my head.

"As you move the ball up, bring your other hand on the side or near the top for balance." She watched me carefully, fascinated. "When you are ready to shoot the ball," I continued. "Remember to flick your wrist in a sharp downward motion as you raise it high above your head. Okay?" She nodded again, watching closely. "Here, you try it," I said. "Just show me where your hands go." I gave her the ball, took a step back and watched her.

She went through the motions, trying to copy my movements.

"Good! Try tossing it toward me." I gestured for her to try it out, miming the flicking motion as if shooting it at the net.

She took her time, doing it step by step.

"Okay, now come on over here." I led her toward the lines on the floor that indicated a boxed in area beneath the net. "It helps to aim for the upper corner of the square on the backboard." I pointed at the mesh above our heads. "Can you see it?"

She nodded eagerly.

I reached for the ball. "Here, I'll demonstrate."

She gave it back to me and watched as I raised it up and pitched it. It bounced off the board and swished through the net perfectly.

"Does that make sense?"

She nodded again, her hands clasped together.

"Do you want to try it?"

She all but yanked the ball out of my hands, anxious to try. Taking her time, she slowly lifted it up, tossed it at the backboard. It bounced off the edge of the rim.

I grabbed the bouncing ball and handed it back to her. "That's okay. I sometimes miss it, too."

She tried it again. It went straight in, swishing through the mesh. She beamed as she looked at me then back at the ball.

I gave her a high five. "That's great! Way to go! Go ahead and keep practicing," I said as I took a step back and let her try out the shots. Her smile grew wider as she became more confident.

I stood nearby, watching and catching errant balls, passing them back to her.

Mrs. Stewart gave the whistle a sharp blast that reverberated throughout the spacious gym. "Okay, ladies, time to go get changed!

She turned on her heel and walked over to me as I was bent over gathering up my books.

"Jessie. That was very kind of you to help out. Thank you."

"Oh. No problem. I like helping out," I said. I shrugged my shoulders nonchalantly. "I guess you could say that I have an idea of what it's like to be in her shoes."

She nodded, understanding my meaning. "Thanks again, Jessie. It was still a very kind gesture," she said before she turned around and marched back to her office.

A few minutes later, the bell rang. I strolled down the polished floors in the narrow hallways to my next class.

The classroom was buzzing with chatter as everyone worked their way into their seats, dropping their backpacks on the floors, books thumping on the desks.

I stopped by Mr. Wilson's desk and handed him the FM system. As he reached for it, his face froze. He looked thoroughly speechless.

When I turned around and moved toward my desk, the classroom went completely silent. You could have literally heard a pin drop.

All eyes were on me, staring at the ugly bruise on my cheek. I sighed as I slunk into my seat, feeling very self-conscious. Some of the students around me began to whisper. Others pointed in my direction.

I guess I should've heeded Mom's advice and stayed home today.

The same thing happened in virtually every class and I had grown tired of it by the end of the day.

I found it became harder to concentrate. My mind felt thick and sluggish as if a greasy fog was impeding on my thoughts.

By the time the bus came to a complete stop at the end of my lane, I was exhausted. As I trudged down the driveway, I kicked at the multi-colored leaves, gleefully sending them flying in every direction. I glanced at the house. I could see Parker sitting in my bedroom window, waiting for me.

Mom was in the kitchen, wearing a flour-covered apron, making supper. The plates were already out, sitting on the table with napkins and utensils beside them.

The table on the other side of the kitchen was covered with large gingerbread cookies in the shapes of either an acorn or a leaf, brightly decorated in warm hues of pumpkin orange and apple green, topped off with colorful sugar sprinkles. The aroma was tantalizing.

She had various cellophane bags and ribbons nearby, ready to package the cookies once they were done. The clear bags were adorned with a simple sticker featuring the words Paige's Pastries in an elegant font.

"Hi, Jessie. How was school?" she said as she turned around to face me, her long, curly auburn hair bouncing as she spoke.

"Well, you were right about me staying home today," I said as I dropped my backpack on the floor with a loud thunk and shrugged out of my vest.

Alarm grew on her face. "What's wrong, honey?"

"Just tired." I played with the edges of the tablecloth. "Everyone stared at me, all day long. It was embarrassing."

"Ah, I see," she said, relief on her face. "Oh! Guess who called today?" She wiped her hands on a dish towel. "Mrs. Stewart! She was so proud of you for helping out in class this morning!"

I groaned, fighting the urge to bang my head on the table. "Mom, it's no big deal."

"If you say so...by the way, supper will be ready in twenty minutes. Could you go find your father and let him know please?"

I found Dad in the study, furiously typing away on the computer, no doubt preparing his notes for this week's classes. His dark blond hair was rumpled as if he had been running his hands through them. He wore a red and black plaid flannel shirt and dark jeans. A cup of coffee, probably cold by now, sat on the desk beside the laptop. He had a large stack of papers, with a red pen sitting on top, near the small antique lamp.

"Hi, Dad. Mom said to tell you supper will be ready in a few minutes."

He looked up from the computer while his fingers still continued to type—an impressive skill that I have yet to master. "Oh! Thanks, Jessie. Whatever she's making smells good!"

After supper, I went upstairs, gingerly carrying a cup of hot tea in my hands, trying not to spill it. I set it aside as I tackled my homework, doing a bit of research online. A few hours later, I'd had enough. I was simply too tired to do anymore, exhausted after such a particularly long day.

I sat on the bed with Parker who was curled up beside me, wearing a sweet smile and purring loudly. I stroked his soft fur, his rumbling purrs vibrating beneath my fingers. "Purrup?" he said as he looked at me, blinking.

"Hi, handsome, I was just admiring your fur."

The sky outside the window displayed a stunning backdrop of deep coral, crimson, and lavender as the sun dipped behind the trees. I sighed wistfully, admiring the beautiful colors. My eyes were growing heavier by the minute. I leaned my head against the soft pillow and gazed out the window.

It was another perfect evening, only this time I was at Ethan's. I stared at the vista in front of me, overlooking Ethan's backyard. Vibrant streaks lit up the sky, the sun blazing a trail as it slipped further down past the horizon. I stood onto the balcony, and inhaled the fresh air, feeling the nip in the crisp breeze, an indication that winter was not too far off.

I could hear the faint sound of trickling water, coming from the fountain that sat in the pond in the backyard.

Ethan stood behind me, slipping his arms around me, watching the sunset.

"Isn't the sky amazing tonight?" I said, feeling his warmth wrap around me like a cozy blanket.

I turned around to face him and my breath caught in my throat as my eyes met his. They appeared to be more green than his usual hazel tonight. He looked as if he'd stepped out of a magazine ad. The warm glow of the setting sun lit up his face, showing off his stunningly-chiseled features. The breeze gently tousled his caramel hair.

He slid his hands along my arms, eventually resting them on my shoulders. I could smell his cologne, a delicious and sensual aroma.

I gestured with my hand. "I love what you did with the decorations, the lights are beautiful."

He had surprised me tonight by covering every inch of the balcony with small, string lights. They were wrapped around the railing, above the french doors and even woven through the grape vine in the Pergola above our heads. They offered a gentle glow that seemed magical, like tiny stars within reach in our personal galaxy. I looked up, admiring their soft glow and feeling very tranquil.

Music played nearby from the portable CD player, Michael Buble's husky voice floating in the air. I was able to make out some of the words, "You're My Everything..."

I laughed, thinking that it was the perfect song for tonight. Ethan leaned down toward me, his eyes sparkling in the twilight, and gave me a gentle kiss. He reached for my hands and began to sway. Gracefully, he pulled me to an open spot on the balcony. We danced under the luminescent lights, slowly spinning around. I leaned into him, feeling his lean muscles beneath my hands.

He twirled me around with one hand. I laughed merrily, feeling giddy. I spun around as he released me, gliding toward the table. On the tabletop was a glass bowl filled with chocolate truffles. Beside it were several lit candles inside frosted glass containers, casting a gentle glimmer all around me.

Smiling, I took a step closer to it, reaching for one of the treats. My hand stopped midway as something caught my eye. Beneath the dish was a crisp white piece of paper, folded in half. I pulled it out, wondering if it was a romantic note written by Ethan. Curious, I pried the edges open.

My face fell upon reading the words. My heart constricted painfully. It was if the air was suddenly sucked out of my lungs. It read, "Goodbye."

Confused, I turned back to Ethan. He was gone. The note slipped from my fingers as I called out his name. "Ethan! Where are you?"

My heart was pounding and my mind swirled with maddening thoughts. I looked frantically around. "Ethan, this is not funny!" The french doors were slightly ajar, swinging in the breeze. I reached for them, grabbing the elegant handles and pulling open the doors, calling out once again.

"Ethan!" His name echoed all around me. Panic shot throughout my body, a sudden cold chill that raced down my spine.

I jerked awake, panting, holding my hand over my chest. My heart was pounding beneath my fingers. I couldn't stop shaking.

Parker was still sound asleep beside me, curled up into a tight furry ball. I glanced out the window. The sky was a deep shade of twilight blue, the stars twinkling in the cold night.

"It felt so real...what did it mean?"

CHAPTER 6

En Garde

I woke up to a delightful scene. Snow fell gently to the ground, glittering in the sunlight like powdered diamonds. As the snowflakes twisted in the breeze, they glinted and sparkled, reflecting all of the colors of the rainbow. It seemed so special and magical.

Parker was sitting on the bench with his tail swishing back and forth, thumping lightly against the pillows, as he watched the birds flutter onto the branches of a nearby tree. Squirrels ran up and down the trunk, chasing each other, swirling around at a maddening pace, taking death-defying leaps across the branches, and shaking off the dusty snow as they bounced on them.

Several large gray doves sat on a branch just outside the window, seemingly keeping a wary eye on Parker. They looked like bodyguards for the flock of chickadees and goldfinches sitting below on the ground as they pecked away at errant seeds.

I rifled through my drawers, searching for heavy winter socks and a long sleeved green thermal shirt. I moved to my sparse closet and pulled out a thick navy-blue knitted vest, embroidered with large white snowflakes. *Perfect*, I thought, happy with my selection. I got dressed, put on my makeup and hearing aids.

As I grabbed my backpack, I could hear Parker chattering, using short little meows as if he was talking to the birds. It was endearing, which brightened my mood even more. I walked over to where he was sitting and looked out the window.

"Purrup?" he asked as he glanced up at me.

"Aren't they a funny bunch?" I said to him as I scratched his furry head. "They'll keep you entertained all day. Have fun Parker!"

I didn't care about the chill in the air as I waited for the bus. It was simply too beautiful outside. I felt giddy, like a kid at Christmas time. I twirled around and glanced up at the sky, watching the sparkling snowflakes fall on my face.

Throughout the day, I kept stealing a peek out the window, watching the snow dance in the wind. As time went on and the teachers handed out more homework, I could feel the straps of my backpack digging into my shoulders. I eyed the straps nervously, wondering if they would snap when I added yet another heavy text book.

Afterward, I marched to the gym for basketball practice. It had been almost two weeks since my concussion, and I decided to give it a try today to see how I fared. Oddly enough, the last few weeks had been significantly stress-free which was a nice change. Unfortunately, the moment I stepped into the changing room and spotted my teammates, all that stress came rushing back at breakneck speed. I could feel the tension in my neck suddenly increase.

I rolled my shoulders in a vain attempt to ease it and blew out a sigh as I walked over to Coach Collins who was waiting for us. His fingers tapped impatiently on the ball that was tucked under his arm. He arched his eyebrows upon seeing me, no doubt greatly disappointed that I was well enough to play.

Oh goody, this will be fun, I thought darkly. I flicked my eyes in the direction of my teammates, Donna, Amber and Jackie, who stared at me with open hostility, their arms crossed over their chests.

"All right, ladies. Let's do a brisk jog around the gym." Coach grabbed the whistle that was hanging around his neck and blew sharply on it. I winced as the shrill sound reached my hearing aids. They amplified virtually every sound and that one came across as a piercing echo.

Our shoes squeaked loudly on the floor as we started our slow jog, going around in a lazy circle. "Okay, on my whistle, you will pick up the pace!" I tried to lip-read him as I ran, a difficult task to do while in motion, so I was grateful that I was already familiar with his tactics. As he blew on the whistle again, we burst into a fast run then slowed again at the second whistle.

We repeated the same motions for several laps and then changed it to running sideways, going backward, and sprints, testing our speed and reflexes.

"Good work!" He blew on the whistle again. "Grab a basketball and line up along the wall."

We all meandered over to the cart full of basketballs. I reached for one. Donna rudely shoved me aside and grabbed a ball, sneering at me as she went by.

Coach Collins blew the whistle again. I winced as he did so. God, he must sleep with that whistle, I thought sardonically, wanting to shove it someplace else.

"Form two lines." He pointed both arms straight out as he stood under the net, facing the length of the gym. "Line one throws the ball. Line two will be the receivers. As you run down the court, pass the ball back and forth to your partner. Is that understood?" He watched us nod our heads in response. "Ready? Go!" And predictably, merrily, he blew the whistle.

I was third in line, thankfully, so that I could watch how to do the drill. I was so intent on watching them go through the motions that I didn't even notice who was next in line until I glanced in her direction. My heart did a little jolt as I realized who it was. Aw, crap, I thought as I spotted Jackie, wearing an evil grin as she held onto the ball.

I groaned inwardly and gulped, my throat feeling a bit too tight. It was now my turn. I started to run and luckily turned my head in the nick of time to snatch the ball out of midair that she had thrown without waiting for me to receive it.

"Cripes," I muttered under my breath as I accelerated madly, stumbling a bit. I barely caught it in time. The ball nearly slipped from my fingers. She continued to force me to work harder all the way down the court. It took an enormous amount of effort to keep up with her antics.

I was panting hard as we stood in line again, waiting for our turn. I didn't dare glance her way until it was time to do the drill again. This time I was prepared. As soon as she started to move, I bolted ahead and kept my eyes on her. It worked. I caught the ball and threw it right back at her as hard I could. She nearly tumbled, grasping it at the last second.

Ha! How do ya like that, eh? Now you know what it feels like to be at the receiving end of your pranks, I thought.

As we ran down the length of the court, I did it again and again. I focused all of my anger and frustration into the ball and threw it at her with all of my strength. She threw it back at me equally as hard, deliberately trying to make me miss it.

Coach Collins caught onto our antics, or so I thought. "Jessie! Over here, now!" He yelled at me furiously.

"Wha..." I blew my bangs out of my eyes as I strode toward him, suddenly feeling nervous.

His face was flushed a bright crimson red, filled with barely concealed anger. "Jessie..." he began as I stood in front of him, puffing and huffing from the exertion of the workout. "What did I say about being careful?"

"Excuse me? Jackie is the one who's being uncooperative!"

I glared at him, hands on my hips, until I realized what he was referring to—the bloody nose incident. He still held a grudge against me for that accident even though I had nothing to do with it. I could feel the heat of the rage rising into my chest as this thought dawned on me. He didn't trust me.

"Wait a minute. Are you talking about when Donna got hit in the face last month? Just to let you know, I was standing beside Donna when it happened. It was Jackie who hit her!" As I spoke, I curled my hands into fists, feeling extremely incensed.

He jerked his head backward as if I slapped him, his eyes flicked past my shoulders toward the players behind me. He sighed loudly, clearly exasperated and walked over to Jackie who was standing by the wall, looking as innocent as possible. As he talked to her, her eyes grew huge. She pouted, twirled her hair and, I swear to God, made her lower lip tremble as if holding back sobs.

I stared at them in shock, completely slack-jawed. "Holy crap, he's totally falling for it!" I slapped the palm of my hand into my forehead, and I shook my head in disbelief, totally dumbstruck by her actions. My hand slid down to cover my mouth as I watched, trying not to gag. His features softened and he even sent a sympathetic smile her way.

I sent dark thoughts in their direction, hoping that he would choke on that stupid whistle. As he turned around, she curled the corner of her lip into an ugly sneer at me from behind his back. He walked right past me, rubbing his fingers on his forehead. His face went back into a dour scowl once again. Not one word of an apology to me.

Wow, that's cold, I thought as I rejoined the group. We continued the practice for another twenty minutes. Coach Collins finally declared it over, and I raced to the changing room, tossing off my damp gym clothes as quickly as I could. Keeping my head down, I dashed out, giving Donna, Amber, and Jackie a wide berth, and stalked back to my locker to pick up my jacket and the rest of my books.

I was glad to be home after such as disastrous basketball practice, relieved to get it over with. Every time I closed my eyes, I kept seeing that sickening vision of Jackie being so coy with Coach Collins. It was simply too much. I didn't how she got away with that kind of disgusting behavior at school. It was appalling.

I sat down at my desk in my bedroom, turned on the lamp in front of me, and thumped down several heavy textbooks—my load of homework for tonight. "Sadistic teachers," I mumbled sullenly.

Parker jerked his head up, startled by the loud thump.

"Oh, I'm sorry, munchkin!"

He chirruped at me as if to say, "That's okay," and settled his chin back onto his paws as he slumbered on top of the bench beneath the window.

I flipped through my notes, grabbed the book I needed, and scanned the text, jotting down the answers, with my head bent forward, focusing on gathering my thoughts.

"So! This is what your room looks like!" A husky voice filled the room behind me.

"Gah!" All of my muscles went into an involuntary spasm, causing me to twitch out of my chair so hard that my pen flew out of my hand and clattered to the floor. I was so intent on my studies that I hadn't even noticed there was someone else in the room until it was too late. I turned around to see Ethan standing in the doorway with his hands in his pockets, grinning.

I put my hand on my chest in shock. I could feel my heart thumping wildly. "Omigod, Ethan! You scared the crap out of me!" I furrowed my eyebrows at him quizzically. "Um, not to be rude, but what are you doing here?"

He bent down and picked up the pen that had rolled to a stop at his feet. Striding over, he handed it to me, looking like the cat that swallowed the canary.

He put his hand over his heart. "What? You don't like me anymore? I'm hurt." He pretended to be sullen and sat on the bench next to Parker, stroking his fur. "I just stopped by and wanted to ask you if you would like to come watch me fence tonight?"

He looked great, sitting on the bench wearing expensive looking jeans that were casually and artfully ripped in various spots, a long sleeved black pullover which revealed a white thermal waffle weave shirt underneath. I had to suppress a happy sigh as I stared at him, otherwise I would've sounded ridiculously smitten.

He gestured with his hands toward my desk and raised his eyebrows. "But, if you're too busy..."

"Hey! Come on, don't pin this on me!" I reached out and slapped his leg playfully. "Seriously? Yes, of course I would love to come!"

His grin spread into a broad smile as he reached out and pulled me up into his arms, giving me a generous hug.

"When do we leave?" I mumbled into his warm chest.

"Oh, how about right now?"

I looked up into his eyes. "Sure!"

He bent down and gave me a lingering kiss. "And, um, what about your homework?"

I glanced at the towering pile of books, my thoughts elsewhere. "Who cares? I'll work on it later." I grabbed his hand and began to tug him toward the door. "Oh, wait! Should I get changed into something else?" I fingered my clothes, feeling a bit plain standing next to him.

His eyes merrily twinkled. "No, I like what you've got on, it's very country girl chic."

"Uh-huh, country girl chic. Now there's a fashion phrase you don't hear every day."

We marched downstairs, hand-in-hand. "Mom! I'll be going with Ethan to fencing tonight!" I yelled in the direction of the kitchen as we went out the door.

"Okay, have fun!" Her cheerful reply came back somewhat muffled as we stepped outside and into his car. Somehow, I got the distinct impression that he had already told Mom about his plans for tonight.

Ethan had told me before that his private school vaguely resembled Hogwarts from the infamous *Harry Potter* books. He wasn't kidding, I thought, as he pulled into the driveway after a twenty minute drive. The school grounds were enormous, surrounded by a vast and well-manicured lawn, protected from prying eyes with a wall of stately and ancient trees. The school itself loomed over us, seemingly old and archaic, standing several stories high. The walls were covered in a thick layer of English Ivy leaves that climbed nearly all the way to the top.

I stared up as we stepped out of the car. "Holy smokes, it does look like Hogwarts."

"Heh! It feels like it, too, right down to a teacher that reminds me of Professor Snape," he said as he pulled his bag out of the trunk of the car.

He reached out and grabbed my hand, intertwining his warm fingers around mine. We strolled up the pathway leading to the majestic doors, and I continued to stare at the building, awed by its size and impressive architecture. "You know, it's funny, it reminds me of a university."

Ethan nodded. "Yes, I can see that too, it has that sense of being timeless."

I touched my jacket, suddenly feeling seriously underdressed and very insecure. This place felt noble and aristocratic. I felt out of place and even out of time, as if I was in the wrong era.

Ethan led me through the hallways and into the gymnasium. It was gigantic. The rafters were filled with championship flags in all sorts of shapes and sizes. I stared at them, marveling at the extensive history that was displayed all around me.

The benches were made out of traditional wood, worn down after years of use. "You can wait here while I go change, okay?" he said and winked at me.

"Um, sure." Momentarily distracted, I stared at the people standing in the middle of the gym. They wore white shoes, strange white pants that stopped just below the knees, and a long sleeved white top that a reminded me of a *strait-jacket*. They were doing stretches and talking to each other, laughing occasionally. Off to the side, sitting on the floor, were gloves, metal helmets, and long, thin bladed weapons.

After a few minutes, Ethan came back in carrying his equipment. He was covered in white garb from head to toe. "Ooh, don't you look snazzy!" I said as he stood beside me.

"Heh, cute, Jessie." He jerked his head in the direction of his teammates. "We usually do a warm-up, some drills, and then a sparring session." He raised his hand and waved at them. "You can sit here and watch."

"Cool," I said as he leaned for a quick peck then spun around to join his group.

Several more guys walked into the gym and joined the original group in the middle, exchanging greetings and witty remarks.

I had to bite back some bubbling laughter as I realized what they reminded me of. Their white outfits gave me a visual image of the Storm Troopers from Star Wars.

A couple strode onto the floor, carrying large bags of equipment. They walked side by side, a slim young woman in her twenties, wearing her strawberry-blond hair in a slick ponytail and a tall gentleman with slightly wavy blond hair.

She greeted them and plunked down her bag. "Hey, guys! How are you doing tonight?"

The group returned her greeting in a chorus. "Hi, Becky! Hey, Matthew!"

I was caught off guard since I wasn't expecting to see a female instructor for these guys. I had this vague expectation of a James Bond type of instructor, with a bit of a mysterious air about him. That told me something—I watched way too many movies.

"All right, guys, are you ready for tonight's class? Go ahead and start jogging around to get warmed up," Becky said as she did up her shoelaces. I sighed, relived that she didn't use a whistle.

They all began running around the gym, interspersed with push-ups, sit-ups, and sprints. Afterward, they lined up on the far side of the court, standing on the red line.

"*En garde!*"

Matthew yelled out this command while Becky walked from one end of the line to other, scrutinizing their postures.

Upon hearing his voice, the boys immediately bent their knees, lowered their center of gravity, and pulled back their shoulders. All of them had their leading foot touching the red line, their back foot pointing outward at a right angle.

"Arms in your *en garde* positions!" He barked out this next command, loud and clear, and watched them change their positions. With military precision, they snapped up their leading hand, as if holding an imaginary sword in front of them.

"Excellent posture, guys! Remember to keep your eyes upfront as we do this drill," Matthew said.

Becky joined him, facing the line to monitor their positions. She started to move backward in a straight line. "Follow me using forward steps." With every step she took, they mirrored her movements. They only moved when she moved, much like puppets on a string. Whenever she picked up the pace, they took quick strides in response.

"Lunge!" She threw out a new command, clearly trying to catch them off guard, and kept a sharp eye on their stances. They immediately took a huge step forward with their leading foot while their back foot stayed glued in one spot. As they advanced, they slapped down their back arm, propelling themselves forward, and thrust out their leading arm, straight as an arrow, at an imaginary target.

Matthew walked around them, checking out their poses. "Good! Nice and strong, guys. And recover forward please." In response to his command, they brought their legs closer together and pulled their sword arms back to their bodies, their elbow nearly touching their rib cages.

I saw Ethan breathe out a sigh of relief as he adjusted his feet. I was guessing that it was strenuous maintaining this particular pose. Sweat was beading on his forehead and his face was slightly flushed.

"And let's continue moving," Becky said as she took a couple of slow steps backward. They followed in unison. Ethan moved gracefully across the floor. His legs looked strong and powerful. He was a natural at this, like a duck in water.

Becky quickly changed course, moving toward them instead. They responded by taking small and quick steps backward while still holding their fighting arms in the ready position. She switched positions again, testing their speed and agility. Matthew followed along aside her, the two of them keeping a keen eye on the students

"Step Lunge!" she yelled as they pounced forward, one quick step then a strong lunge in her direction, seemingly trying to poke a hole in the air with the thrusts of their arms.

They continued this exercise, back and forth along the length of the gym, going faster and slower, backward and forward while she threw the occasional surprise at them.

"*Fleche!*" The word sounded foreign to me but it held a distinctive air of power. All of them suddenly leapt across the floor, pushing off their legs and were propelled forward a long distance.

"Good job guys! I know that's not an easy one to do but it can be useful to catch your opponent off guard," Matthew said as he looked at them, nodding in approval. "Go get a drink and put on the rest of your gear."

The group broke apart, bending over and grabbing their water bottles from their bags. Ethan strolled over to me. Smiling, he picked up his drink and gave it a squeeze. He took several gulps before he knelt down in front of me, placing his hands on top of my legs. "So? What do you think so far?" he asked, looking a bit sultry.

"It looks like hard work. Doesn't it hurt your legs to hold that pose?"

He thought about it then said, "Um, sort of. My legs do feel the tension which is a good sign that I am doing it correctly. If I ease up too much, I'll be off balance. It reminds me that I'm in a stable position."

"Do you know what's interesting about that stance? I kept thinking that it's similar to the one we do at the dojo, it's like one of our moves. It's so familiar."

His eyes lit up as he responded, "Yes! It's a great match. Karate and fencing complement each other. That's why it feels so right."

His grin broadened and he eyes twinkled as he spoke, clearly enjoying this moment. "Oh hey, would you like me to show you some moves after class?"

I nodded, intrigued to try it out.

He picked up his glove, slipped it on his right hand, snatched up his mask, and pushed it onto his face, then did up the Velcro straps at the back. I could barely see his eyes through the tiny metal grid work. I didn't know how he could possibly see his opponents.

"Ethan, how can you see anything through that mask?"

"Ah, you get used to it," he said as he adjusted it. "It's very much like a hockey mask. You learn to see beyond it."

He pivoted around to walk back to his group, casually carrying his weapon in front.

"Okay, guys, partner up! We are going to work on your Parry Ripostes!" yelled out Matthew, beckoning them closer to him with a wave of his hand.

They paired up and faced each other, listening to him patiently.

"I've noticed that some of you are having trouble blocking the overhead strikes. It takes time to develop those reflexes for that particular action. Therefore we will focus on that tonight. You will strike the top of your partner's head and bring it immediately back to protect your head as your partner repeats the same motion."

Becky and Matthew split up and wandered around them, observing their movements and correcting them when necessary.

I watched Ethan intently as he practiced his strikes and blocks, carefully and efficiently. I could hear the sound of a metallic ping when he came in contact with his partner's mask. It was almost comical, looking like Larry, Moe, and Curly as they hit each other.

After several minutes of practicing the maneuver, Becky stopped the group. "Good! That's much better! Now, we will work on your Banderoles." I saw Ethan pump his fist in a hurrah motion, evidently pleased to have the chance to practice this particular move. I'll admit that I was curious to see what kind of technique it was.

Becky continued with her instructions. "You do a feint toward your partner's head, and then follow up with a Banderole strike across their chest. Remember to roll the wrist for a smoother motion." She mimicked the rolling gesture with her hand to demonstrate.

Everyone faced their partners again in the ready position. Ethan delivered a quick fake head strike then did an

elegant slashing motion along his partner's chest. My heart
picked up the pace as I watched them perform these
strikes. I thought it was a totally cool move. I had a mental
image of Johnny Depp as a swashbuckling pirate, slicing
and dicing the bad guys on his ship.

"Nice one Ethan!" Becky called out as she and Matthew
roamed around the gym, watching the students' motions.
Ethan nodded in response and continued with his strikes.

"And break! Okay, take your places on the floor with
your partner. While you guys are sparring, I want you to
think about what you've worked on tonight and incorporate
it into this session. Ready? *Allez!*" yelled out Matthew while
he strolled around them.

They split up and spread out across the gym floor.
Ethan faced his sparring partner, stood upright, pulled his
weapon straight up to his face then sharply yanked it
downward off to his right side. I perked up as I realized
that it was a lot like how we bow to our opponents before
we spar in karate, *That is so cool!* I thought.

They switched to the *en garde* position, squaring off with
each other, waiting for someone to move first. Ethan took
the first prompt, moved several paces and delivered a su-
per-fast slash to his partner's leading arm. It appeared to
have counted as a point since they took several steps back
to their starting positions and faced off again. His partner
lunged at him, trying to take a swipe at his chest. Ethan
swiftly knocked it aside and rapidly followed up with a
strike to his head. The tempo of the match was fast and
furious, electrifying to watch.

Both of them moved apart and squared off again, back
into their *en garde* stance, ready to go again. They moved
back and forth, taking hard swipes at each other, striking
the arm, head or chest in an attempt to gain a point. The
sound of clanging metal filled the air. It was an exhilarating
experience and I loved every minute of it.

They swapped partners and continued the matches, going at each other with tenacity, strength and dazzling speed. At the end of the session, Ethan faced his last sparring partner, took off his helmet, tucked it under his arm and shook hands, smiling and said, "Well done, mate."

Ethan walked over to his instructors and exchanged a few words then looked in my direction and strode over to me.

"Jessie, this is Rebecca and Matthew," Ethan said as he gestured in their direction with his hand. "Both of them have been on the National Fencing Team, and between them, they have over 20 years of experience!"

"Wow! It's great to meet you both." I reached out and shook their hands, honored to meet such high-ranking competitors.

Rebecca smiled at me. "So, what did you think?"

My smile grew broader. "I loved it! It was awesome! It's so exciting to watch!"

"Ha! That's great, Jessie!" She looked at Ethan. "You know what? We may have a future competitor here," she said as she flicked her eyes in my direction and nodded her head.

Matthew chimed in, "Ooh, yes, we could potentially have some fresh blood here."

"Heh, yes, literally," replied Rebecca.

"That wouldn't surprise me one bit," Ethan said, grinning.

"I'm going to go put this stuff away. Nice to meet you, Jessie!" Rebecca said as she and Matthew started to walk away.

"Thanks! You, too!" I called back.

Ethan stood in front of me, his face red with exertion, sweat beading all over. He looked exhausted but pleased with his performance. "Wanna try it out?"

"Um, sure." I gulped as I said this, wondering what I was getting myself into.

"Here, try holding onto the sabre to see how it feels."
He placed it my hands, the grip was warm and spongy, covered in a neoprene material. The metal guard sat like an upside down tea cup, covering my hand, the metal surface was crisscrossed with nicks as if it had seen a lot of battles. The blade was nearly as long my leg, and about as thick as my finger, cut in an angular fashion like a triangle with a groove down the center. It was much lighter than I anticipated, considering how long it was. It felt very strange to hold it and I wondered what it felt like to use it and strike out at an opponent.

"This is amazing," I said in awe as I held it, swishing it through the air gently, gauging its feel.

"Here, I'll show you how to stand. It's called the ready position or *en garde*. You know how we do the three point stance in karate? It's a lot like that." He moved around me, shifting my body into the right position with his hands on my shoulders and tapping my foot with his toe. "Take a step back with your left leg, turn on the ball of your foot and pivot it outward. Really bend your knees and lower your weight."

"Oh holy—I can feel my legs burning already," I muttered as I tried the stance.

"Place your left hand at the back of your hip, keeping it out of the way so it doesn't get hit by an errant strike. Tuck the elbow of your right arm close to your ribs." Ethan said as gently moved my arm into the right spot.

"Now, hold your sabre upright, almost like a knight. Fabulous. And now..." he said, wearing a mischievous smile, "...move forward."

"Uh? What? I'm not even sure I can move!"

"Take a step forward with your right leg. As soon as that foot moves, let the back leg follow."

I tried it out, moving gingerly, taking the first step, then another. It was harder than it looked as I concentrated on the steps without falling over or looking like an absolute klutz. "Whoo! This is hard work! Is my leg on fire? It sure feels like it."

"Now try moving backward." said Ethan as he watched me, amusement etched all over his handsome face.

I let out a wheezy laugh in response to his request. "Okay, here goes." I nearly stumbled in the process, trying to get my feet to move in quick succession the way he did it earlier tonight.

"While we are at it, wanna try on the helmet? It's likely to be too big but at least this way you get to see what I see."

"Sure," I said, feeling my legs tremble from the exertion of holding the pose.

He slipped it on under my chin, and then slid it over my forehead, tightening the straps at the back. It was a bit wet from him wearing it and as he suspected, a bit loose. It was an odd sight to behold. All across my field of vision was a mesh of tiny lines, very much like looking through a screen on a window. It felt dark and slightly claustrophobic.

"How can you possibly see anything in this?"

He moved into my line of vision. "You'll see, follow me as I go backward."

I focused on him, trying to keep up with his movements. He was right, the dark mesh gradually faded into a light gray background as I looked past it and locked onto Ethan. "Oh yeah. I see what you mean. You get used to it and simply see the person in front. It's kinda like mind over matter."

"Neat eh?" he said as he nodded at me.

"Yeah, thanks for letting me try it out and for inviting me over tonight," I said as I took off the mask and gave it back to him.

My eyebrows creased in thought as I pointed at his weapon. "I thought these were called a foil."

"Ah. Good point. Heh, get it?" he said as he waited for me to get the joke, referring to the tip of the sabre.

I sighed and tilted my head sideways in exasperation, raising my eyebrows at him, prompting him to answer my question.

He conceded. "This is one of three weapons that we use: foil, sabre and epee. The foil is more common and widely used. The sabre is gaining popularity, especially among the female competitors."

"Really? Why?" I asked curiously.

"They wouldn't allow sabres to be used in tournaments for the women's division until a few years ago."

I balked at that, spluttering, feeling a bit incensed. "What is this? The dark ages?"

"Anyway," Ethan said, trying to steer me off topic, knowing full well that I could debate on that subject for days, hence driving him crazy. "With the foil, the target area is limited to the chest, toward the heart. It relies more on the thrusting motions and swift turns of the wrist for counter moves. It's more classical and precise and appears quite elegant."

"Do you use the foil?" I asked him, wondering why he used the sabre instead, although I had a sneaking suspicion that he liked the thrill of the pace.

"Occasionally, although all of us were trained to use the foil first before switching over to the sabre. It gave us a better idea of the physical differences between them, such as the mindset and reactions. It's like night and day."

He continued speaking, "The sabre has more target areas such as the arm, head and chest. It's much more direct in terms of strikes and the blocks are so similar to the ones we use in Karate such as the side to side motions. Plus, I like the speed of it, it suits my aggressive nature."

Aha, I thought so.

"Regarding the epee, I haven't met very many people using it, primarily because I focus so much on the sabre in competitions. We tend to stick with a certain group based on our choices in weapons."

"Wow. All I can say is wow. I loved what I saw tonight. You were impressive." I stepped up to him and gave him a soft kiss on the lips as a thank you.

"Well, I should go get changed and then we can go back home," he said as he reluctantly released me from his embrace.

CHAPTER 7

Veil

As I stepped out of Mom's car, I was assaulted by a blast of frigid air and icy crystals. They whirled around me and stung my eyes as I walked across the parking lot toward the dojo.

The warm glow filtered through the windows, casting a cheerful square of light onto the soft blue snow in the waning light.

As my fingers gripped the handle of the door and swung it opened, I turned briefly and waved at Mom. She drove away. I was supposed to help Ethan tonight with the kids to help them get ready for their grading. Several of the younger ones were going to be tested for their yellow belts and he wanted them to have an opportunity to test out their kicks on the shield, namely making me fun target practice for them. I could already see them eagerly delivering a high pitch shout of triumph as they hit me with all their might.

I walked past the main desk and strode into the changing room. I tugged on my white pants, t-shirt and white top and wrapped my green belt snuggly around my waist. There were three stripes on the end of my belt—a mark of progress and an indication that I was ready to step up to the next level, the blue belt. Within minutes, I was standing outside the classroom beside the doorway, stretching out my arms and legs, trying to loosen up my muscles, tight from sitting at my desk at school all day.

I took a step toward the edge of the door, stood, and bowed at the waist, slapping my arms on the outside of my legs—a sign of respect and courtesy before entering the room. I did it sharply, acutely aware of how the young students picked up on it. I knew they looked up to me. I tried to watch my language around them and was often forced to dumb down some words since they didn't understand yet. But, for some strange reason, they understood the meaning of sarcasm and could always tell when I was being silly.

I was greeted by a chorus of greetings from the little ones, all in the range of six, seven, and eight. They were as cute as pixies and loved learning something new every time they came here.

"Yay! Jessie's here!" said one kid.

"Hi Jessie!" said another as they surrounded me.

Some waved at me. Others smiled broadly. Two of them came running at me and wrapped their little arms around my waist, gripping me tightly in a bear hug, squealing in delight.

I feigned gasping, wheezing as if I was out of breath. "Ugh! Geez, can you squeeze me any tighter? I can't breathe!" I tried shuffling my feet across the floor with two kids latched on to me. It turned out to be an impossible feat. "Great. I don't think I can move. You guys are heavy!" I squeaked out the word "Help" breathlessly, pretending to look around the room in vain, not finding my dashing hero to rescue me. "Where's Sensei Ethan? Maybe he could rescue me."

They promptly let go, tugging at my uniform, prompting me to bend down and look at them, eye to eye.

"He's not here!" one little girl with big blue eyes, who wore her blond hair in two ponytails, said. She pouted and crossed her arms like a spoiled brat. "Hmph!"

"What do you mean he's not here?" I asked her as I tugged on her adorable ponytail. "He was going to help you get ready for your yellow belt test."

I looked up, panic surging through me. Did I make a mistake? Was this the wrong night? He was nowhere to be found as my eyes scanned the dojo.

"He had to go away. We're stuck with Sensei Jake." A skinny girl, with brown eyes and long brown hair braided at the back, interjected, pointing her chin at Sensei Jake who was going through the attendance cards by the wall. She pouted miserably. "I don't like him...he's mean."

I'll admit that he did look imposing, especially with his spiky, raven black hair sticking straight up like miniature mountains. He was incredibly fit, and I got the impression that he worked out on weights to bulk up. The sleeves on his uniform were covered with all sorts of badges, a sign of his immeasurable talents. I'd never liked him and tended to feel nervous around him. I hadn't been able to pinpoint why I didn't trust him. It was more of a gut feeling. Even though he was generally polite, he could be rather terse at times, as if he had a short fuse. There was that and the way he looked at me, he could be creepy at times.

"Oh, hush. It won't that bad." I hope, I thought. "I'm here, aren't I?"

They beamed and bobbed their heads at me. "Okay? I'll be with you in a minute. I'm going to talk to him for a sec."

I had to literally pry their fingers off my hand as they continued to grip it tightly, not wanting to let go. I finally made my way across the floor, feeling the cool tiles beneath my toes, and stood beside Sensei Jake.

He looked up from perusing a list of drills in a binder, notes for the instructors for each class.

"Um, I have a question for you," I said, feeling somewhat intimidated by his presence.

"Sure, anything for you, darling," he said and threw a sly smile my way.

It made the hair on the back of my neck stand up. I sighed inwardly, desperately holding back a tart reply to his derogatory use of "darling." The way he said it unnerved me.

"The kids just told me that Sensei Ethan is not here tonight. Is that right?"

"Yep." He drawled out that word.

I gestured with my hands for him to elaborate. "And?"

He sighed and shrugged his shoulders. "They were asked to help out at a tournament in the US for several days since they needed more judges and referees."

"Oh! I didn't know that. Well, that's great news for them."

"Yeah, I guess so." He sighed dismally, looking as though he wished that he was with them. His eyes held a faraway look. I couldn't help but wonder if he felt hurt or left out. He blinked, looked at the clock on the wall, and clapped his hands together. "Well! It looks like it's time to start the class, eh?" He glanced at the kids, watching them as they sat on the floor doing their own stretches or kicking the air at an imaginary opponent.

Both of us walked over to the front near the floor to ceiling mirrors. He called out to them, "*Keske!*"

They all jumped up and ran up to him, forming a line. Students wearing white belts stood at one end of the line which progressed to higher levels of colors, looking more like a rainbow, featuring yellow, orange, green, blue, red, and brown belts at the far end.

They stood still as they faced him, with their feet apart and hands out in front, ready to bow. I stood at the back with another assistant who wore a brown belt. The two of us lined up in the same fashion, from lowest belt to highest.

Sensei Jake barked out, "*Keske! Rei!*"

Everyone suddenly snapped their feet together, slapped their arms quickly to their sides, and bowed to him. He spoke in a loud commanding voice. "Now, how many of you are getting graded this month? Raise your hands."

At least seven of the fifteen students jerked their arms straight up in the air. "Great!" he said as he nodded his head at them, mentally grouping them according to their belt rank. "I want you to think about what you need to work on tonight, and we will help you with it, okay?"

They nodded back at him, looking a wee bit nervous. He pointed his arm out to the right side. "Everyone start running that way!"

We did the usual drills, running side to side, backward, push-ups and sit-ups. Then we moved on to the laborious stretching which included trying to do the splits. While I was on the floor, stretching alongside with them, Sensei Jake tapped me on one shoulder and beckoned me with his finger to approach him. I stood up and followed him over to one side of the room, away from the group. He put his hand on my shoulder which made me uncomfortable. I had to work hard to not twitch it off.

"Jessie? Could you do me a huge favor and the take the white and yellow belts and work on their kicks and blocks?"

"Sure. I like working with them."

"Good, because I sure don't. They drive me crazy."

I sucked in a quiet gasp, realizing his true nature. He thought that they were beneath him, not worthy of his attention.

He slapped me brusquely on the back and practically shoved me in their direction. Then he clapped his hands together loudly and said to the class, "Okay, is everyone all warmed up?" He looked down at them as he spoke. They nodded in response. "Yeah? All right, everyone stand up, and I will organize you into groups." He gestured with his hands for them to rise. "White and yellow belts will go with Jessie. Orange and green belts will go with Logan." He pointed at the other assistant who nodded in response. "Blue, red and brown belts will work with me. Off you go."

As he finished speaking, the white and yellow belts practically ran over to me, jumping up and down gleefully.

"Yay! I get to work with you guys!" I knelt down to see them eye to eye. "We will need two items, a foam blocker and a kicking shield. Who wants to get them?"

As I'd predicted, they all promptly put their hands up. I picked the little girl with adorable freckles on her nose and pig tails to get the blocker and chose the sturdy boy with a yellow belt to get the shield. They dashed off to the wall full of various pieces of equipment.

"Aw nuts!" said one despondent kid with dark spiky hair. He looked like a mini duplicate of Sensei Jake which I suspected was intentional. That thought scared me. I really didn't think the world needed more Sensei Jakes.

"Oh, don't worry, you may get chosen next time." He perked up slightly when I said that although his features were still set in a scowl.

Both students came scampering back, happy to help out. I nearly laughed out loud as I watched the tiny girl carry the giant foam blocker. It was nearly as tall as she was. She had a little bit of trouble bringing it to me, but she was absolutely determined to do it by herself.

"Thanks guys! That's awesome! You can put them on the floor beside me." They plunked down the equipment and rejoined the group. "So what kind of kicks do you need to work on?" I asked them.

One boy raised his hand and quipped, "Side kicks."

Another said, "Roundhouse."

"Aha!" I gestured at him, nodding. "That's a toughie. Let's focus on that one, okay?" I rested my elbow on my knee. "And what about blocks?"

The girl with her long hair tucked into a braid raised her hand and said cheerily, "Low block!"

A perky girl with curly blond locks piped in, "High blocks!"

"Ooh, so many choices! Tell you what, everyone gather around me in a giant circle and go into a horse stance."

They immediately surrounded me, eager to practice their techniques.

"We will do some low blocks and then switch to a high block. Here we go!" I said and stood inside the circle, watching them.

"Start with your right arm." They briskly moved their right arm into their chest, fist near their chin, while the other arm shot downward to protect the groin. "That would be the other right arm, Trevor." He giggled as he switched hands. I rolled my eyes skyward. "On my count, switch arms. *Ichi*!" I barked out the first number as they swiftly slid their right arm downward and pulled the left hand backward to sit on their hips, ready to do a follow up punch.

After a few minutes of doing low blocks, I had them switch to high blocks. They moved their arms up at a right angle to their heads, just above their foreheads.

"This time, I'm going to test you to see how strong your blocks are. Don't let me hit your head!" I grinned as I said this, knowing that they loved it when I used the giant foam blocker. I picked it up from the floor, gripping the handle, carrying it like an Olympic torch. "Ready?" They all nodded, eager to do this drill. "I might surprise you!" I added.

I went around the circle, aiming the blocker at their heads, tapping them on the arm. Then I dashed off to the other side of the circle, trying to catch them off guard. They laughed and giggled as I tested their reflexes. Their eyes grew wide when they realized it was their turn.

"Wow! You guys are fast! And...shake it off, loosen your legs a bit," I said as I put the blocker back on the floor. I bent down and picked up the large blue foam kicking shield, gripping the straps on the sides, and held it against my hip. "This time, let's work on your front kicks as I go around the circle with the shield."

They all stood facing me in the circle, totally ready to kick the crap out of the shield. I was thankful that it was just the little kids and not the older group. I lunged at them with the shield, trying to get a quick reaction out of them. Their first response was important, a sign of how well they reacted when suddenly surprised. I moved back and forth within the circle, darting from one kid to another, randomly. They threw their weight into it, delivering a loud, "*Hiyah!*" in the process, determined to put a dent in the shield.

"*Keske!*" Sensei Jake's yell echoed loudly in the dojo. "Bow to your to your instructors and line up!"

My small group promptly snapped their feet together, bowed to me, and dashed to the front of the class, facing the mirrors. Sensei Jake strolled over to them as I picked up the pieces of equipment and carried them back to their respective spots. He stood in front of the students and clapped his hands together. "Was everyone happy with this opportunity to work on their skills?" They bobbed their heads in response. "Good! Keep practicing them at home! *Keske! Rei!*" he yelled. Everyone did a snappy bow to him. "And dismissed!"

They all ran out of the dojo, bowing out at the door before going to their changing rooms.

"So, Jessie...I hear that you will be getting graded for your blue belt soon, eh?" he said as he ambled in my direction. I nodded and walked over to the wall that featured see-through containers, all filled with cards the same colors as the belts. I rifled through the light green attendance cards, found mine, and plucked it out of the box. I looked at the list, running my finger down the names of the required techniques for the next level. Nearly all of them were checked off, except for sparring which was delayed as a result of my concussion.

Sensei Jake snatched the list out of my hand. He scanned the list and flicked his finger at it, wearing a smug smile. "Oh ho, it looks like you're not quite ready yet. We are going to have to do some sparring tonight."

I gulped, not sure what to think about this. I was nervous about getting back into a sparring session and would've preferred to have practiced with Ethan. "Um, sure, I guess..."

"Looking forward to it!" he said and gave me back my list. The adult students filtered in, picking up their cards. They strode over to the front, ready to line up.

I quickly bowed out and went to the changing room to grab my sparring gear. I bowed back in and placed it at the back of the wall along with several other students' equipment.

"*Keske!*"

Everyone in the room scooted close to the mirrors, facing Sensei Jake. Even though this was technically the adult class, many of them were the same age as me. There were four older students, pretty much the same age as my parents. It was a fairly small group tonight with no more than twelve of us present.

"*Keske! Rei!*" Sensei Jake yelled out the next command, prompting us to bow at him crisply.

"As most of you already know, we will be grading some of you soon for your next belt. Tonight's class will focus on that aspect, getting you ready for it." His eyes roamed across their faces as he spoke. His gaze locked on mine, making me feel uncomfortable. "All right folks, start running in that direction," he said as he gestured toward the right.

We went through the same warm-up and stretching drills that we had done earlier, only with a bit more oomph to it, namely a lot more sit-ups and push-ups, including grueling leg stretches with our partners. Then we spread out on the floor, facing the mirrors as Sensei Jake barked out the numbers while we worked on our strikes, blocks, and kicks in unison. Afterward, we split up and worked on our katas, going through the motions, making it seem as if we were fighting an imaginary opponent. I stumbled at one point, missing a step, and had to start over again, my frustration mounting.

I spotted Sensei Jake watching me when I began the kata. He sent a sly grin my way. Embarrassed that he saw me fumble, my face grew warm as I turned red. He marched over and stood in front of me, watching every move I made. Suddenly, I felt nervous and my legs felt a little wobbly. I concentrated on my steps as I went through the routine, throwing a kick here, a punch there. I bowed at the end and stood facing him, waiting to hear his critique.

"You certainly know the moves which is great. However..." My heart sank upon that dreadful word. "You need to be much more precise with your strikes, especially your kicks. Really snap them out, make them look more deliberate. You need to show me that you are hitting an opponent. This is what the judges look for at a tournament. They have no idea what your Kata is supposed to look like. They want you to prove to them that you are aware of your opponents and are defending yourself. They want to feel it. If it helps, add a 'Kiai' at the end for a final emphasis."

I nodded, trying to absorb his comments without feeling hurt. It wasn't necessarily what he said, it was the way he said it. He was cold and indifferent toward me. He was thinking like a judge, very critical and nit picking, taking every little thing apart and scrutinizing it to death.

"I want you to continue working on it for a few more minutes, and then we will move onto sparring okay?" he said as he started to move on to the next student.

After practicing the moves for the umpteenth time, I was growing weary and losing my focus as I grew more frustrated. I couldn't wait for this class to be over. It was a very different atmosphere without Ethan. It felt more military than anything else, cold and technical.

"Everyone grab your sparring gear and a seat on the floor once you are ready." Sensei Jake gestured toward the middle of the room as he spoke.

I grabbed my bag, pulled on my shin pads and padded foot gear, put the mouth guard over my teeth, and slipped the gloves onto my hands. I turned down my hearing aids a notch, otherwise they would've squealed under my helmet.

I was about to sit down when Sensei Jake called out my name and motioned for me to stand in front of him. He called out another student, a lady about the same age as Mom, wearing an orange belt. She had long red hair tied up in a ponytail and her face was adorned with freckles. As we faced other, it was at that moment that I had a flashback to the tournament where I lost my memory. She looked so similar to the opponent who had kicked me in the head so hard. I froze, suddenly feeling very afraid. I gulped loudly and my hands shook. I wanted to back away and run out of the room.

"Ladies, bow to me," said Sensei Jake as he gestured with his hands toward himself and then at us. We bowed to him, then to each other. She took a step back, raised her fists, eager to begin.

I held my position, willing myself to take the same stance, having a mental argument with my body to cooperate. I could feel myself starting to panic.

"Jessie. Jessie?" He was snapping his fingers at me impatiently. "Come on! Let's go!"

Upon hearing his words, I obediently stepped back into a fighting stance, acutely aware the whole class was watching me.

Sensei Jake held his hand between us, a signal to wait until he gave us the command to start. "*Hajime!*" He said as he quickly pulled his hand away.

My partner lunged at me with a roundhouse kick, the same kick from the tournament. I slapped it away in a sloppy manner, feeling terrified. She threw another kick at me. I stepped apprehensively out of the way, not putting much effort into it. I basically danced around her, keeping a wary eye on her body language.

"Oh come on, Jessie, I've seen you do a better job than that!" said Sensei Jake in a scolding tone.

Feeling a surge of anger from his remark, I threw a side-kick and followed up with a back fist strike. I kept going, sending another kick at her with my opposite leg, sent a punch toward her ribs, adding a loud *kiai* for good measure. She backed away, disappointed that I was able to deflect her moves. We continued to exchange a variety of punches and kicks, deftly avoiding them as we danced around each other.

"And...break! Have a seat, ladies." He pointed at two students that sat nearby. "Okay, next group, up and at 'em!"

After several matches, Sensei Jake looked up at the clock on the wall and stopped the sparring session. "Sorry folks! Time's up! Take off your helmets but leave the rest of your gear on and we will bow out," he said as he started to move toward the front of the class.

I removed my helmet and mouth guard and stood in line facing him.

"*Keske! Rei!*"

We quickly bowed out and I was just bending down to remove my gloves and foot gear when Sensei Jake stood beside me.

"Jessie, I would like to work on your sparring. Your timing seems a little bit off."

"Ah, that's because I took several weeks off from any physical activity. Sorry about that."

He winked at me as he proceeded to pick up his bag. "Well then, you've got some catching up to do! Put your gloves and helmet back on while I suit up."

I felt uneasy and trapped but didn't want to cause a scene. I couldn't help but wonder if he would be acting this way if Ethan had been here. I stood up and adjusted the straps on my helmet and clamped down on my mouth guard. He walked back over to me, tapping the ends of his gloves together, clearly ready for a fight. I looked at him, feeling apprehensive but determined to prove that I could stand up to him.

"Ready?" he said as his eyes slowly slithered down the length of my body as if he was mentally undressing me.

Ugh. I had to suppress a shiver from his disgusting body language. I just wanted to take a shower to wash off his slimy advances. He seemed to exude an underlying, greasy layer of darkness. I blew out a breath and stepped near him and bowed.

"Wait," he said as he reached over and tapped his glove against mine, much in the way a boxer would. *How macho*, I thought. I did a mental eye roll and reminded myself to wash off that glove afterward.

He began to jab punches in the air near me, an obvious attempt to disarm me. I took a skip backward to avoid his punches, waiting for an opening. I aimed a kick at his midsection. He easily pushed it out of the way, a light effort for him.

He kept egging me on, trying to get a rise out of me. "Come on, go for it. I can take it."

I did a side kick with my right leg, then a back fist strike. I followed up with another punch with the opposite hand. He blocked all of them, dancing away with a smarmy smirk on his face. I was getting irritated and knew that he was just toying with me, taunting me with his "Me Tarzan, you Jane" attitude. I clamped my teeth down even tighter and narrowed my focused, trying to ground myself. Fine, if that's the way you want to play it, I thought.

He swiftly threw a roundhouse kick at my abdomen then pulled it back and aimed it at my head, nearly hitting me. I sucked in a gasp and tilted my head away from it, moving out of his range. We prowled around each like two lions ready to pounce at any given moment.

He pretended to look at his wrist as if checking his watch. "Any day now, Jessie."

I lunged at him, which was a mistake and exactly what he wanted. He did a sidestep then kicked me in the ribs. That left me stunned and slightly out of breath. I staggered backward. "Hey! Take it easy!"

He smirked at me. "That's life. Get used to it. No one's gonna pull their punches on the street are they? Don't be such a wimp!"

We squared off again, exchanging kicks and punches. He increased the tempo and strength of the strikes, deliberately trying to bruise and weaken me. He kept hitting my arms which began to throb painfully. He stared at me ruthlessly, circling around me like a hungry shark. I wanted to prove to him that I was not some sort of wilted flower that would have a panic attack over a broken fingernail.

As he prowled around me, he kept mocking me, trying to undermine me. "Is that all you got?" His smarmy attitude was infuriating. "Don't you bat those baby blue eyes at me. That won't work on me. I know all about you, Jessie, how you play the helpless cripple, getting Ethan to fall for that old trick."

"*What*? Are you crazy? He loves me for who I am!"

"Right." He continued to lash out at me as we moved around. "Did you really think you were his type? I mean, come on, have you taken a look in the mirror lately?" He scoffed at me as he dashed forward, coming at me with a back fist strike, forcing me to stagger backward, momentarily caught off guard. He was trying to get under my skin and it was working. I was shaken by his crude remarks.

"You didn't seriously think that he loved you, did you?"

I bit down hard on my mouth guard to prevent myself from saying anything I might regret. It was painfully difficult to hold back my raging thoughts. I gathered all the anger and confusion and redirected it into my kicks and punches. I tried desperately not to let go of the smidgeon of control I had left. The last thing I wanted to do was walk right into his trap.

He pounded at me with his kicks, aiming them at the side of my legs, dangerously close to my knees. I tried in vain to block them with my shins but he still managed to get through. Then he switched tactics and aimed for my elbows, relentlessly. Frustrated, I resorted to slamming my elbow hard onto his foot as he tried to strike me in the arm.

"Oh! Son of a..." He limped slightly trying to shake it off. He sucked in a long breath, drew his beady eyes at mine, his gaze burning.

Crap. I thought. I brought my fists close to my body into the fighting position.

He brought up his left leg with another roundhouse kick, hard at my elbow.

Pain suddenly shot through my arm as he came in contact with the nerve on the funny bone. My arm hung uselessly by my side, throbbing with blinding pain. I'd had enough of this and decided to end it now.

"You know what I just realized? My ride will be here shortly and I really need to get changed." I took off my helmet, my arm screaming in pain. I bowed at him and picked up my bag on the way out, feeling intensely angry at him for taking advantage of me.

"Oh sure, that's just an excuse to get out of this," he said, his voice tinged with malice.

I sat down on the bench in the changing room, whimpering every time I moved my arm. When I stepped out and went through lobby, I could see him sparring with another assistant instructor, the two of them exchanging barbs at each other amidst a flurry of strikes, gleefully enjoying the adrenaline rush.

Mom was already in the parking lot. I groaned slightly as I slid into the seat and placed my bag on the floor, rubbing my elbow. She glanced my way, slightly concerned. "What's wrong, honey?"

"Nothing, just a tough sparring session. Guess I'm a bit out of shape," I said, trying to put her mind at ease.

She nodded as she drove. "Well, that's certainly understandable after taking a break."

I nodded as I looked out the window, watching the streetlights cast strange shadows in the car as we sped past them. The wipers went back forth on the windshield with an audible thunk that wore on my unsteady nerves with every swipe as it tried to remove the stubborn wet snowflakes. As I gazed out the window, the cityscape whisked by in a blur of colors. My mind was being tormented by a swirling storm of all of the awful words that had been thrown into my face tonight. I began to doubt myself, wondering if there was even an ounce of truth in them. I cradled my sore arm, wriggling my fingers to ease the numbness and tingling sensation.

I ran upstairs as soon as we got home, anxious to take a shower. I wanted to quell the storm of angry thoughts that were flying around in my mind. It wasn't until I stepped out of the steamy bathtub that I truly saw the extent of the damage from the blows that I'd absorbed. I gasped as I saw the angry purple splotches on my legs and the dark red marbling on my upper arms. The most shocking was how black the bruise on my elbow appeared—the most painful one of all. It was grotesquely swollen all around it, making my elbow look a bit deformed.

I slowly and carefully pulled on my pajamas and padded back to my room. I gratefully sat down on the bed, resting my elbow on a soft cushion, leaned back and closed my eyes.

CHAPTER 8

Reveal

I plunked down my stack of books on top of the long wooden table in art class, head bent down as I searched for the FM system in my pencil case. *Aha!* I thought as my fingers gripped the small blue box.

Striding over to Mr. Brown's desk, I placed it in front of him. He looked up as he reached for it and placed the clear loop over his head, letting the box settle on to his chest.

He nodded at me, smiling. "Thanks, Jessie."

He was always polite to me, impeccable in his manners, and usually in a good mood which was rare around here. Most of the teachers wore a tired expression, a sign that they were already weary of the winter season.

As I walked back to my seat, I glanced out the long bank of windows at the back. The sky was gray and overcast, making the classroom seem darker than usual. It had been snowing nonstop since this morning. Large flakes of wet snow filled the landscape, creating a serene feeling, like a soft hush. When I had waited for the bus this morning, it was eerily quiet, as if the snow had somehow dampened the acoustics. The silence around me had been deafening.

I sighed deeply, feeling a bit dispirited. The bruises along my arm and elbow were still painfully sore from the pounding I had taken from Jake in sparring. The dark purple discoloration stood out in stark contrast against my light skin. As the day wore on, I struggled to carry my heavy books. The strain was getting to be too much for my tender elbow. I rubbed it gingerly, feeling the muscles in my forearm cramp from doing so much writing today.

I hadn't gone back to the dojo since that fateful night, and I didn't dare step foot there without Ethan or his father. Jake was too mean spirited around me, and I no longer trusted him. It baffled me that he had been allowed to teach there, especially around the young kids. For the life of me, I couldn't figure out how he'd gotten away with it for so long.

I was so deep in thought that I didn't realize that Tiffany was standing beside me, apparently talking to me. I blinked and looked in her direction. She had one hand on her hip, the other pointing at my wrist. As usual, her outfit was immaculate, straight out of a fashion magazine. I had heard a rumor that she was a model for one of the local agencies which I suspected was true.

"Hmm? Oh, I'm sorry, what did you say?"

Exasperated that she had to repeat herself again, she rolled her eyes and sighed dramatically. "That bracelet," she jabbed a bright pink fingernail at my wrist. "Where did you get it?"

I quickly cast my eyes downward and tugged the sleeve of my shirt over it. The last thing I needed was another reason for her to berate me. I cleared my throat for it had suddenly become very dry. "Um, it was a gift." I glanced back at her as I spoke. "My boyfriend gave it to me. Why?"

She had this look of shock and horror as if she didn't believe what she was hearing. After a moment of stunned silence, she abruptly started laughing. It was a soft wheezy sound and she slapped her thigh as if I had told her a hilarious joke.

"You?" she said in between wheezy gasps. Several of my classmates looked in our direction, curious about the commotion. I quickly glanced away and covered my face with my right hand, pretending to fuss with my hair. "A boyfriend?" she continued as tears formed in her eyes from laughing. Clearly she found this amusing. I scowled at her which set off another bout of near silent laughter.

I blew out a frustrated sigh and began to rifle through my stack of books, deliberately ignoring her. The attention she was giving me was deeply embarrassing. I was mortified by her reaction. My face had been growing warmer by the minute and I was positive that it was beet red by now. I pulled out my notebook, slapped it down and started flipping through the pages. Tiffany stood up and wiped a tear from the corner of her eye.

"Yeah right, like anyone would want to go out with you. I mean, come on. Look at you." She flapped her hand up and down at my body, disgusted by what I was wearing.

While, granted, I did look more like a tomboy in my sweatpants and hoodie, she had no right to be so cruel. Apparently, she was really enjoying the spotlight as a model, and clothes, in particular, had taken on a whole new meaning for her. She was even more obsessed than usual about how I looked. Simply passing each other in the hallway would prompt a snarky riposte from her about my attire for the day. She always found something to nitpick about as if it was her mission in life to make me feel unbelievably small and dimwitted.

I tilted my head to the side and glared at her, my arms crossed in front of my chest. "Remember that self-defense class that we had last year?"

She shrugged her shoulders at me. "Yeah? So?"

"Do you recall the instructors?"

Her trimmed eyebrows drew together into a quizzical frown. "Uh-huh, you mean the old guy with the moustache? Ew!"

I sighed, wanting to smack her forehead with the palm of my hand to knock some sense into her. "No, the good looking one. His son, Ethan."

Her eyebrows shot up beneath her bangs. "Him?" she scoffed. "Yeah right, in your dreams, darling."

"But I'm telling you the truth!"

Too late. My words fell on deaf ears. She sharply turned around and marched over to her gang of fashionistas.

Once she sat down, she leaned into their tight circle and began to whisper, occasionally pointing in my direction. At one point, they all jerked their heads my way and burst out laughing loudly.

I tucked my head farther into my notebook, hoping that the class would start soon.

Mr. Brown stood up, his chair scraping loudly across the floor, and strolled around the room. He stood behind Tiffany's gaggle of Barbie look-alikes and cleared his throat brusquely, throwing a stern look their way. They promptly shut up and found a way to suddenly become busy with their books.

"Ahem. Everyone grab your Art History book and turn to chapter eight on page sixty seven. Today we will take a look at the Art Deco period."

There was the sound of numerous books thumping on the tables, of pages being rapidly flicked around, and of pens scattering on the smooth surface.

Mr. Brown stood in the middle of the room, holding the book in one hand as he waited for everyone to find the specific page. "Found it? Good. Now, Art Deco period was considered to be the age of the machines, the evolution of modern technology and travel. This was the era of promoting elegant travel on trains, ocean liners, and eventually planes. It was all about luxury and leisure. Throughout the

1920 and '30s, there was an explosion of advertising posters featuring sophisticated men and women, overlooking majestic vistas." He lifted the book to show us two pages of richly decorated travel posters.

"They often utilized large sleek fonts to grab the viewer's eyes, with simple shapes and strong use of color. The intention was to create a futuristic and aerodynamic look. Even though the technology was becoming more proficient at mass producing these ads, lithography was still a tricky field. There was only so much that could be done at the time in terms of shading, layers of colors, and fine details."

He flipped to another page and held it up. "Take a look at this one. Notice how bold the ship is against the rich blue background? It dominates the poster with its simplicity. It gets right to the point. The overall composition is well balanced and appealing to the eye.

"Here's another one," he said as he chose another page. "This is from the Canadian Pacific Railway." It portrayed a woman with a dazzling smile and rosy cheeks skiing in the Rocky Mountains. "The CPR went to great lengths to promote their services. They wanted to showcase the beauty of Canada, including luxurious resorts and untouched wilderness, to entice millions of people to visit our country."

I looked down at the image in front of me. Even though the style of the clothes was old fashioned, I could see why the poster would be appealing with its scenic background of fresh snow. She looked so happy to be there. Even I wanted to go skiing.

"I want everyone to read pages seventy-three to seventy-nine, then write down the answers to the questions that are listed on the blackboard." He turned around and pointed at the list. "I will give you fifteen minutes to do this. Will that be enough time?" He looked around the room and watched everyone nod their heads. "Excellent! Go ahead and start reading."

I began to scan the pages. Occasionally there would be a full page featuring a stunning poster that I admired. I took a moment to observe its bold use of simple colors. After several minutes, I was ready to answer the questions. I wrote down the first question into my notebook and added my response beneath it. I added more information as I went back to the first page, scrolling through various paragraphs.

Suddenly, I could swear that I heard a soft voice. I stopped with my pen poised over the paper and listened again. What in the world? I thought to myself. I heard it again. "The answer is on page seventy four." Surprised, I glanced up across the room at Mr. Brown who was smiling, laughter clearly evident in his eyes. He was whispering into the microphone!

My eyes darted around the room, everyone else was deeply engrossed and busy flipping through the pages of their books. I looked back at him and did a quick sideways motion with my head, smiling at the same time. His grin grew even wider. I looked back down and continued writing down the answers, feeling lighter and amused by our little private joke.

Once we were finished with that task, he continued his lecture, flipping through more pages to demonstrate his point. Finally, the bell rang. I quickly slapped the book closed, added it to my giant pile of textbooks and scooped them up, mindful of my tender elbow. On my way out, I snatched up the FM system and strode through the doors into a sea of students marching down the hallway. The chatter around me increased in tempo as everyone piled out of their classrooms and rushed to their lockers. Shoes squealed on the slick floors and the hall echoed with the metallic clang of the lockers being slammed shut.

I quickly made my way to the small office with the recharging station for the FM system and plunked down the blue box into its designated slot. I took off the plastic boots from my hearing aids and the receiver for the FM system and placed them in a small box to protect them. Relieved that the day was finally over, I turned around and strode over to my locker. I yanked off my shoes, stuffed them into my backpack, and quickly pulled on my winter boots. I stashed several books that I didn't need on to the top shelf, grabbed my jacket from the metal hook, and shrugged it on. Satisfied I had everything I needed, I slammed the door shut and clicked the lock into place. As I walked toward the main entrance, I pulled on my gloves and wrapped my green and white scarf around my neck.

The wet snow clung to my hair as I trudged through the slush to the bus. I climbed up the muddy steps and sat down with a huff, not looking forward to the long ride home. After several minutes of waiting for the rest of the students to clamber aboard, the bus lurched forward onto the road. I rifled through the backpack and pulled out my Art History book. I flipped through the pages until I reached the Art Deco section and took my time gazing at the travel posters, anything to distract me from the never ending taunts from the guys behind me. I ran my fingers over the vibrant images, trying to imagine what the world was like back them.

After what seemed like an eternity, the bus rolled to a stop in front of my red mailbox. I quickly stomped down the grungy steps and landed in the deep, slushy snow. The snow continued to fall in thick layers all around me, creating a hazy view of my house. There were fresh tire tracks in the lane. I walked in the groove all the way down, finding it easier than dragging my feet through the deep snowdrifts. As I got closer, I began to see more clearly through the curtain of snowflakes. A shock of recognition went through me as I realized whose car it was parked in front of the house. I stared at it, feeling perplexed and curious. I shook off the snow from my boots as I stepped onto the porch and pulled open the door. I came to abrupt halt once I spotted who was in the kitchen. My backpack fell to the floor with a loud thud.

"Ethan! What are you doing here?" I proclaimed, still stunned by his surprise visit.

"What? No 'hello, how are ya?' Gee, I can really feel the love in this room," he said in a jocular tone as he smiled.

"Fine...so, how was your trip?" I conceded, grinning back at him.

"It was okay, pretty straight forward, you know...nothing exciting," he said as he casually placed his hands behind his head, stretching out his long legs in front of him. His tall figure looked a little bit too big for the chair. "How about you? How was your week?"

"Oh, just the usual," I said as I took off my boots and hung up my jacket in the closet.

"Uh-huh. You know what's odd? When I got back to the dojo and went through the attendance cards, yours was conspicuously blank for this week."

I froze momentarily as he said that.

He got up and walked lazily toward me with his hands in his pockets.

"I found that rather strange for you. You practically live at the dojo. Are you sure you're okay?" His gaze pierced mine, searching for an answer. I gulped loudly and averted my eyes while I bent down to pick up my backpack and proceeded to go up the stairs toward my room. I had my hand on the post when Ethan reached out and grabbed my elbow. I sucked in a loud gasp, cringing at the fresh pain that shot through my arm.

Alarmed, he rapidly withdrew his hand and took another step closer to me. "Jessie, what's wrong?" he asked imploringly.

"Nothing, it's just sore," I said as I quickly climbed the steps to my room.

He followed behind me and sat down on the bench by the window as I dumped everything out of my backpack onto the bed. I winced at the newfound pain, feeling a rush of anger toward Ethan for setting it off.

Feeling a bit too warm, I gingerly took off my hoodie and reached for the soft pink flannel shirt that my brother gave me last year. Ethan gasped loudly when he spotted the dark bruises on my arm. He stood up and strode across the room to me. He gently placed both of hands to the sides of my face as he asked, "Jessie, where did those bruises come from?" His eyebrows were deeply creased in concern as he looked into my eyes.

"It was Jake from sparring. I kept telling him to stop being so rough with me but he kept calling me a wimp and said that I needed to face the real world."

He looked as if I had slapped him in the face. "Jake? Wha—No, that's not possible. He would never do that."

I reached up and held on to his arm, needing to feel safe and grounded. Something strong to hold onto. "He kept hitting me harder and harder and wouldn't stop."

Ethan gasped and took a step backward, clearly at lost for words. The warmth of his hands faded from my skin as he moved away.

"I've known him for years. I mean, sure, he can come across as being too strong at times but he has always been careful about that." Ethan turned around, running his fingers through his hair. He was completely stunned, acting as if the floor had fallen out from beneath his feet.

"Ethan, he was a completely different person when you weren't around. He became mean to me as if he resented me. I don't know why he behaved that way. I've never said or done anything even remotely harsh to him."

He turned around, gently grasped my fingers, and took a long look at the bruises. Then he leaned down and gave me gentle kisses all along my arm, as soft as a cloud.

When he looked up at me, I could see tears welling in his eyes. Pulling me into an embrace, he said, "Jessie, I'm so sorry."

After a minute or two, he reluctantly pulled away from me. Anger blazed across his features now. "I'm going to get to the bottom of this, Jessie. He had no right to that to you. As a Black Belt, he should have exercised far more control than that."

His hands shook as he spoke. "We have a class together tonight. I'll confront him about it." He leaned in and gave me a lingering kiss on the lips before pivoting around and walking out of my room, his feet clomping loudly down the stairs.

"Ethan, wait!" I said as I ran after him.

He was already at the bottom of the steps when he came to a stop. He looked up at me. "Will you be coming to the dojo this week?"

"I don't know, maybe?"

He nodded. "That's okay. Just give your arm a chance to heal first. Bye, Jessie."

My heart dropped like a stone. I had a bad feeling about this.

I ran down the stairs but by then it was too late, the car was already partway down the lane. I sat down on the bottom step, feeling completely despondent.

CHAPTER 9

Verity

I bowed to Sensei Jonas and accepted his heartfelt congratulations as he handed over the blue belt. I immediately took off my green belt and placed the new one over top of my white gi, checking that both ends of the belt were even and tightened the knot.

Sensei Ethan stood beside his father and nodded at me. He shook my hand and said, "Way to go, Jessie, I'm proud of you."

Funny, he didn't look all that enthusiastic. In fact, he had appeared somewhat somber throughout the night. At first I thought he just being professional about it, simply focused on doing his job while he helped with the grading. However, as the evening progressed, it became acutely obvious that there was something else going on. His mannerism seemed a bit too stiff and formal. In a way, he conveyed a sense of coldness toward me as if I was just another student at the dojo.

It bugged me because I'd had to work up the courage to come tonight. I was anxious to return after taking some time off. Ethan had been right that I literally lived at the dojo since I was there so often. It seemed so strange to have spent so much time away from it. Now that I was back, the atmosphere felt different to me. Something had changed. I frowned, feeling a bit puzzled by Ethan's odd behavior.

After we bowed out of class, I started to walk to the changing room when Ethan's voice rang out across the floor. "Jessie! Wait a sec!" He took a few quick strides toward me and placed his hand on my shoulder, gesturing for me to follow him. A sense of relief surged through me. I guess he was being professional after all.

He pointed to the office. "Let's talk in here."

I sat down on the couch expecting him to sit beside me. Instead, he leaned against the desk and stood there fussing with the papers beside him.

My blood ran cold and my heart stopped beating for a solid moment. A terrible feeling of despair washed over me. My fingers gripped the edge of the cushions in fear.

"Jessie..." He began to speak, and then stopped as he struggled to compose his thoughts. "I talked to Jake about what happened."

I stared at him, waiting for the other shoe to drop.

"He said that you fell in the parking lot after class. That you tripped over one of those concrete curbs."

My jaw fell open in shock. I was beyond being upset as rage shot through me like hot gasoline. I shouldn't have been this surprised, though. It was exactly the kind of thing Jake would do.

"Wha..." I was flabbergasted that Ethan would have fallen for his lies. "And you believed him?"

He raked his fingers through his hair nervously. "Jessie, I've known him for years, trained side by side with him, and taught many classes with him. It seems a little out of character, even for him."

I shot out of the couch as if I had been sitting on coiled springs. "Ethan! How can you even say that? You weren't even there!"

He looked at me, his eyes filled with sorrow. He placed his hands on top of his belt and shrugged his shoulders as he spoke. "Exactly. I don't know who to believe. I want to believe you. My heart tells me to but my mind says otherwise. I don't know what to do."

I raised my hands at him, exasperated. I could feel him pulling away from me, the distance starting to grow between us like a vast frozen lake, the ice cracking loudly as it formed. I was afraid to lose him to Jake in this ridiculous war of "he said, she said" but I feared it was too late.

"Ethan! You know me. Why would I lie about something like this?"

He shook his head somberly. "I don't know, Jessie. I don't know what to say or do. Frankly, I'm completely torn."

He crossed his arms on top of his chest. He glanced downward for a moment then looked up at me again.

My heart thudded painfully against my chest as I realized what he was going to say next.

"I need time to think about this..." He blew out a frustrated sigh. "I think we should take a break from each other."

He could've knocked me over with a feather with that remark. He sounded so cold and emotionless.

I stood there feeling rejected, devastated by this sudden turn of events. It should have been a night of celebration instead of this ugly confrontation.

Too stunned for words, I turned sharply around and stormed out of the office into the changing room. My hands shook violently as I struggled to pull on my clothes. It wasn't until I got home and stepped into my bedroom that it truly hit me. I've lost Ethan. He's gone, I thought as I sat down in front of my laptop. I opened the lid and logged onto the internet. I checked my messages, hoping that there would be a letter of apology from him, something, anything, that said he'd made a mistake.

My eyes welled up, turning the bright screen into a sparkly, blurry mess. It felt like there was a giant chasm in my chest, deep and hollow. I shivered, feeling utterly cold. I managed to grab a warm blue sweater from the closet before collapsing on the bench in a torrent of tears. They stung my eyes, and I furiously blinked them away. Instead, it just made them fall faster and harder. My head began to ache as I glanced out the window at the twilight sky. The last remnants of pink were fading quickly.

Parker jumped up onto the bench beside me, pushing his head under my hand. "Purrup?" he said as he gazed up at me with his bright green eyes. He seemed to smile at me for a moment.

"Oh, Parker, you're so sweet!" My voice sounded raspy. I pulled him into my arms, snuggling into his warm fur, feeling the rumbling purrs on my face. "Thanks Parker. I needed that," I mumbled into his soft fur.

After I showered and brushed my teeth, I padded back into my room and sat down at my desk, resting my chin in the cup of my hand as I leaned on the edge. I took a long look at the corkboard in front of me, filled to the brim with various photos and handwritten notes. There were shots of Ethan and me from the beach, at the dojo. Some were from his house with his family, and some shots were of us smiling at the camera with our faces pressed together, cheek to cheek, deliriously happy. I reached out and began to pluck them off, one by one. My throat constricted painfully and fresh tears began to fall. I opened the drawer and placed the pictures inside. My eyes roamed over the bracelet on my wrist that Ethan had given me with the inscription "Believe." I immediately unclasped it and threw it in the drawer on top of the photos. I didn't want any reminders of him. I couldn't bear to look at him again nor think about him. It was just too painful.

I didn't believe in anything anymore. I felt lost. It was as if I was surrounded by a sucking black hole of nothingness, its dark wispy tendrils trying to pull me in deeper. There was this huge void in my life and I didn't know what to do.

With shaking hands, I took off my earrings, the long strands of tiny stars that Mom had given me for my birthday. I traced my fingers over them, feeling the shape of the metallic stars as they glittered in the light. I glanced up at the board and seized the birthday card she had given me. It read: "To reach the stars, all you have to do is believe." More tears suddenly welled up, turning the words into a blurry streak. I placed the earrings and card on top of everything else and closed the drawer with a bang. They were painful reminders of a different life that I couldn't handle right now. It was simply too much for me to bear.

As I clambered into bed and pulled the blanket over my shoulder, Parker jumped up and curled up beside me, sending rumbly purrs my way. I reached over and gently stroked the soft fur between his ears. My eyes grew heavy quickly. I was deeply exhausted from all the crying.

A swirl of stars surrounded me, twinkling and shimmering. A feeling of immense joy wrapped around me like a warm and cozy blanket. I felt deeply loved and very happy. As the glittering facets of the stars faded from my vision, Parker stood before me in the form of my spirit guide. As usual, he appeared more like royalty since the surface of his body shimmered in gold. His shield was strapped across his body along with his majestic sword. I got the impression that he was timeless and so very wise. However, his eyes stood out the most as they revealed his true soul. They were very much like the eyes of Parker, who remained sound asleep beside me.

He raised his hands and held them out to me. They formed a cup. Inside it rested a large star. It seemed so alive, like a flame dancing before me. The light was dazzling as I leaned in for a closer look. It glinted like a diamond.

His voice was husky. I felt it in my body and mind rather than heard it as he spoke. "All you have to do is seek the brightest star and follow it. There, you will discover the truth."

"Great, another cryptic message. I just love trying to solve these puzzles. Thanks," I said somewhat sarcastically, feeling a bit miffed. "How am I supposed to find this magical star that you speak of? I can't even figure out what to do with my life right now! I feel so...lost." My voice nearly gave out on that last word.

"Don't worry, the answer will reveal itself," he said as his voice started to fade. He raised his hands to his face, illuminating his golden sheen into a brilliant, sparkling sea of sunlight. He blew into the cup of his hands that held the star. As the wind of his breath touched it, thousands and thousands of tiny, glittering stars flew up like confetti, falling like snow. Laughing, I reached out catch them, swirling around, letting them fall gently onto my face.

CHAPTER 10

Serendipity

I woke up to a bright morning. The sun glinted off the snow and bounced the light in to my room. Squinting and shivering as I climbed out of my warm bed, I strolled over to peek out the window. In the middle of the lawn stood a tiny and scrawny tree, its bare branches sticking outward. As it swayed in the breeze, something glinted in the sun. I continued to stare at it, wondering what it was that caught my eye. Then I realized what I was seeing. They were chunks of ice clinging stubbornly to the ends of the branches. They hung heavily on them, pulling the thin branches downward. They sparkled like Swarovski crystals in the morning light. It reminded me of a Charlie Brown Christmas tree, so forlorn and lonely, making me feel sad again.

Curious and desperately searching for a hopeful sign, I sat down and logged on to the internet. My eyes roamed through the messages as I scrolled down the screen. My heart sank even farther as it dawned on me that it was truly over. Still in a deep funk, I slunk downstairs into the kitchen and munched on my cold cereal without really tasting it. I felt Parker's paw on my leg as he stood up and reached out to tap me gently while meowing loudly.

"Sorry, Parker, it's just cereal," I said glumly as he sat down with a huff and continued to stare at me, turning his head from side to side. He ran over to the large window and stood up on his hind legs to peer outside, twitching his tail madly. Again, he reached up and touched the window, looking over at me as if trying to send me a message.

Hmm, that's strange. Why is he doing that? I thought as I watched him while I ate my breakfast.

Insistent, he came back over to me and reached up to tap my leg again. He pawed the air as if to say, "Hello? I'm right here!" Then he turned around and padded over to the door.

Okay, now that's odd. I stood up and strode over to the door, where Parker sat, and opened it. I stood there stunned as the wind blew a gust of frosty snow across the threshold.

I knelt down to look closer at what was in front of me. It was a small and scrawny cat, not quite a kitten but not really a full grown cat. It sat there shivering in the frigid air surrounded by a pile of snow. The bones of its hips stood out prominently, a clear sign it was starving. My hand went to my mouth in shock. I quickly went back inside, grabbed a bowl, filled it with kibble, and placed it gently beside it. Despite the wind and snow, I sat down cross legged to keep it company. It looked up at me and uttered a weak meow. It came out as a high squeaky sound, kind of like a mouse. It broke my heart in two. After a minute or two of munching on the cat food, it slowly walked over to me and began to purr. Then it rolled over, clearly at ease with me. It got up and crawled into my lap, exhausted, resting its chin on my knee. I gently gathered it into my arms and brought it inside, Parker padded along beside me, watching every move I made.

I sat down on the couch where it remained curled up in my lap purring as I stroked its soft fur. Parker leapt up beside me and sat down, softly touching the cat's head with his paw as if to reassure her. Mom came into the living room with a cup of tea in her hand and came to complete stop in front of me. Startled, she sloshed some of the hot liquid over the brim of her cup.

She let out a shocked gasp as she stared at the tiny cat. "Oh! Jessie! It's beautiful! Where did it come from?" she asked and knelt down in front of me.

"Parker...he was the one who told me to look outside. It was sitting in the snow, shivering."

"Oh my! Poor thing! It's funny though, it seems quite content here. It must belong to somebody."

Just then it woke up and looked at Mom, sending a squeaky meow her way "Meow?"

"Aw! Aren't you adorable? I love that cute little meow of yours!" she said.

Her eyebrows creased in concern. "I wonder who she belongs to." Mom slowly reached out and gently stroked its fur between the ears. "Tell you what, I'll take it to the vet's office so that they can check for an ID and make sure it's healthy, okay?"

I was reluctant to hand it over to Mom, but it was the right thing to do. I couldn't bear the thought of it being away from its family. I shuddered as I imagined Parker being in the same position, lost and away from me, and it scared the crap out of me.

After I got dressed and while I waited for Mom to come back, I checked my messages again. Nothing. I sat down on the bench and idly flipped through a glossy fashion magazine, not really reading anything. My mind was too far away to even begin to appreciate the spring fashions cropping up in the ads. My eyes wandered outside the window, anxiously waiting for the car to show up. Parker sat beside me on top of the cushion, also peering outward, his tail twitching impatiently, thumping against the surface of the bench. Finally, Mom's car appeared and slowly made its way along the snow covered driveway.

I ran downstairs as Parker pounded down the steps beside me. I opened the door for Mom as she gently carried the new cat inside.

"Well? Is she okay? It is a 'she' right?" I asked anxiously as I picked it up and held it in my arms. Somehow, I'd suspected that it was a female, for it seemed to be so full of poise and grace. There was an air of elegance around it, a sense of feminine pride.

"Yes, it's a 'she.' The vet said that she's quite weak and recently suffered a miscarriage. We were lucky to have found her otherwise she could've died. She would not have lasted another week in this weather."

I stared at her dumbfounded. "We saved her?" I said as I felt my eyes began to well up. I was deeply touched and my voice sounded raspy. "Does she have a home?"

"The vet couldn't find any ID on her and there were no reports of her missing. I even checked the lost and found board," she replied as she took off her jacket and hung it in the closet.

"I'll make some calls today and ask around to see if any of the neighbors are missing a cat or know if she belongs to anyone."

I nodded and went upstairs to my room, cradling her in my arms. I sat down on the bench and placed her gently onto the cushions. She promptly curled up and went to sleep, purring. Parker sat down beside her and looked up at me as if to send me a telepathic, "Thank you."

As the sun shone on her fur, it turned into a shimmering sea of silver, revealing an extravagant pattern of dark swirls. It reminded me of Italian marble. Her tail lay limply around her, appearing crooked part way along it. It looked as if it had been damaged at some point. She was broken and lost, just like me. My breath caught in my chest in a choked sob.

I don't know why but I felt such a deep connection to her. I swiped away a tear from my eye as I stroked her silky fur.

Mom had no luck. She called everyone she knew in the area, but no one claimed her. We waited for a week and placed posters, featuring a photo of her, everywhere but there was no response.

"It's a shame. She is such a beautiful cat," Mom said as she looked down at me holding the sweet little creature in my lap. "Well, what do you think, Jessie? Should we adopt her?"

I glanced up and laughed. "Um, I think she's already adopted us."

Mom laughed in return. "You know, I think you are right about that," she said as she reached out and playfully touched the cat's nose. "Have you decided on a name yet?"

I shook my head. "I don't know. Maybe Serendipity? I don't think it's a coincidence that she landed in our lap like this."

"It seems like a big name for such a little cat. Why don't you shorten it to something like Serena?"

It was perfect. "I love it!" I looked down at her as she watched us in awe. "What do you think, Serena?" She answered with a squeaky meow. "Yep! That'll work!"

I held her in my arms and gave her a kiss on her furry cheek. "You're my little star, Serena!"

Serena gradually became accustomed to our home and routines. At night, she and Parker slept side by side on my bed, curled up alongside me like two furry caterpillars.

She was a bright star in an otherwise bleak time of my life. Every day, I continued to check my messages for a sign from Ethan. But there was nothing from him, no indication that he even noticed I was gone.

I hadn't gone back to the dojo since that night. I had told Mom and Dad that I wanted to take some time off from Karate. They grew concerned and noticed my broody moods, aware that something lurked deeper in my thoughts. It was a struggle to focus on school, the days seemingly so dark and hollow. I kept mostly to myself, looking forward to spending time with Serena and Parker, enjoying their mellow company.

I trailed behind Mom at the hardware store, while she shopped for new faucets for the kitchen sink. I strode past rows of old holiday merchandise, sitting forlornly on the shelves, looking rejected and depressing. I rifled through a nearby bin full of ornaments and pulled out a handful of small, mirrored stars, holding them by their ribbons. They were on sale at a huge discount. I admired them as they twirled in the air in front of me, wondering how they would look in the window in my room. Remembering my strange dream about following the brightest star, I decided to get them.

As I walked down the aisle, randomly looking around, I idly plucked some paint chips from the bright display, pairing a warm rusty orange with a deep fuchsia purple. Mom casually strolled up to me, parking the shopping cart in front of us. "Those are great colors, Jessie. I like the way you paired them together like that."

I held them up as I deliberated. "Really?"

"You know...they would look fantastic in your room. Did you want to get them?"

"Oh! I don't know. I was just looking at them." I stammered, surprised by her remark.

"You don't have to paint all of the walls in one color. You can do two or three in orange, and one wall in purple." She continued talking as she pushed the shopping cart. I had to run to keep up with her so I could lip-read and follow the conversation. "We could even get some pillows that match. Would you like that?"

"Um, sure." I was still somewhat taken aback by her offer to redecorate my room. I knew that money was tight and that a can of paint was costly. This spoke volumes about how much she was willing to help me snap out of my blue funk.

When we got home, I placed the two cans of paint on the floor in my room and walked around, trying to decide which walls should be painted in orange or fuchsia. I stared at the paint chips, holding them at arm's length, trying to imagine how it would look. I loved the warmth of the orange, it seemed so cozy. I decided to place it on the three walls I would see while lying in bed and settled on having the wall *behind* the bed in fuchsia. I clapped my hands together eagerly, ready to start painting.

I grunted with effort as I pushed my furniture into the middle of the room. I went over to my closet, yanked out my old clothes, and pulled them on. Quickly going around the room, I put painter's tape along the edges of the door, windows, and baseboard. Then I turned around, picked up the drop cloth, and placed it on the floor, along one wall. I grabbed the pail of orange paint, opened it, and stirred it, before dipping in my brush and outlining the door, windows, top, and bottom of the walls. Then I switched to the roller and began to cover the surface. It was lovely as it began to take form. It was remarkable how it changed the overall mood of the room. It just felt so right. I continued around the room, delighted with the results. Once I was done with the orange paint, I switched to the purple paint for the last wall and was surprised that it didn't take very long to finish.

Exhausted, yet pleased to have gotten the first coat done, I sat down and checked my messages on the lap top. Disappointed to find nothing from Ethan, I closed the lid feeling more than a little glum. Sitting on the desktop lay the shiny stars, their mirrored surfaces picking up the light. I grasped one of them and hung it in the window. Perfect, I thought as I took a step backward, to check the positioning of it, and proceeded to hang the rest of them.

I turned around and froze. I stood there, stunned, as my eyes spotted purple paw prints on the floor. I gasped, mortified. I quickly snatched up a towel, bent down, and began to scrub them off the floor, and then stopped, curious. I stood up and followed the trail out through the door. It faded by the time I reached the top of the stairs.

"Jessie! What's the meaning of this?"

Crappity, crap, crap, I thought as I looked down at Mom who was standing at the bottom of the stairs holding Serena and a wet towel in her hand, covered with streaks of purplish paint.

"Sorry! I just found out myself! Is there paint down there, too?"

"Not anymore. I cleaned off Serena's paws," she said in an exasperated tone, clearly not amused.

"Aw, is she okay?"

"You're more worried about the cat than the floors?" A tiny smile grew on her face as she began to see the humor in it.

I went down the stairs and picked up Serena, giving her a kiss, and went back up to my room as a giggle started to form. Laughing, I stepped into my room, following the paw prints on the floor. It was a perfect fit. I decided to keep them there. She looked up at me and said, "Mew?" her purrs growing louder by the minute.

"You are such a silly girl, Serena!" I said as I stood in the middle of the room, taking in the colors. I couldn't believe the difference it made. It felt so right...it was me.

I tackled the room again later in the week after the first coat of paint had completely dried. It was really coming together, like the pieces of a puzzle falling into place. I was just putting the last strokes of paint on the final wall when Mom came in.

"I have a surprise for you, Jessie."

I spun around and strolled over. She opened the bag she was carrying and pulled out a creamy white bedspread cov-

ered in rich orange blossoms and pillows elaborately decorated with bold patterns of orange and fuchsia. I gasped
with delight as I saw them.

"Oh wow! They're perfect! Thanks Mom!"

Just then Serena burst out of my closet, dragging a long
pink feather boa. It trailed along behind her as she ran
down the stairs, tufts of pink feathers flying off. It was hilarious and I laughed so hard that tears formed in my eyes.

Mom clapped her hand over mouth, trying to hold back
the bubbling laughter.

"Ha! She must've been going through my box of old
costumes and found it!" I said as I ran after her, watching
her zip across the floor in glee. It warmed my heart to see
her so happy.

CHAPTER 11

Touch

I sat on the bench by the window sipping a hot cup of tea with Parker and Serena curled up beside me, their furry cheeks puffed up in sweet smiles, as if having the most wonderful dream. It had been raining nonstop for the last couple of days creating an eerie spectacle of floating mist over our backyard as the snow melted quickly. It resembled ghosts, hovering in the air, more than fog. Today, the sun broke through the clouds, warming up my room. I began to giggle as a couple of ladybugs crawled on the window. Despite the chill outside, they were determined to go for a little jaunt. I reached out and touched the window where they roamed. It was warm to the touch.

I glanced down at Parker and Serena and sighed. They looked so perfect together, like Yin and Yang. It was as if they were made for each other. I sighed again, feeling a sudden pang in my heart.

I stared outside, watching the birds flit around, going from one branch to another. A sudden gust of wind blew across the lawn, producing a mini-tornado and blasting the old leaves across the driveway.

Feeling a little bit somber, I leaned over my desktop and pulled the laptop toward me. I flicked it open and logged on to the internet, waiting for it to load. As the messages appeared on the screen, one by one, my heart jolted when Ethan's email popped up.

Feeling a sense of dread, I clicked on it. It read: Hi Jessie. It seems so strange not to see you at the dojo anymore. Even Dad said the other day that it was odd not having you around to help out. I feel kinda bad about what happened. Would you consider coming in tonight to give us a hand? Ethan

What the...I stared at it dumbfounded. What kind of letter was that? It wasn't an apology and it really didn't welcome me back. I couldn't understand why he felt bad about it since he put me in this position in the first place. I stood up and walked around the room, thinking about it, then sat down, and sent a terse reply that I would help out. My stomach twisted in a knot as I responded, and I began to feel anxious about it. More than anything, I wanted to continue taking classes for myself. It tore me apart to stop at the blue belt level, I wanted to keep going and eventually get my black belt.

It wasn't easy for me to step back into the dojo. I had to summon the courage to walk through the doors. I tried to avoid making any eye contact with the students in the changing room and felt distinctly uncomfortable about being away for so long. I took a long deep breath before bowing at the door, then stepped inside the class, and proceeded to line up like everyone else. In the mirror, I could see several people sneaking glances at me. My face started to burn and grew redder by the minute.

Then I saw Ethan stroll into the room and I became very still. My heart thudded madly against my rib cage and I could swear that everyone around me could hear it. Sensei

Jonas and Sensei Jake followed behind him, all three lined up in front, ready to bow us in and begin the class. As Ethan walked past me, I spotted him sneaking a glance at me. His face was unreadable and my heart sank. He was all business tonight. I couldn't feel any personal connection to him.

"*Keske! Rei!*" barked out Sensei Jonas, bowing crisply as we all followed his motions. "It's wonderful to see so many of you tonight! We have some new beginners and familiar faces that have come back to join us." He winked at me and I instantly felt more at ease.

"Sensei Ethan will lead you through the warm-ups. Please follow him," he said as walked over to the side.

As the class began to run around, Sensei Jonas gestured at me with his hand to stand beside him. "Jessie, may I speak with you for a moment?" His eyes sparkled as he spoke. "It's great to see you again."

"Oh, thank you. I missed being here." I felt a little bit shy, like a brand new student.

"I just wanted to say I'm so sorry for any misunderstandings that may have happened. The last thing we want is for you to lose out on your chance to train with us and continue to get your belts."

He seemed genuinely apologetic and I felt much more at ease. Much of the anger and sorrow that I was carrying around in my heart was beginning to lift. The pain was starting to fade. My throat constricted painfully and I just simply nodded at him.

"Would you mind helping us with the new students tonight?"

I cleared my throat. "Um, sure. That's fine." I was surprised by his request. However, I suspected that he was trying to heal the rift between Ethan and I. I began to wonder if he was the one to make the suggestion to Ethan to have me come to the dojo tonight.

I joined the group in their warm-up and stretches. Afterward, we were split up into small groups to work on our Katas. I was assigned to two white belts who were a few years younger than me. I showed them a few moves, repeating the motions as they followed me and then took a step back to let them practice on their own for a few minutes while I watched. My eyes focused behind them as I saw Sensei Jake struggling to teach a yellow belt the next sequence.

He was becoming more flustered by the minute as she kept stepping in the wrong direction. Eventually, he began to raise his voice so loud that even I could pick it up.

I could see why he was having trouble with her. She was developmentally challenged which required an immense amount of patience. I had worked with her before and knew that she could only handle small bits of information at a time. He was trying to show her far too many steps and moves all at once which only confused her. She cringed when he spoke too brusquely at her. I could see the beginning of tears forming in her eyes. At that point, I'd had enough of his rude attitude and made my way over to them.

I could hear more clearly as I moved closer to them. "No, no, no! That's wrong! You need to step to your left, do a low block, step forward with the other leg, and deliver a punch with the right hand!"

"Sensei Jake? Would you like me to go over the kata with her? Perhaps break it down into smaller segments to make it easier for her to remember?"

His face immediately flushed bright crimson. "Excuse me? That's fifty push-ups for you, right now!"

I was beyond shocked and deeply embarrassed. Tears welled up in my eyes before I could even stop them. I briskly went down to the floor and did the push-ups, sniffling loudly and trying to stop the tears from falling.

Sensei Jonas came over and asked Sensei Jake what was going on. Sensei Jonas told him to lower his voice and started to pull Sensei Jake away from us, leading him toward the back of the room.

Furious and close to shouting, Jake shook his head at me, sending dark thoughts my way. "She won't listen to me or follow my instructions. Why do you even have her in this class? And what is Jessie doing here? I don't want her in my class!" His voice was filled with venom, sending a clear message that he did not want me in the dojo. He stood there glaring at me with his thick muscular arms crossed over his chest.

Sensei Jonas became very still then leaned into Sensei Jake's face, his voice in a loud whisper, brimming with anger. "First of all, this is my class and you are to watch your manners in the dojo. Let's continue this discussion in my office, now." He jerked his head in the direction of the office, prompting Sensei Jake to follow him. He stormed away like a petulant child having a temper tantrum.

Sensei Ethan came over to me. His eyes filled with concern, he placed his hand on my shoulder to reassure me. "I'm sorry about that Jessie. That was not your fault in any way." He nodded at the girl wearing the yellow belt. "Could you work with her? She seems to be more comfortable around you." As he spoke, he gently touched my cheek with the palm of his hand, a warm and familiar gesture. I suddenly felt a pang of sadness in my chest. I hadn't realized how much I'd missed his gentle touch until now.

I nodded and went over to her, still reeling from Sensei Jake's outburst. I plastered on a smile and approached her, trying to look as if I was unfazed by what just happened and eager to help her with the kata. "Okay! Are you ready to work on some moves?" She smiled back at me, keen on trying again. I showed her three simple moves, allowing her to follow me. Then I had her try it out at her own pace, letting her find the rhythm. Once she got the hang of it, I showed her another move and let her get used to it. She would stumble once in a while but was determined to get it right and started over again, going through it, step by step. I was pleased with her progress and admired her spunk for trying so hard.

At the end of the class, I felt Ethan's hand on my arm just as I was going out the door. "Jessie? I just wanted to say thanks for being here tonight. You...uh...did a great job." He seemed a bit sad. He paused as if gathering his thoughts, and started to say something but stopped.

"Thanks Ethan. It feels great to be back. I'll admit that I was nervous about coming here." I laughed, trying to keep the conversation alive between us. It was an awkward moment. I kept expecting him to reach out or say something meaningful. There was nothing but empty silence.

I took that as my cue to leave and get changed. I bowed at the door and went into the changing room, disappointed that he hadn't made an effort to step forward and apologize. Ethan was going around the dojo, turning off the lights, and putting away the equipment when I stepped out. As I walked over to the main door, I saw him look in my direction briefly then snap his eyes elsewhere as if he didn't want to have anything to do with me. I could feel this huge chasm between us, and it tore me pieces. I felt so ashamed that he wasn't interested in being with me anymore.

As I pushed the door open into the parking lot, Jake appeared out of the shadows on my right side, completely catching me off guard. He stormed toward me, shaking his finger at me. His face was flushed and his eyes blazed with intense anger. "You freak! It's all your fault that I've been suspended! Happy now?"

A shock of cold fear ran through my body as if I had been doused in ice cubes. I was confused. I didn't understand what he was talking about. "What? I don't know what you mean—"

Suddenly, he grabbed my lapels, nearly lifting my feet off the ground. "Don't you play dumb with me. That trick you did in class, to make me look like an idiot, worked."

My breath came in short gasps. I started to panic, deeply terrified. He shook me roughly and yelled at me incoherently. I placed my hand on his chest, shoved my fingers into the cleft of his throat, and tried to push him away. He started to gag and loosened his grip. I pushed even harder, and he finally released one hand, coughing from the pressure to his throat. His other hand still held on to my lapel. I cupped my hands and slammed them over his ears. Stunned, he staggered backward, finally releasing his grip.

"Christ, Jake! What's the matter with you?" Ethan grabbed Jake and pulled him away from me. Incensed, Jake immediately swung around and delivered a hefty blow to Ethan's ribs. He danced out of the way as much as possible but still took a portion of the hit. In a blind rage, Jake kept coming at Ethan, swinging hard. They exchanged a flurry of blows, blocking some of them, others getting through. Eventually, Ethan was able to grab a fistful of Jake's jacket and slam him into the wall. "Stop it, Jake! It's me, Ethan! Look at me!"

Both were gasping for breath. Jake's hands were shaking, and there was a trail of blood trickling down the side of Ethan's face from a cut on his forehead.

After a minute or two of sucking in some air, Jake finally spoke, his eyes now filled with shame. "Your dad suspended me for that stupid stunt in class tonight. And it was your girlfriend's fault! If she hadn't shown up, this never would've happened!" He jabbed his hand in my direction, showing me the blood on his knuckles.

"But, Jake, I just wanted to help, that's all. I'm sorry if I offended you."

He scoffed at me and looked the other way. "Yeah right..."

Ethan released his grip on Jake and took several steps away from him. "Jake, please go home. This is not Jessie's fight."

"Yeah, whatever." He flapped his hand at Ethan as he walked away, searching for his keys in his pocket.

Ethan was by my side in seconds, his eyes roaming all over me, searching for injuries. "Oh my God, Jessie. Are you okay?"

My hands were shaking, and I felt so cold, as if the core of my body had been plunged into the Arctic. I was so shaken up that I felt like crying. "I think so..." I said as my teeth chattered loudly. "I don't understand. Why did he go after me like that?"

We each took a step back toward the door as Jake's car roared past us, nearly clipping us in the process. Even his driving was aggressive.

Ethan's hands were on the sides of my face as he looked at me. "Jessie, there's something you don't know about Jake. He comes from an abusive home. He had a rough life growing up. I thought he'd gotten past all that. He promised me, promised me, that he wouldn't be like his father. I had no idea that he had so much anger toward you. I'm so sorry."

I gripped the back of his neck and leaned into him as I began to lose control, sobbing. It was as if all of the emotions that were building up to this point finally broke through. After a minute or two, I was shivering so much that I slid my hands beneath his jacket and grabbed him in a bear hug, seeking out the warmth. He wrapped his arms around me, pulling me in closer.

A few minutes later, we broke apart, feeling very exposed even in the dark parking lot. The cold air made the tears on my face suddenly seem like ice. I looked up and saw that the cut on his face was still bleeding. "Ethan! You're bleeding!" I started to reach up to his forehead but he grasped my hand and pulled it to his chest, as if not wanting to let go.

"It's okay Jessie, believe me, I've had worse cuts than this. Dad can patch it up when we get home," he said. He stared at me as if memorizing my face, his voice soft. Pulling my hand to his mouth, he gave it a gentle kiss. "Oh, Jessie, you have no idea how much I missed you."

"Same here. It was one of the darkest times of my life. I thought you were gone for sure. I have never felt so lost...so empty," I said, remembering the unbearable pain. "What did I do to deserve this?"

"Jessie, look at me please."

He trailed his fingers along my jaw, tucking a long strand of my hair behind my ear. I looked back at him, seeing the sadness in his eyes. I could see that he was hurting. "I didn't mean to cause you any pain," he said. "I'm sorry I decided to break us up. I should have believed you." He leaned in and gave me a feather light kiss on my forehead. "I was so torn that it felt like my soul was being ripped apart."

He continued his kisses downward, eventually landing on my lips with a passionate fever, the pace growing in intensity. I grabbed his jacket and pulled him closer to me, hungry for more. I hadn't realized how much I missed kissing him until now. My lips tingled from his eager touch and the heat of his lips. I didn't want to stop.

Gasping, Ethan gently broke away, easing us apart with his hands on my arms. "Will you ever forgive me?" he said, his voice breaking as if he were barely able to speak, and brushed away the tears on my cheeks with trembling fingers.

I reached up and intertwined my fingers with his, embracing the warmth of his hand. "As long as you promise me that you won't do this again. I can't stand the thought of you being apart from me."

Just then, a shooting star streaked across the night sky behind him. I gasped. Ethan turned around quickly and looked up, following my line of sight. "What? What are looking at?"

"It was a shooting star! It's a sign!"

Confused, he looked back at me, his eyebrows creased. "What are you talking about?"

"I guess it means that we're meant to be together. Maybe the stars are telling us what to do? In a way, you're my Northern Star."

He stared at me, his eyes wide. "Uh-huh. So...that means I'm forgiven?"

We both looked back up at the sky as I said, "Of course." Then he pulled me into a tight embrace, letting the warmth of his body seep into mine.

CHAPTER 12

Illumination

My body felt weary by the time I reached history class late in the afternoon. It had seemed like an unusually long day. The teacher's voice had a hypnotic effect as he droned on as if he was speaking to us in Latin. I had to fight to keep myself from falling asleep. The lights in the room were dimmed for viewing the images on the screen and that was lulling me deeper into a trance. I had this mental image of my head plunking loudly down onto the desk, and I tried to stop myself from falling into that trap. It was sorely tempting to just relax as the warm spring air wafted in from the open windows nearby. Instead, I focused on jotting down some points of information, absentmindedly following Mr. Makena's lecture. Part way through, my brain suddenly tuned in and I jerked my head up to really listen to what he was saying.

"Shamans had this belief that part of our life energy could become lost. Specifically, a part of our soul could break away due to a traumatic experience such as illness, or when someone close to us suddenly dies." He pointed to the screen which depicted a strange drawing that vaguely resembled someone on a bed with a ghostly figure floating above them.

He continued on as the image changed. "Even children could lose a part of their soul. I want you to think back to when you were very young during a blissful time in your life. Perhaps you loved to run through the grass barefoot or sit at the base of your favorite tree and stare at the clouds. As you got older, something changed, and life suddenly didn't seem so free anymore, did it? Something happened. Could that be a sign that you'd lost a part of your soul? This is what Shamans look for, a major change in your life. It's essentially a clue."

The image changed again as he walked to the other side of the screen. "The universe strives for balance. It needs to remain in harmony. If there is a void, it tries to find a way to fill it. Shamans believed that if a part of the soul separates itself from the body, it leaves a gaping hole. As a result, the body becomes unbalanced and something else will fill it, like an illness.

"Shamans will journey to an inner spirit world to retrieve the lost part of a person's soul and bring it back to help restore the harmony. They often used tools to help them go into an altered state of consciousness by focusing on the rhythm of a drum or using quartz crystals which are also known as stones of light. What's interesting about the particular drum rhythm used for this process is that it's considered to be the heartbeat of the earth."

A new image filled the screen depicting a flowing river and forest filled with animals. "Shamans also believed that all humans have a guardian or two to help guide them. They sometimes appear in the form of animals that have very distinct personalities. When Shamans go on this journey, they enter a different reality where animals can talk and even the trees can come to life and offer wisdom. They may visit strange cities made out of sparkling crystals or fly high in the sky as far as the stars. They search through this realm for the missing soul. Sometimes the lost soul can appear much younger, perhaps at the age of three or four, hiding in some dark place, still trembling with fear which is a sign that something scared them away from their body. Once they are found, the Shaman will try to reach out to them and encourage them to come home, to restore the balance and allow the body to become whole again."

I blinked. A suspicion was suddenly confirmed. Parker was my guardian. The more I thought it, the more I began to remember—the strange palace filled with crystals that held the flickering life forces, the cryptic messages from Parker. He'd been a tremendous comfort at the most difficult time in my life last year, at the traumatic birthday party—it was when I felt as if a part of my soul was being ripped from me—and then again when I thought I had lost Ethan. The more I remembered, the more certain I became. It all made sense. It hadn't been an easy year. First there were all of my injuries, then the concussion, and finally, the experience with Jake.

As I listened to Mr. Makena talk about lost souls, I began to search through my memories, going backward to a younger version of me. As I sat at the desk, resting my chin on my hand, the slow wispy edges of a happy memory began to form and crystallize into a clearer picture in my mind. It was like watching a movie of myself as I skipped gleefully across the soft lush grass toward a towering tree. Its branches were covered with thick leaves, fluttering in the gentle breeze. I felt gloriously happy and so free. I sat on the swing, rocking back and forth, feeling the wind in my hair. Then the image faded to be replaced by a duller view of the same girl. The edges were obscured, appearing somewhat dusty. The colors were less vibrant, with more of a dull-gray overtone. I was just a few years older, sitting forlornly on the swing set at a school playground. All around me, kids ran, squealing with delight, but their voices sounded muted and hollow. My head hung low as my fingers gripped the steel chain and I dragged my dirty shoes in the dirt, feeling completely alone. *I wonder...*I lost my hearing when I was five. Had I lost a part of my soul back then?

The school bell rang loudly. I nearly jolted out of my chair in shock. Abruptly, the vision of that sad, lonely girl vanished.

In my bedroom, later that night, a cold beam of moonlight shone through the windows, painting bright panes of light across the walls and floor. The moonlight bounced off the mirrored stars that hung in my window and reflected their images on top of my blanket. Serena and Parker lay curled up side by side along the length of my body, taking up a good portion of the space, essentially leaving me with a small margin of the bed. Trying not to disturb them, I snuggled deeper under the sheets.

After a while I began to relax. The stars on the bed began to shimmer and multiply. They rose up in a lazy swirl of sparkling lights. I gasped quietly as I admired the magnificent light show. Millions and millions of tiny stars stacked upon one another, gradually forming a shape.

Standing before me was an elegant woman, maybe twenty years old, majestically adorned with long, silver curly hair, gleaming in the moonlight, nearly turning white. I stared at her face, since it seemed so familiar. There was something about her eyes. Serena! They looked just like hers!

She inclined her head toward me, nodding in agreement as if she could sense my thoughts.

"Indeed, my darling. I can read your mind." Her voice came through in a gentle and soft tone filled with a sense of kindness and love. I reached up to touch my ears, I didn't have my hearing aids on, and yet I could hear her clearly.

She raised her hands to cover her mouth as she giggled, finding my confusion rather amusing. As her arms moved, the cloth that covered her body seemed to shift like waves of water, as if it was completely fluid. Her simple dress looked like a Roman toga, draped across one shoulder, falling down in a curtain of tiny glimmering facets. Her face and arms looked pale as if bathed in a beam of the moonlight.

"Wow. I had no idea you were this beautiful, Serena."

"Thank you for your kind words and hospitality. I am forever grateful for your intervention. You saved me, and you will always have a place in my heart."

"How could anyone abandon you like that? It seems so cruel."

"Perhaps it can be construed as a test to determine what is the correct placement," she said as she folded her hands in front of her body. As she moved, some of the glittering stars fell from her body and disappeared, like sparklers.

"But you almost died! That's a horrible test!"

"I understand your predicament and feel your sorrow. Some things in nature happen for a reason, to find harmony and balance."

I pondered on that for a moment, beginning to make some sense out of this puzzle.

She leaned over me and reached up. A long sparkling sash appeared in her hands. She bowed her head in a regal manner. "As a token of my thanks, I'm honored to present you with this gift."

She gently placed the sash over my head and let it fall across my shoulder. The sash seemed to shine brightly as if filled with sunshine and joy. I could feel the energy radiate out of it and into me. It literally glowed with tingling warmth. It warmed my heart as it quivered with amazing energy and vibrated with intense love.

"Remember to bring more sunshine into your life. In your world, wear yellow to brighten your soul for it craves positive and nurturing light."

"It's beautiful, thank you." As I replied, I wondered what to do next.

Pleased, she closed her eyes and smiled then suddenly clapped her hands together. The sound echoed in my mind as millions of stars exploded over me in a breathtaking display of shimmering fireworks. As the sparkling pieces fell down, the glittering embers disappeared into Parker and Serena's fur.

I awoke with a jolt to a bright sunny day, I touched my chest where the sash had been, feeling a bit sad that it wasn't there anymore. I got up and strolled to the window. As I opened it, a rush of warm air floated in along with the delightfully sweet scent of fresh blossoms. Curious, I looked around the yard, wondering where it came from, and spotted a short tree near the house, covered with vibrant yellow flowers. Feeling giddy, I ran outside in my pajamas to admire them. As I reached out to the soft petals, a gentle breeze suddenly shook some of them loose, sending them dancing in the wind, surrounding me in a swirl of yellow, like golden butterflies.

CHAPTER 13

Possibilities

Ethan and I were sitting on the wooden swing by the porch, rocking it back and forth with our feet as we intertwined our fingers. It was a beautiful warm Saturday and both of us felt too lazy to do anything else. I closed my eyes, feeling luxuriously sleepy as the sun warmed my face. I could feel the gentle breeze in the air as it blew through my hair, tossing stray curls onto my cheeks. Ethan shifted his weight beside me, and I felt his warm fingers on the side of my face as he tucked a strand of hair behind my ear.

As he leaned in closer, I could smell the intriguing scent of his aftershave that reminded me of fresh pine trees. My heart skipped a beat as he leaned in even closer to me. A flush of warmth filled my body when his lips gently caressed my cheek. He slowly reached up with his hand and placed it on the back of my neck as his soft kisses trailed nearer to my lips. I couldn't help but moan and lean into him. He grew more passionate as his tongue roamed over my lips. A sigh escaped my lips. My fingers gripped his soft hair, pulling him much closer to me. I could feel the heat of his skin as I eagerly explored his lips.

Suddenly a door slammed behind us, breaking our sensual trance. I opened my eyes in shock, still feeling woozy from our mesmerizing kisses. He was panting slightly as he pulled away and licked his bottom lip, appearing somewhat dazed.

I heard Mom's voice and felt her feet pounding on the wooden floorboards. They creaked and groaned loudly as she came around the corner of the porch. "Jessie? Are you here?"

"Over here, Mom!" I called out as Ethan ran his fingers through his hair looking a bit flustered.

"Oh! There you are. I was looking all over the place for you!" She came to a stop in front of us, wiping her hands on a bright yellow dish towel. Her multi colored apron was covered in flour. She'd been baking all morning in preparation for a client's birthday party. "Well this is a lovely spot! And aren't you guys adorable!" she said as she looked at us and then gazed out over the front yard, taking a moment to relax.

Ethan's face flushed beet-red. He quickly turned away for a moment but I saw a wicked smile appearing on his handsome features.

"I wanted to ask if you could do me a favor?" Mom said, smiling and inclining her head at us.

"Sure, what is it, Mom?" I said.

Ethan looked up at her questioningly as he rested his hand on my shoulder.

"Can you go to the store and pick up some more supplies for me? I'm worried that I may not have enough ingredients for the next batch."

I could smell the rich aroma of spice cookies that surrounded her as she spoke. I looked at Ethan. "What do you think? Do you want to go?"

He nodded and chimed in, "Certainly. It's not a problem."

"Oh! Thank you, you're a life saver!" she said and pulled out a sheet of paper from her jean's pocket. It was completely covered with her handwriting and had cooking smudges on it. "Okay, here's the list and some money."

She gave it to me and went briskly back inside. As Ethan and I got up and stretched, he wrapped his arms around my ribs and gave me a big hug. I looked up into his eyes, "You know that Mom adores you, don't you?"

"Yep. For some reason, little old ladies seem to like me. Maybe it's because of my charm and good looks."

I rolled my eyes at him and regretfully pulled away.

"Shall we go?"

"We shall...just give me a sec to grab my purse." I scampered away and deftly plucked the strap from the hook on the wall by the door. "Okay! Let's go!"

We strode off to his car, holding hands. As the trees blurred by the window on the way to the city, Ethan reached forward and turned down the radio.

I looked at him quizzically. "What? Something wrong? Too loud?"

"Hmm? Oh! No, I just wanted to talk to you about this summer."

Dread rushed through me like ice.

He must have seen the look of alarm on my face and quickly added, "I was wondering what your plans were?"

"Um, no idea actually. Why?"

"Well, for the last few years Dad and I have spent the summer at Camp Balsam, near Algonquin Park, teaching Karate. Dad can't go this year and Sensei Jake was originally slated to help out but obviously that won't happen." He looked at me and continued on. "I was wondering if you would be interested in joining me as my assistant?"

I was speechless, beyond shock. I never expected this. "Seriously? But I'm not a Black Belt like you."

"That won't be a problem. What matters is how you treat the kids. You're so great with them, Jessie."

"Wow, I don't know what to say." I looked out the window and tried to gather my wits.

"Trust me, they'll love you."

I had a thought and narrowed my eyes at him suspiciously. "Why? What does that mean?"

He smiled as he briefly glanced at me. "Many of the kids at this camp have a learning disability of some sort. Once they see you with your bright hearing aids, they'll embrace you. You'll fit right in."

"What kind of disabilities?" I asked, my curiosity growing by the minute.

"A wide range, such as ADD, ADHD, OCD, Tourette's, and many more."

"Was that English?" I asked feeling confused by the long list of letters.

"Heh. Attention Deficit Disorder, Attention Deficit Hyperactive Disorder, and Obsessive Compulsive Disorder."

I gestured with my hand impatiently for him to continue. "Which means?"

"Um, ADD generally means someone who has a very short attention span. ADHD is someone with a short attention span and who is quite hyper, literally unable to sit still. They need to be doing something all the time. A person with OCD tends to repeat things like counting, washing their hands constantly, or doing something over and over. It can be really hard to tear them away from something like that."

"And Tourette's?" I prompted.

"It's an uncontrollable urge to speak out loud or do inappropriate things. They can't stop themselves. It's like their mind suddenly takes over their body and does whatever it wants. It's embarrassing for them because it's not their fault."

I tried to envision these kids with those symptoms. It baffled me. "Wow."

"Oh wait—it gets worse," he said with a sly grin as he watched the traffic.

"Worse? Worse than that?" I asked, not really believing him.

"Some of them have several of these symptoms at the same time. They could have OCD and Tourette's or ADHD and something else." He looked at me for a moment when the light changed to red. "They're nice kids, though."

"How do they get it? Are they born like that?"

"I don't know. Some are born with it. For others it's an environmental problem. I asked Luc that same question and he said that it was different for every kid. Some are allergic to certain kinds of food and that sets them off, makes them go out of control."

"Luc? Who's Luc?"

"You'll like him, Jessie. He's a bit like your brother Ken. He loves working with kids, teaching them camping and canoeing. He's the director of Camp Balsam, in other words he's our boss."

"Ah, I see," I said, feeling a bit overwhelmed and suddenly very scared about going to a camp filled with hyperactive kids.

We pulled into the parking lot and walked into the grocery store. Ethan grabbed a cart as I read Mom's list. As we strolled down the aisles, I continued to ask him questions about the camp.

"So what's it like, the camp I mean?" I inquired as I grabbed a large bag of organic flour.

"Oh it's beautiful. There's a sparkling lake called Balsam Lake. We have a mascot named Bucky the Beaver. Lots of old fashioned wooden cabins and trees that go on for miles. It's peaceful...when the kids aren't screaming their heads off," he said wistfully.

"Did you go there as a kid?" I asked slyly, nudging him with my elbow.

"Who, me? What are ya saying? That I have problems?" he replied playfully, his face filled with mock surprise. "No. Dad was asked to teach up there a few years ago. He discovered the hard way that the kids were a handful. When I was old enough and had enough experience teaching, he had me help out."

He looked at me, holding a hand over his heart with his face filled with pride. "It was a life changing experience, Jessie."

I got goose bumps on my arms as he said that. "In that case, maybe I should go. I gotta say this though...I'm scared out of my mind and excited about it at the same time."

He rubbed his hand on my arm. "I know, It was like that for me too when I started out." He pushed the cart down the aisle. "So, what else is on that list?"

I was in a daze on the way back home, thinking about camp. I was so nervous about what to say to Mom and Dad and wondered how they would react.

"Jessie?"

"Hmm?" I said blinking my eyes, trying to snap out of my reverie.

We were at a stoplight and he was waiting for the red light to change. "Did your brother go to camp or work at a camp?"

I tried to remember what his summers were like. We rarely saw each other anymore. "Yeah, he did for two summers as part of some course requirements for University.

"Did he talk much about it?"

"Um, yeah some, mostly about the guys he worked with and the things they did. He was a bit of a practical joker. He taught Ecology and survival stuff, how to use a canoe, set up a tent, start a fire...you know. I can remember how much he loved being out there. He often took the kids on nature hikes and taught them how to use a compass, stuff like that." I thought about it some more. "He said that he had a great time."

Ethan nodded his head in understanding. "Did he ever encourage you to go to camp?"

"Oh no, my parents couldn't afford it."

He quickly sucked in a breath as he realized his mistake. "I'm sorry, Jessie."

I shrugged my shoulders, "No it's all right. I guess I'll just make up for that this year."

"Heh. No kidding."

"Do they have any counselors that were campers who actually stayed at that camp?"

"Yep, a couple. They've been going to the same camp for almost ten years."

I gaped at him, shocked. "Really? Wow!"

The tires crunched loudly on the gravel as the car rolled to a stop in the driveway. We grabbed the grocery bags and went up the steps and into the kitchen. As we plunked down the bags on the dining room table, I yelled, "Mom! We're home!"

Mom popped her head out of the of the laundry room door. "Oh! Perfect timing! I was just about to work on the next batch of cookies!" She walked down the hallway and into the kitchen, grabbing the apron, and tying it around her waist.

I deliberated for a moment, trying to decide how to break the news to her.

She looked up from rummaging through the bags. "You look like you have something on your mind, Jessie."

"I do? I do!"

She continued to rifle through the bags, laying out the items that she needed, putting others in the fridge or cupboards.

I pulled out a chair and sat down, spinning the grocery list around and around in my hand. "Huh. How do I say this?"

Ethan looked down at me as he casually leaned against the doorway, resting his arms across his chest.

"I guess I have a summer job at a camp this year." I said not quite believing it.

Mom slapped her hand on the counter, startling me. "Ha! I knew it!"

I looked at Ethan who wore a smug smile on his face, clearly enjoying this spectacle.

Mom pointed her finger at Ethan. "His father called us a few weeks ago asking us if we thought you would be interested in working at summer camp, teaching karate."

My jaw dropped to my chest, "You knew? That's so not fair!"

"Well, I did say that it was up to you." She leaned on the counter with her arms on top of it. "So? What do you think?"

"Yeah, I think Ethan swayed me on that topic." I said stunned that I had committed to it.

She squealed with delight and came over to give me a huge hug. "I'm so excited for you, honey! Ken thought you would be perfect for it!" She moved over to Ethan and gave him a hug also.

"What? He knew too?" I stood there feeling like a fool, being the last person to know about it.

Mom went back to rifling through the groceries. "By the way, Ken sent a list of camping items that you'll need. He said that most of it is in the closet by the fireplace."

I stared at both of them, my eyes darting back and forth between them. Somehow I got the impression that they had planned the whole thing.

I threw up my hands in the air. "Oh great! My whole life is a sham, a complete farce!" I said somewhat sarcastically.

"Oh don't be silly! That's just your hormones doing the talking. Now shoo! I need to work here," Mom said.

I stuck my tongue out at Ethan as I grabbed a warm cookie from the baking rack and marched outside to sit on the porch.

Out of the corner of my eye, I saw Mom give Ethan a couple of cookies before he followed me.

"So are you hiding anything else? Any more tricks up your sleeve?" I asked as I bit into the cookie and he sat down beside me on the steps.

He sat there smiling, munching on his cookies as he stared across the lawn.

CHAPTER 14

Camp Balsam

I was frantically pulling various knickknacks out of the closet and tossing them aside as I searched for a Coleman lantern and life jacket. On the floor beside me in a towering pile were a sleeping bag, compass, canoe paddle, my swimsuit, beach towel, and bath towel. My large suitcase was filled with T-shirts, tank tops, a pair of shorts, two uniforms, lots of underwear and sports bras, socks, pjs, jeans, plaid shirt, thermal shirt, a pair of sturdy sandals, running shoes, raincoat, a couple of pairs of sweatpants and sweatshirts, plus a thick, heavy pullover. I couldn't fathom wearing the heavy pullover since it was hot and muggy but it was on the list so I managed to stuff in it with the rest of the items by sitting on top of the suitcase. It was a struggle but I eventually won.

"Aha!" I exclaimed as my fingers gripped the handle of the lantern and yanked it out. I clicked on the button, hoping that it would come to life and fortunately it did. Now, if only I could find the friggin' life jacket, I thought to myself as my hands roamed through the bottom of the closet. I could feel a piece of strap within my grasp. I leaned farther in and managed to get a tenuous grip on it and inch it out to me, tugging it through the mess. One final pull...there! It came flying out. I nearly toppled over as it came loose. I shrugged my arms into it and zipped it up, testing to see if it fit. Perfect!

"Oh my! Jessie, Ethan's going to be in here any minute and you're not ready?" Mom exclaimed as she stood beside me, surveying the giant mess all around me.

I unzipped the life jacket and tossed it on top of the pile with a pleased smile. "Yes I am. That was the last thing on the list."

"Uh-huh." She placed her hands on her hips and narrowed her eyes at me. "Did you remember to pack your pajamas? Toothbrush? Hearing aid batteries, lots and lots of batteries?"

"Yep, yes, and oh yes," I said smugly.

"In that case, here's a gift for you." She held out a small box in shiny mint green wrapping paper with a pink ribbon tied into a bow on top.

"Oh! What's this?" I was not expecting this at all. It was hard enough to walk away from Parker and Serena who were sound asleep on my bed upstairs. My heart broke as I had looked at them before going downstairs, knowing that I wouldn't see them all summer.

"You'll see," she said with a twinkle in her eyes.

I tugged at the bow, ripped off the wrapping, and lifted the lid. Inside was a smooth round white object, just a little bigger than a hockey puck. In the center was an LED screen featuring the time, the seconds blinking away.

Confused I pulled it out and rested it in my palm, it nearly covered my entire hand. "Um, what is it?"

"That's a Sonic Shaker. It's an alarm clock." She gestured at it. "Try pressing the little button at the top."

Gingerly I touched the button and it suddenly began to vibrate. I nearly dropped it in shock. "Sweet! That is so cool!"

"You can tuck it under your pillow so it will wake you up in the morning. This way, you don't have to get up early to keep checking your watch."

Curious, I pressed the button again and giggled as it shook beneath my fingers.

"Okay, that's enough, you don't want to kill the batteries before you get to Camp Balsam. And no practical jokes young lady. I know what your brother did when he was at camp." Mom looked around as if mentally tallying every-thing up, "Where's your pillow?"

Dang, I knew I'd forgotten something. "Oops! I'll get it right now!"

I dashed up the stairs, snatched it off the bed, and gave Parker and Serena a quick kiss on their furry foreheads. Then I thumped back down with the pillow in my hands and tossed it on top of my suitcase.

"There! I think that's everything. I hope."

I started putting the stuff I'd taken out of the closet back in when the doorbell rang. "Crap. That was fast." And I began stuffing everything in faster.

Mom went to the door and opened it. Standing on the porch were Ethan and his father, wearing big grins. "Jessie, they're here!" she yelled in my direction, gave each of them a hug, and let them in.

Ethan strolled over to me. "Ready to go?" As he came to stop beside me his eyes roamed all over the floor and couch. "Geez, what happened?"

I knelt back down feeling somewhat defeated. It was a close contest between the closet and me and it seemed to be winning. "Ugh! I don't know how Ken put all this stuff in here!"

Mom came over with Ethan's dad, "Oh, don't worry about that, honey. We can put that away. It's time to go anyway."

I blew out a nervous breath, feeling the impending pressure of being totally committed to going to camp. It was now or never. I'd had this battle going on in my head for the last week or so, debating whether I could do this. The last thing I wanted was to regret it if I didn't go. I had received an email from Ken a few weeks ago congratulating me and offering some advice on what to do at camp. His last words were, "Just go for it and be yourself. It's like being a part of a big family. I had a great time and you will, too!"

I stood up and reached for my suitcase. Ethan beat me to the punch and hefted it by the handle. He grabbed the pillow and tossed it at me. "Here, you can carry the heavy one."

I smacked him playfully with it. "Ha, ha, very funny."

I picked up the paddle and life jacket and proceeded to walk to the door. Mom came over to me, grasped me in a tight hug, and gave me a quick kiss on my cheek. "Bye, honey, have a great time!"

My throat constricted painfully and I could feel my eyes watering. "Thanks," I said in a whisper, afraid that my voice would crack if I said anything more. I looked down and saw Parker and Serena standing beside the door as if waiting to go with me.

My mind wanted to go forward but my body was trying to betray me. It wanted to go back in. I took a deep breath and marched out to the car, determined to be strong. It was like a parade with the three of us towing my stuff and packing it in the trunk.

I climbed in the back as Ethan's dad slammed the trunk shut and made his way around the car. As Ethan sat down beside me, I looked over his shoulder at the front door,

Mom and Dad waved at me. Serena and Parker stood on the porch steps beside them.

Willing myself not to cry, I waved back at them as the car started to roll away down the lane.

When I twisted around to latch my seatbelt, I felt an odd buzzing on my hip. I gasped loudly and jolted back, frantically digging my hands into my pocket. I had forgotten that the Sonic Alarm was in my pocket.

"What's the matter?" asked Ethan.

I laughed at the reaction on his face and pulled out the vibrating alarm.

"Ohh...kay. Dare I ask what this is?" he said as I placed it in his hands.

I sputtered, laughing breathlessly as he held it, wearing a bewildered look.

"It's a Sonic Alarm! You know, for people like me." I grinned as I said this.

"Oh! I see, so instead of noise that you can't hear, it moves so that you can feel it. Dang, that's cool." A wicked smile spread on his face and I had the feeling that I knew what he was thinking.

"Uh no. Mom said no practical jokes."

He let out a theatrical sigh and rolled his eyes as he gave it back to me. I saw his dad watching us through the rearview mirror and grinning.

It was a long drive which took most of the day on the 401 and 400. We eventually joined Highway 11 that took us through the Muskoka area, past Gravenhurst and Huntsville. The scenery changed dramatically the farther north we went. High walls of solid rock loomed on either side of us. Hillsides featuring farmland turned into thick stands of trees the closer we got to Algonquin Provincial Park. The roads were damp and slick and the sky had turned dark from the storm clouds that loomed overhead. There was wispy layer of fog that floated over top of the road, making it disappear and reappear as we drove. The opaque mist looked like strange ghosts that swirled and writhed across the surface.

My eyes had begun to feel drowsy and I was beginning to fall into a gentle slumber when the car suddenly lurched to the side. I snapped my eyes open and gripped the edge of the seat.

"Wha the—" Ethan and I exchanged worried glances.

"Gah!" Ethan's father was muttering and jerking the steering wheel side to side. "I've heard of it raining cats and dogs but frogs? This is crazy! There's too many of them!"

The car lurched to the other side as he swerved madly.

I began to giggle and mouthed at Ethan, "Seriously?"

He arched his eyebrows at me and nodded.

I glanced over his shoulder at the road to see what he was talking about. The road was indeed covered in frogs, hopping all over the place. I had never seen anything like it. It must've been the rain that attracted them.

"Why are the frogs crossing the road?" I asked.

Ethan laughed. "Is that a real joke? Because I don't know the answer to that one."

"Too bad we can't just whip out our wands to save them."

Ethan grinned mischievously at me. "Big *Harry Potter* fan?"

"Ahhh! This is insane!" The car jolted to the side again as Ethan's dad attempted to avoid squishing them. I cringed and squealed as I watched him drive past the poor frogs.

I could see behind us that some them were not as lucky as others. They were beyond saving. "Ew."

I rolled down the window and yelled, "Sorry!"

Ethan and I burst out laughing.

After another hour or so of driving, we began to approach our destination. We went past a large lake with a row of yellow and green canoes stacked beside a simple two story hut. We slowly followed a narrow winding road to the campgrounds and emerged through an archway created two posts with an upside-down, bright yellow canoe perched on top featuring the words "Welcome to Camp Balsam" in bold green letters.

There was a clearing off to our left. We veered off in that direction and came to a stop. I looked up at the sky as the clouds receded. It appeared that the worst of the storm was over. I shivered as I stepped out of the car. The temperature in the air had dropped dramatically.

I glanced at my surroundings. Tall balsam, pine, and birch trees loomed overhead. They seemed generations old with thick trunks.

I picked up my pillow, paddle, and alarm clock and waited to grab more of my stuff, but Ethan and his father snatched up the rest of it.

I could smell the sweet scent of pine as we walked to the cabins. The pathway was covered in golden pine needles, creating a plush walking surface.

The closer we got to the main cabin, the more I could detect the rich scent of wood smoke. As we approached it, I could see a plume of smoke coming from the chimney. By the time we reached the porch, there was a man standing in the doorway wearing a broad smile. He was tall, with an athletic appearance, strong, and healthy. He had thick, brown, wavy hair, graying at the sides, and a hint of rosy cheeks. He wore a bright red plaid shirt, beige cargo pants, and gray hiking shoes.

"Ah! You made it!" He said as he stepped forward to help out. His voice sounded as if it had an accent. "Come on in! There's a bit of a nip in the air because of the storm, it brought a little bit of a cool wind with it."

He gestured at the wall on our left side, "You can pile your stuff here while you get warmed up and acquainted."

Once we'd dumped everything on the floor, he made his way toward us with an outstretched hand, eager to say hello. "Jonas, it's wonderful to see you again. It's been too long!" he said as the two exchanged manly hugs. "Ethan, oh my! You've become a strapping young fellow! I've think you've grown another foot this year!" He shook his hand and pulled him into a hug, giving him a hearty slap on the back.

He ambled in my direction and pumped my hand enthusiastically, "And this must be Jessie. Jonas has told me so much about you. I'm thrilled that you have decided to help out this year!"

He tilted his head to the side and gazed at my hearing aids. "I love the color of your hearing aids. They are simply fantastic!" My earmolds featured bright green streaks mixed with white which produced a swirling marbled effect.

"Thanks, I love them, too," I said humbly, feeling a bit shy in his presence.

"They suit you very well! The kids will certainly adore them when they see you!" he said.

"I'm Jean Luc by the way but you can call me Luc. Everyone else does." He pronounced it as Sean Looc.

Curious I asked, "Why Luc?"

"Heh, it's French Canadian and spelled as J-E-A-N. Once they see how it's really spelled, they have a tendency to go around calling me Jean..." He nudged me with his elbow and gave me a wink while wearing a silly grin.

I nodded. "Ah I see, good point."

"Okay, since this is your first time, I'll give you a brief tour. This is the dining hall and meeting room. He gestured at the room. "This is where we have our staff meetings and meals."

The fire crackled warmly behind us as I looked around. It was a large banquet hall with walls of rounded wooden logs and beams that arched above me. There were rows of tables stacked against the walls, waiting to be unfolded and used. In the middle of the room were six long tables placed together to form the shape of a U. The walls were covered in small wooden plaques, all brightly decorated in paint, featuring the names of the campers and the dates. I stared at them in disbelief, there were so many of them and the dates went as far back as the 1970s.

"The kitchen is at the back through those double doors. I'm afraid it's the chef's night off, have you had anything to eat?"

Ethan spoke up. "Yeah, we ate at Tim Horton's on the way up."

"Jessie, since you are new here, the food is rationed so I'm afraid no impromptu snacks are permitted. Meals are served at 8:30 a.m., 12:30 p.m., and 6:00 p.m. There are drinks for the staff such as tea, coffee, and hot chocolate as well as juice and water. You can have those at any time you wish. Just to let you know, sugar is off limits to the children and is kept hidden in a cupboard by the tea and coffee," Luc said with a fatherly smile.

"Um, I'm curious, why is sugar not allowed?"

Luc nodded at me and clasped his hands together in a relaxed manner. "We have found that some of the campers can't tolerate sugar. It can make them extremely hyper or more uncooperative than usual."

"Oh! I didn't know that. So they are quite different from us?" I asked.

"In some ways, yes, they function at a different level. Many of them are very smart but have trouble reading, understanding rules, or being able to relate to people properly. As a result, their peers or teachers have treated them rather badly. Our job is to find ways around their issues and embrace them for who they are. After a few days, they really shine, and we get to see their true personalities. It's a wonderful experience."

I was in awe and in a way understood what he meant, "I know what you mean about the teachers. They were cruel to me at times when I couldn't hear them. They thought I was too stupid to understand them and they would yell at me."

"You know what? That's probably a good thing because the kids will connect with you since you lived through it. You can relate to them better than most of the staff."

I'd never thought of that and felt somewhat more at ease.

"Don't worry, you'll do fine," he said reassuringly. "Okay, ready to see your cabin?"

I nodded and grabbed some of my stuff as we followed him outside. Luc walked down the well-worn path, past a large cabin on the right side with a big deck and Muskoka chairs. Sitting on the lawn out front was a large tower with a cast iron bell inside it.

He gestured at that cabin, "That's where I'm staying. It's also the headquarters for some of the meetings and a place for when a kid needs a time out."

"The cabins on the right are for the female staff. The ones on the left are where the guys stay. The cabins in between are for the campers so there will always be staff around them. I'll give you the official tour tomorrow since it's starting to get too dark tonight to appreciate our campgrounds."

He stopped at the second cabin past his, and there were two more after this one. "Jessie, this one will be yours." He pointed at the small, simple log cabin with steps leading up to the door with railings on other side. As I started walking to it, Ethan and his father veered off the path over to the other cabins.

"Come on in and I'll show you where you can put your things." Luc pulled the screen-door open, the hinges screeching loudly. He pushed open the second door which was made of solid wood with a little window at eye level. The screen-door slammed shut with a bang as we ventured inside. He turned around and flicked on two switches, one for inside lights and the other one for the outside porch light.

"Since you are the first one here, you get to pick which bed you want." I stared at the sparse room. There were five beds and three tall dressers. The beds were pushed up against the wall or tucked into a corner, and there was barely enough space for a path down the middle of the room. There were small open shelves above each bed on the walls next to the windows.

"Each staff member can use half of a dresser plus the shelves and under the bed for storage if necessary. Be careful about where you put your things otherwise someone may trip over them. It will get crowded once everyone arrives."

I looked around. It was already too crowded for me and I was feeling a little bit claustrophobic. I chose the far left bed and placed my paddle on the wall beside the shelf, tucked the lifejacket under the bed and laid my suitcase and pillow on top.

"Go ahead and unpack. Once you are finished come on over to my cabin. Ethan and Jonas will join me in a few minutes. I'm going to go check on them." He promptly turned around and marched down the steps, his feet clomping loudly on the way out.

I sat down on the bed and looked around the cabin. It was just a little bit bigger than my room at home and I tried to envision it filled with more staff members. It was an impossible feat. I unzipped my suitcase and began to pull out everything, wondering where to put it all. After several minutes, I figured out how to organize everything and put it away. I unrolled my sleeping bag and placed my pillow on top. I grabbed some of my books, make up, shampoo, soap, face towel, and flashlight and stored them on the shelves above me.

Satisfied, I made my way back to Luc's cabin and spotted Ethan sitting in the Muskoka chair waiting for me. He grinned as he saw me and stood up, draping his arm around me as I stopped in front of him.

"So, what do you think?" he said smiling, his eyes twinkling in the fading light.

"It's small."

"Small? What? The cabin?" He let out a wheezing laugh. "Well, it is a camp for kids. You should see my bed. My feet hang off the edge and it's the longest bed they have here."

"Really? Oh, wow," I said feeling like an idiot for complaining.

"Believe me, it's better than the one I had last time. The bed was shorter than this one."

I looked at the window off to the left side of the door. The lights were on, casting a soft glow onto the wooden deck. "It looks like your dad is already inside, chatting with Luc. Is he staying in the same cabin with you?"

"No, he's staying here with Luc. There are two bedrooms in this cabin plus a bathroom and kitchen."

I stared at him, slack jawed. "Seriously? How come he gets a bathroom? And speaking of which, where are the washrooms?"

He gestured with his head and looked over my shoulder. "The washrooms are over there, not far from my cabin."

I turned around and looked. There was a large building, bigger than my cabin but smaller than the dining hall. There were two doors on either side with ramps leading up to each one.

I raised my eyebrows at him questioningly. "Um, and where would the showers be?"

He nodded again. "Same building."

"Oh great. That's lovely, something to look forward to tonight," I said sarcastically.

"Heh, don't worry. If it gets to be too much, you are more than welcome to use Luc's washroom."

He grasped my hand and gently tugged me toward Luc's cabin. "Why don't you come sit with us for a while? Luc has lots of stories to tell and he would be more than happy to answer any questions you have."

CHAPTER 15

Bonjour

As we sat down, Luc was strolling toward Jonas with a steaming cup and handing it to him. He smiled at us and said, "Can I get you anything? Juice, water, tea?"

I nodded, "Tea is fine."

He tilted his head at Ethan. "How about you?"

"I'll have the same, thanks."

"Luc? Can I ask you a question?"

He looked in my direction as he plugged in the kettle and grabbed some mugs. "*Oui*, what's on your mind?"

"What's the bell for that's outside, in front of your cabin?"

He raised his eyebrows and smiled. "Ah, that would be the camp's version of an alarm clock. Not everyone wears watches around here. When you hear the bell, it means that it's time to wake up, begin the next session, meet in the dining hall, or gather for a special event."

I thought about that for a moment and said, "But I don't wear my hearing aids to bed, I'm literally deaf without them."

"Ahem!" Ethan wriggled his eyebrows at me and held out his hand miming something in it.

Oh yeah...the Sonic Alarm. I wanted to smack my forehead for forgetting that little detail.

"Never mind. So will I be able to hear it if I'm by the lake or somewhere else?"

He nodded enthusiastically. "Oh yes, it's quite loud. Have you ever heard the chime of church bells?"

I nodded, remembering that I could hear their distinctive metallic chimes echoing clear across town.

"That's what it's like, loud."

"Cool."

Once the tea was ready, he carried over the mugs and handed them to us.

"Oh thanks!" I said as I grasped the handle. The steam curled up from the hot tea. "When does everyone else arrive?" I asked as I blew on the surface of the cup.

Luc frowned for a moment as if recalling the schedule in his mind. "Let's see, most of them should be here by noon. Three of them can't make it until later in the evening. The majority of them worked here last year so it should be an easy transition for everyone. I think you'll like this group, Jessie. They're good people, very eager and easy going."

As he sat down beside Jonas, the two of them switched to French. I tried to make out what they were saying but it was nearly impossible. They spoke so fast and Luc had a strong accent.

I looked around the room as I waited for my tea to cool down a little. We sat on the left side of the room, facing Luc and Jonas, on one of three couches that formed the shape of a U. Large windows, reaching nearly to the floor, were right behind and on the left side of the wall. On the right was a small oval dining table with four wooden chairs around it. Behind it was a simple rectangular counter, a small island used for serving meals. Around that were shelves, a stove, sink, and a refrigerator. There was a short hallway behind it, and it looked as if there were two small bedrooms and a bathroom back there.

"Ethan? How long have you and your dad worked here?"

He pursed his lips and his forehead crinkled as he thought about it. "Um, maybe five years I think."

"That's impressive. You must really enjoy being here."

The crinkles disappeared as he smiled and raised his eyebrows. "Yeah, it's fun. The kids are amazing, and I like meeting new people. Some of them are good friends. It will be great to see them again." His eyes held this faraway look as if recalling good times.

I felt a little jealous and a bit surprised at his remark. Since we didn't go to the same school, I really had no idea who his friends were or how many he had. This was a side that I was not familiar with. I wondered if any of them were his former girlfriends. My stomach tightened in anxiety as I thought about it. The last thing I wanted to have to do was prove to them that we were a couple.

Before I could say anything about that, he broke into my thoughts. "I should warn you that it will get crazy. Halfway through the summer, you will feel tired from working so hard. It's a tough schedule."

Luc turned to us. "Ah! Speaking of schedules, I will be handing them out tomorrow when everyone else is here. Jessie, just to let you know, wake up time is at 7:30 a.m. and breakfast will be served at 8:30 a.m."

I nearly choked on my tea. "Ahem. Okay," I said in a harsh whisper. I didn't expect to get up that early, especially during the summer. It was bad enough that I had to go through that for school.

"Ethan, you may want to give her a little tour before it gets too dark." He looked at me and gestured at my tea, "You can take that with you during your walk. Just bring the mug back when you're done."

"Oh! Thanks, I'll do that." We rose and ventured out the door.

I looked at Ethan as we started to walk on the deck, "Nice cabin, it's cozy."

"Yeah, it's a great place to hang out and get away from the kids from time to time. As much as we like them, there are moments when it gets to be too much."

"How long has Luc worked here?"

"Hmph, maybe eleven or twelve years? I don't know the exact date."

"Twelve years? Holy cow, I couldn't imagine doing that. That's impressive!" I said feeling stunned.

"Yeah, he strongly believes in keeping this place going for the kids. He went to a camp like this when he was a kid and it had such an incredible impact on his life that he made a promise to himself to run a camp for future generations. I can remember one summer when we had a major cash shortage and we all thought it was going to be the last year. He thought he was going to have to retire but we made it through. Generous donations make a big difference here." He paused, pointed. "Okay...let's go this way and I'll show you the washrooms."

We walked straight ahead across the open space along a well-worn path. There were two tall lamp posts standing on each side of the building, illuminating more structures on either side. On the right side were five more cabins lined up in a row stretching down the field. On the left were two smaller buildings, a little bit bigger than the regular cabins.

I sipped my tea as we strolled across the grounds, getting closer to the ramp. I could hear the crickets starting to chirp loudly all around me. Once we reached the top, I took a quick peek into the girls' washroom. It was brightly lit with a row of sinks and mirrors along the left wall and a row of stalls on the other wall. A few feet in and off to my right, hidden from view, there was a small room, a little bigger than a closet featuring two shower stalls. I gaped at the narrow space, feeling very claustrophobic. There were no windows in this section, just a row of lights above, towels racks and couple of hooks on the side wall.

I walked back out and stared at him, slack-jawed. "Wow, we are really roughing it aren't we?"

He nodded as he tipped his head to drink the last bit of tea. He gestured at the doorway. "When the kids are here, there's usually five or six of us keeping an eye on them. We stay by the doors to remind them to brush their teeth or hurry up. Some like to stall, delaying as long as possible. And some of them are afraid of the dark, so we're here to escort them back to their cabins."

"Oooh, night patrol. How sexy. Do you get to wear a uniform?" I asked slyly. "I'm afraid of the dark. Is there any way I can get a good-looking staff member to escort me back to my cabin?"

He delivered a snappy military salute with his fingers and offered the crook of his arm. "Sure can ma'am."

Acting like a tour guide, he gestured broadly at the building on the left side of the washroom. "On this side, we have the nurse's station and office. On the right side are the quaint and oh so rustic cabins for the guys."

We turned around and strolled toward my cabin. "As you can see, the cabins down in this section are for the lovely ladies. Beyond them, is the Arts and Crafts Building and rock climbing wall."

I squinted past the large building at the end and could barely see the outlines of a tall rectangular structure near the edge of the woods.

"Also located in that area is a swimming pool." He said following my gaze.

I could see a tall chain link fence all around it. Curious I asked, "What's with the fence?"

"Ah! Excellent question! Some campers have suicidal tendencies. It's for everyone's safety."

Shocked I queried him, "But why? They're too young to even think about that!"

"It depends on the kid. Some are under enormous peer pressure at school because of their disability or have problems at home. In some cases, it's from the medication they take. It can be too much for them. They feel like they've lost a part of themselves."

I looked back in that direction. The setting sun cast a brilliant coral glow onto the clouds above the trees and lit up the leaves behind the cabins. It cast a golden halo around everything in its path. It was a beautiful moment as I watched the leaves shake in the breeze, appearing like glittering orbs.

He walked up the steps and pulled open the door. "After you, ma'am."

I giggled. "Aw, gee thanks."

I marched in and sat on the bed and turned on the little Coleman lantern. He sat down beside me and cradled his arm around me.

"So? Ready for the big day tomorrow?" he asked as he leaned his head toward me, resting his forehead on mine.

"Heh, no, not really."

He caressed my back as he gave me a gentle kiss on my cheek. "Will you be okay for tonight? It might be a tad spooky with no one else here." I could feel his body rumble with his words.

I gulped, trying not to reveal just how truly scared I was. I felt as if I was six years old again, totally afraid of the dark. "Um, yeah, I think so. I have this lamp so it should be okay. I'm going to take a shower and brush my teeth before I go to bed though."

"Hey, tell you what, I'll meet you over there so that we can say goodnight."

"Sure."

"Oops, I'll take that mug to Luc for you," he said as he grabbed the handle.

"Oh! Thanks!"

As he left, the door slammed shut with a squeaky bang.

I began grabbing various items: towel, toothbrush, pajamas and a little plastic box of soap. I was about to go out the door when I realized I didn't have my flashlight with me. I quickly snatched it up and pounded down the steps, striding over to the washrooms.

I didn't see Ethan and assumed he was still with Luc and his dad. As I stepped into the little cubby with the shower stalls, I stared at them, dumbfounded. They were so small, smaller than anything I'd ever seen. I turned around and searched for a place to put my stuff. All I saw were a couple of racks for the towels and hooks for the clothes. Since there was no place to put my hearing aids, I took them off and stuffed them into my pockets. I hung up my towel and stripped down, hanging my clothes on a little hook.

Pulling aside the flimsy curtain, I leaned in and turned on the tap. I reached out to test it and instantly pulled my hand back. It was freezing. I waited for nearly a minute, standing stark naked and feeling very self-conscious. I tested it again. It was warm, and I stepped in holding onto the bar of soap. I lathered up, washed my face and stood under the cascading water, letting it fall across my shoulders. The soap suddenly slipped from fingers and fell, landing between my feet. Crap! I bent down to retrieve it and promptly banged my head on the wall. Cursing, I rubbed my forehead. It was impossible to bend down in the stall. It was so frickin' small, and there was just enough room to turn around. I sighed and gave up. I turned off the water and stepped out. At that point, I was able to snatch up the soap, fumbling with it as it tried to escape from my fingers again.

I felt unbelievably vulnerable being out in the open like this and quickly dried off with the towel. The air was cold. I shivered, rubbing the towel all over my body. Fast. Goosebumps formed on my arm as I pulled on my jammies. I reached over and yanked my clothes off the hook. To my horror, my hearing aids fell onto the wet floor. I quickly snatched them up and dried them off, hoping that they hadn't gotten too wet. I put them back into my ears and turned them on. I heard the sound of the crickets chirping away outside. Relieved, I strode over to the sink and brushed my teeth, looking out the open door and watching the sky turn indigo blue.

Satisfied, I grabbed everything and made my way outside.

"Boo!" Ethan jumped out in front of me, startling me. I uttered a piercing shriek.

"Ethan!" I shifted my clothes, towel, and lamp to my other hand and smacked his arm. "You scared the crap outta me!"

He smiled impishly. "Need an escort?" He held his hand out to and I linked my fingers with his.

"Gladly," I said, my heart still pounding from his prank.

We strolled in the darkness, except for the glow of my little lamp which formed a spotlight around us. As we reached the main pathway, we came to a stop.

Ethan kissed me, his soft lips lingering on mine. I didn't want it to stop.

When we finally broke apart, he said, "Mmm! Minty fresh! I'll see you in the morning, bright and early."

I groaned, not looking forward to getting up that early. "Ugh...see you later, handsome."

We released our hands and walked away in opposite directions, back to our cabins. Once inside, I shut the doors and placed my towel by the dresser to dry, set the lantern on the shelf above me, and put my clothes away. I turned off the light, placed my hearing aids on the shelf beside the lamp. Lifting the pillow, I grabbed the Sonic Alarm, entered the wake up time, and tucked it back underneath the pillow. I wriggled into my sleeping bag, trying to get comfortable.

I looked around the room. It felt so strange to be surrounded by empty beds. It was dark and spooky. I crawled deeper into the sleeping bag and zipped it up as tight as possible, resisting the urge to whimper and suck on my thumb like a three-year-old.

For an hour or so, I kept tossing and turning, shivering. The cabin had gotten really cold. I turned on the light and looked around for a thermostat or heater. There was nothing, the walls were bare except for a few outlets. I shivered again, marched rapidly over to the dresser, pulled out a pair of socks, and yanked them on. I rummaged through the drawer, pulled on a thermal shirt, and quickly crawled back into my warm sleeping bag.

After what seemed like hours, the shivering finally stopped and I started to fall asleep. Out of habit, I rolled over and felt nothing but air. I fell to the floor with a thud.

"Stupid camp bed!" I muttered as I frantically struggled to get out of the sleeping bag and back onto bed. It was so narrow that the sleeping bag pretty much covered it. But I slapped it down and slithered back in.

It took a while to calm my beating heart and fall back asleep. I nearly rolled off the bed again but managed to grip the edge of the mattress in time. I scooted closer to the wall to give myself a little bit more room just in case.

I jerked awake to violent shaking, thinking that there was an earthquake. Then I remembered the Sonic Alarm. I reached under the pillow and turned it off. With a sigh, I unzipped the sleeping bag and climbed out, shivering in the cold morning air. Faint light filtered through the windows, bringing some solace into a dark room.

I dashed over to the dresser and grabbed the warmest clothes I had and pulled them on, feeling very exposed despite the fact that there was no one around. I kept glancing over my shoulder hoping that no one could see me through the windows.

Grabbing an elastic band from the shelf, I pulled my curly hair into a ponytail and tugged it into place. I rubbed my arms, trying to get warm and walked outside. The sun was rising, and there were scattered clouds floating in the crisp blue sky. I could smell wood smoke in the air. I inhaled it, savoring the scent. As I marched down the steps, I saw Ethan emerge from his cabin, walking toward me and carrying a toothbrush in his hand.

"Good morning, Jessie! Sleep well?" he remarked with a smile.

Feeling sour, I grumbled a reply. "No, not really. It was too cold and I fell off the bed!" I said as he pulled me into a hug.

He chuckled as he embraced me. "Aw, I'm sorry. Heh, heh."

I looked up at him. "What's so funny?"

"So did I on my first night here."

"Really?"

He nodded. "You get used to it."

"Why is the cabin so cold? Where are the heaters?" I asked.

"There aren't any. These cabins are quite old. Don't worry, it will warm up soon. You won't even need a blanket," he replied as we stood in the sun, getting warmer by the minute. "Feeling better now?"

I nodded. We pulled apart and held on to each other's hand as we sauntered over to the washrooms and dining hall.

CHAPTER 16

Impressions

The large wooden doors were already open as Ethan and I stepped onto the porch and into the Dining Hall. I made a beeline to the crackling fireplace and immediately warmed my hands in front of it, sighing happily.

Ethan's father sat at the table near the fire beside Luc. The two of them were chatting earnestly, in rapid French, nonetheless. Their eyes snapped in our direction as we strolled in.

"Ah! Bonjour, Jessie!" said Luc, beaming, his robust cheeks glowing in the morning sun. If he'd had white hair and a beard, he could've easily been mistaken for Santa Claus, especially with the joyful glint in his eyes. His soul seemed to exude a sense of the inner child bursting through with glee.

"Bonjour," I said shyly and nodded at Jonas as well. I was particularly thankful that I remembered some French that I took as a junior.

"Oooh, *parlez vous francais?*" he asked. Translation: Do you speak French?

"*Non, un petit peu, desolé*" I replied, no, a little bit, sorry.

I switched back to English. "I wasn't supposed to take French at school. My counselor discouraged me from taking it."

Luc gasped loudly as his eyebrows knitted together. "May I ask why?"

"He thought it would be too much for me. He told me that hearing impaired students should not learn other languages, including French. He claimed that it was too advanced for someone like me." I raised my hands in the air, miming finger quotes.

He scoffed. "*Mon dieu*! Excuse me. He had no right to hold you back like that or tell you what to do with your education."

"I know. That's exactly what I said to him. It made me even more determined to take it."

He reached across the table and gave me a high five. "Ha! Good for you, Jessie!"

"That's the kind of attitude I like to see in young people. Nothing holds you back!" He leaned back in his chair, sipping on the liquid in his cup as wisps of steam curled upward in the sun.

Ethan stood beside me with his hands on a nearby chair, leaning on it casually and smiling as he watched our banter.

"I presume you are ready for breakfast?" asked Ethan.

"Yep. Do I go in the kitchen or is it served out here?" I thumbed over my shoulder at the double doors.

"Ha! I like this girl...served out here," Luc said as he clapped his hands together, laughing quietly.

I looked at Ethan then back at Luc and Jonas. They all smiled at me as if I'd made a joke. "What?"

"No, no, it's definitely not served out here. Follow me and I'll introduce you to the chef." He gestured with his hand to go with him. He walked over to the doors and pushed them open. The chef turned around, holding a spatula in midair over the grill. A long steel table sat in front of us, separating us from the cooking area. It was spotless. On the far right side stood a stack of plates with the utensils in a bin beside it. "Jessie, this is Jamie, he is the head chef for this summer."

"Hey, Jessie, hope you're hungry," he said with a smile as he waved at me with his spatula and went back to flipping the pancakes.

They smelled heavenly and made my mouth water. He wore a black and white bandana, white chef's uniform and loose black pants.

I nodded. "Starving. They smell great!"

"Yay! My first fan!" He deftly slid the spatula under the pancakes on the grill, plunked them on a plate, and passed it to me.

Steam rose from them as I picked it up and grabbed a fork. "Thanks!"

He nodded and continued to dole out more pancakes. We all made our way into the dining hall and sat down. I grabbed the small jar of maple syrup and poured it lavishly over top of the pancakes. I took a bite and moaned. "Mmm! So good!"

Luc chuckled as he glanced my way and stabbed his fork into his pile of pancakes.

In between mouthfuls, I uttered, "Geez, what time did he get up to already have these done?"

Luc swallowed. "Usually between 5:30 or 6:00 a.m. It depends on what he's making."

Stunned, I let my fork stop in front of my lips. "Wow, that's early."

He nodded again. "The assistant chef will be here shortly to help with the meals when the rest of the staff arrives."

He looked at his watch. "As a matter of fact, some of them will be arriving this morning."

I could feel the butterflies fluttering in my stomach. Suddenly, I was feeling nervous.

Jonas looked at Ethan, jabbing his fork toward the doors. "Have you shown Jessie where your classes are held yet?"

"Oh! There's a dojo?" I asked and then creased my forehead in concentration. "I don't remember seeing one."

Ethan stopped short of sipping his tea and grinned. "That's because there isn't one. It's outdoors, beside the nurse's station. It's not ready yet."

I smirked, seeing the irony. "Was it put there on purpose?"

"Heh, nope. It's just a good flat area with some shade."

"Speaking of which, you'll need to put some new rope around it. The old one is too frayed to use this year. Perhaps after breakfast, you and Jessie can get it ready?"

He nodded in assent. "Sure, no problem. I had another project in mind which will give me the chance to show her the workshop."

I stared at them. "You have a workshop, too? Wow!"

Luc spoke up. "It's where we also keep the extra camp beds."

I was already beginning to feel warmer after breakfast and sitting by the fireplace.

I scraped my plate clean, mopping up the maple syrup with the last piece of pancake. I stood up, holding the plate in my hand. "Um, where do I put this?"

"Ah! Finished? You can put it in the plastic bin by the window. It's already filled with soapy water." He gestured with his fork at the table by the kitchen doors along the wall. "Utensils go in the other one beside it."

I strode over and placed the dish in one bin, my fork in the other. Looking out the window, I stretched and rolled my neck, trying to loosen it up. All that tossing and turning had made it stiff, and falling off the bed certainly didn't help. Ethan joined me, dumping his plate and fork into the soapy water.

He turned around and looked at me. He placed his hands on my neck and began to massage it with his blissfully warm fingers. "Sore neck?" he asked.

I nodded, enjoying the sensation of his hands on my skin. It felt amazing and I sighed happily.

He chuckled as he saw my face. "Happy now?"

"Mm hmm," I mumbled, not wanting him to stop.

I could feel the tension beginning to ease out of me as his fingers worked their magic. I was supremely disappointed when they stopped.

He turned around and walked over to his father who was still sipping his cup of coffee.

"Dad? What time are you leaving?"

He looked up at Ethan. "Probably within the hour."

Ethan nodded at him. "Okay, we will either be at the workshop or putting up the rope."

He walked over to me, grasping my hand as we marched down the steps. I could feel the warm sun on my face as we went outside. We turned left onto the dirt path meandering past tall trees and onto the road, through the canoe gateway.

He looked at me, briefly pointing down the lane. "It's near the watch tower by the lake," he said as if reading my thoughts when I wondered how far away it was.

I glanced at him. "Okay." It loomed on the horizon, about 60 feet away from me on the left side of the road. It was a simple structure with a large rollup metal door and a smaller doorway on the side. We went in through the small door. Ethan flicked on the lights. In front of me stood a long wall of tools, all lined up in military precision. It was filled with an assortment of screwdrivers, saws, hammers, and wrenches. On the counter sat rows of clear glass jars filled with nails and screws, organized accordingly to size. Beside them was a stack of masking tape, paint brushes and a couple of paint cans. Underneath the counter sat a gasoline jug, garbage can, stacks of smooth, flat square pieces of wood and a chainsaw.

Ethan followed my line of sight and pointed at the wood, "Those are for the kids to paint and put on the wall in the dining hall for each session. Each cabin gets to come up with their own theme. It's a yearly tradition."

"Oh! Very cool. I love the dining hall like that, it's amazing," I said as I looked around. "You know, this place is organized, and I'm mean really organized."

Ethan chuckled knowingly. "Heh, yeah that's Luc."

I got the impression that there was something else about Luc that he wasn't saying but I shrugged it off.

All along the back wall were rows of beds and mattresses, all waiting to be used. I shuddered, thinking about the mice that were lurking around and likely crawling all over them. On the left side of the wall, by my side, were stacks of wood in various thickness and lengths. Ethan went straight for them and began rifling through them. With a grunt, he pulled out three short pieces, nearly an inch thick and two feet long, and held them out to me. "Jessie, can you hold onto these for me, please?"

I walked over to him and picked them up, stacking them in my arms. I stared at him, wondering what he was up to. "What are these for?"

He grinned slyly. "Ah, you'll see...I have an idea," he said as rifled through the longer pieces, running his fingers over them. He stopped and began to yank out a long and thick beam and dropped it onto the floor with a clatter. Hands on his hips, he muttered, "Yep, that'll work." He hefted it up onto his shoulder, strode over to the counter, and picked up a hammer and box of nails with the other hand. "Oh! Before I forget, can you grab that rope from the top of that box?" He gestured with his head toward it.

I walked over to it. I managed to shuffle the wood into the crook of my arm and, with my free hand, snatched it up.

"Perfect! All righty then, let's go to the dojo. Don't forget to close the door otherwise the mice will get in."

I shuddered, reached out, and yanked on the doorknob, slamming it shut with a bang. We marched down the road, our feet crunching loudly on the gravel. By the time we reached the nurse's station, I had worked up a sweat and gratefully dumped the wood onto the ground. I pulled off my heavy pullover and placed it on the steps that led up to the office door.

"Okay, I'll bite...what are you making?" I asked as sweat beaded on my forehead.

"Isn't it obvious?" he replied. He laid out the three smaller pieces of wood, several feet apart in front of me.

He placed the heavy, long beam on top of them and began to mark the wood at three intervals with a pencil he pulled from his jeans pocket.

I gazed at it, recognizing the pattern and pointed at it, "Is that a balance beam?"

He nodded. "Yep. Thought we could teach the kids how to do some kicks on it, you know, make it more challenging."

"Yeah, that's a great idea!"

He moved the beam off to the side and placed one of the smaller pieces on top where he had made a notch on it. "I should show you where the rope goes. Come on over here." He waved with his hand for me to go with him.

I grabbed the rope off the ground and followed him around the corner of the building. There stood four trees off to the side, about fifteen feet apart providing a neat square surrounding a smooth clearing in the middle.

He pointed to one tree off to his left. "You'll see a large round eyelet on each tree. Tie the rope at this end, pull it tightly, then loop it through the other three to the other one over here." He gestured at the tree on my right side. "We'll leave this area open between the two trees, sort like a doorway." He spread his arms out and spun around. "This will be our dojo."

"What happens if it rains?"

"The classes will be held in the dining hall."

"How come we don't have all of the classes there?"

"Oh no, no, no. That would require putting away the tables and chairs to use the room and then setting up everything again to be ready for lunch and dinner every single day. It's a giant pain in the butt and it drives the kitchen staff crazy. We tried it a few years ago and it was a disaster. We had a lot of rainy days that summer," he said as his eyes took on a faraway look.

I began unraveling the rope, trying to find one end. "Ah, good point. Okay, I'll work on this."

He turned around, went back to the beam, grabbed the hammer, and began nailing in the flat piece of wood, hitting it with a sharp bang.

A few minutes later, Luc and Jonas strolled over to watch us. Ethan's dad held a gray duffel bag in one hand and let it drop to the ground. "Aha, hard at work, eh?"

Ethan pounded in another nail and grabbed another piece of wood as he looked up at his father.

"Ethan, I'm going to head back home now."

Ethan stopped hammering and stood up, giving his dad a hearty hug. "Bye, Dad, have a safe trip home."

"Thanks, Son." He strode over to me and gave me a quick hug. "Have a good time Jessie!"

"Thanks," I replied shyly.

He bent down, retrieved the bag, and marched toward the parking lot behind a row of large, majestic trees.

I tightened the knot on the final hook and took a moment to watch Ethan pound in the last nail. He hit it with a satisfied bang and stood up to analyze it. "Perfect!" He picked it up and carried it over toward me, looking at the roped in area. "That's great, Jessie." He put the beam down on the ground. "Okay, try it out and see what ya think."

I gingerly stepped on the end. It was strong and sturdy.

"Okay, try taking a step forward and add a kick or two," he said as he watched with his crossed arms resting casually on his chest.

"Sure." I proceeded slowly, taking a step then snapping out a quick kick. I nearly lost my balance momentarily and decided to do it more slowly. "Whoo! It's harder than it looks!"

He nodded. "I think one of us should act as the spotter to help the kids across, otherwise it should work fine, eh?"

I went back and forth, trying out different kicks, experimenting with ways of doing it. Just as I got to the end of the beam, I heard a yell behind me. It was too far away for me to decipher. To me it sounded muffled. Once I stepped onto the ground, I turned around and saw a tall person struggling to carry her gym bag and suitcase. She wore a bright orange zip-up hoodie, green shorts, and hiking boots. Her long brown hair was tied back into a ponytail that swayed as she started to jog to Ethan. Her face was suffused with joy.

"Ethan!" she yelled again. "You made it! I can't believe you're here!"

Ethan's face lit up like a light bulb. "Maggie! Ha, ha! You came back!" He zipped out of the dojo and strode to her, arms outstretched, "Whoo! It's so great to see you!"

She dropped everything and ran into his arms, giving him a huge hug. He nearly toppled over. "Oh my God! I can't believe it!"

They broke apart and stood there, staring at each other. I stood there flabbergasted. I had never seen this side of him before. I could sense that there was a strong connection between them. I scrutinized them, wondering if there was more to what I saw.

"Hey...love your hair," he said as he gazed at her.

"Oh! Thanks! I wasn't sure how it would look this long." She reached up and grasped her ponytail, twirling it between her fingers briefly.

"Is Rick coming too?" Ethan asked.

"Yeah, yeah, he should be coming sometime this afternoon."

"All right! Man, this is going to be a fun summer!"

I came to a stop beside him, reached down, and intertwined my fingers with his, sending a clear signal to her.

"Oh! This is Jessie. She's my assistant instructor this year."

Assistant instructor? Uh, hello? Yoo hoo, girlfriend here, I mentally ranted at him.

"Jessie, this is Maggie. She's the climbing instructor, in charge of rock climbing and ropes."

I reached out with my other hand, which she gave a friendly shake.

"Hi!" she said wearing an easy going smile. "Is this your first time here?" She beamed as bright as the sun.

I nodded. "Yes, Ethan convinced me to join him this summer."

"Oh wow, Jessie. You're in for a real treat. Everyone is like family here."

"Uh-huh, he said that, too," I remarked as I tilted my head toward him. "How about you?" I asked curiously.

"It's my third year. There is just something about this place that makes you want to come back."

Ethan chimed in, "Heh, yeah no kidding! Even though there are moments when you just wanna wring someone's neck, you find out what makes them so special." He mimed choking actions with his hands and scrunched up his face.

Her eyes went wide with excitement. "Ha! That's right! Remember when Barry did that huge belly flop into the pool ?"

"Oh hell yeah!" He slapped his thigh as he laughed. "Ouch!"

The two of them chattered animatedly as they began to walk over to her luggage. She bent down and picked up the suitcase and was reaching for the duffel bag when he intervened. "Let me get that for you."

"Oh, thanks, you were always a sweetheart!"

I mentally held back a growl, feeling the panther inside me grow more defensive.

"Which cabin do you have this time?" Ethan asked her.

"Um, I actually don't know. Guess I'll have to ask Luc."

I stood there feeling like an idiot as they continued reminiscing with each other.

He turned around and looked at me. "Jessie, can you be a darling and go ask Luc which cabin Maggie is staying in?"

Darling? Where did that come from? "Uh sure, do you know where he is?"

"Check the dining hall and his cabin. He's bound to be in either of those places."

I gripped my hand into a fist, trying to hold back my temper. I felt as if I was being rudely shoved aside like an old toy when Maggie showed up. Now I knew how Woody felt when Buzz came on the scene in Toy Story. It was the same thing with Maggie who was clearly in the spotlight in Ethan's eyes.

"Sure, no problem," I said cheerily, wearing a fake smile.

"Oh, thanks, Jessie!" She smiled again, showing off dazzling white teeth. Even though she wore no makeup, she was still beautiful and oh, so perfect.

I sighed deeply as I marched to the dining hall. I peeked in through the doors. The place was dark and empty. I spun around and clomped off the porch over to Luc's cabin. I knocked on the door and waited. I saw some movement by the window on my right side. Luc appeared in the doorway and pulled open the screen door. He held a clip board in his hand and I could see that the kitchen was covered in binders, folders, and paperwork.

"Jessie, what can I do for you, dear?"

"Maggie's here and she wanted to know which cabin she is in."

He chuckled. "Easy one, she's in cabin two, same as you."

I nodded, not really sure what to say at that moment. "Oh, okay. I'll go tell her."

"Excellent. I presume that the dojo is ready?"

"Yep, just finished."

"*Tres bien*!" Very good, he said and glanced at his watch.

I stepped back out and did a little jog over to Ethan and Maggie.

Ethan raised his eyebrows and bounced on his feet as I came to a stop in front of them.

"Well? What's the verdict?" he said.

"Same cabin as mine."

She grinned. "That's great news. It'll give us a chance to get to know each other better!"

He smiled broadly. "Cool! Two of my favorite ladies in one place!"

She laughed. "Oh Ethan. You were always so charming."

I rolled my eyes—once I turned around and started walking back to my cabin. As I reached the door, I held it open for them.

"Thanks, Jessie, you're so helpful," she said as she went through the doorway and looked around.

She laughed again and pointed at the bed beside the door on the right. "Ha! I slept here in my first year!" "This brings back so many memories!" Her eyes glinted joyfully as she gazed at the room. "Ooh, I think I'll try sleeping over here for a change." She placed her suitcase by the far right wall, across from my bed. "Ethan, you can put my bag on top here.

"Sure." He walked across the floor and dumped it top of her bed.

The screened door slammed with a bang and we all turned around. The girl who entered had short spiky black hair and wore dark green sweatpants with purple flip flops and a purple tank top. She screamed as she saw Ethan and Maggie.

"Ahh! It's you!" She dropped everything she was holding and leaped into Ethan's arms. Her legs gripped his waist as he held onto her. Maggie ran over and hugged both of them.

I stood there and stared at them, completely stunned.

She jumped back down onto the floor with a thud as she wiped away tears of joy from her cheeks. "Is Rick coming too?" she asked enthusiastically.

Maggie nodded. "Yep!"

"Aw! It's so great to see you guys!" Her eyes roamed to me past Ethan's shoulder. "Hi! I'm Dani."

She walked over to me with an outstretched arm. I reached out my hand and she gave it a generous pump. Ethan came over and placed his arm across my shoulders. He introduced us with a wave of his hand. "Jessie, this is Dani. She's our lifeguard, but we call her the pool chick."

I looked at her, thinking that it seemed like an impolite title. "Pool chick?"

"Hey, don't worry, I'm okay with it. It's all in good fun and the kids get a kick out of it," Dani said as she placed her sunglasses on top of her head. She turned around the room, checking out the beds. "Hmph, I think I'll take this spot." She bent down and picked up her bags and practically pranced over to the bed beside mine.

"Well, I think I'll leave you ladies alone and let you unpack, and you know, catch up." Ethan said and headed for the exit. "Hey! Ryan!" he yelled out the door.

Both Dani and Maggie made a beeline to the door, squishing Ethan as they waved their arms out the door, screaming Ryan's name.

I couldn't even see out the door. Their bodies completely filled the doorway, casting long shadows into the room. I could hear him say something back at them but it was too faint for me to understand what he said.

"Isn't this great?" said Maggie as the two of them turned around and walked back to their beds. Ethan went outside to join Ryan, yelling at him excitedly.

I sat on my bed and crossed my legs, watching them unpack while they chatted. They seemed to have picked up where they left off from last time they were together. I didn't get much out of it. They were talking so fast and moving around too much for me to lip-read.

Maggie went over to the dresser and yanked out the top drawer. "Oops! Looks like you claimed this one, Jessie." She smiled and closed it.

I nodded. "Yeah, is that okay? Did you want me to move my stuff?"

"Oh no, no! Don't worry about it. I'll just use the lower half," she said and reached for one of the drawers closer to the bottom.

"Are you sure?" I asked feeling concerned. I didn't want to ruffle anyone's feather's here, particularly since they seemed to know each other so well.

"It's fine, Jessie. It's kind of you to offer though," she said as she began stuffing in her clothes and mumbled something else as she looked down. I missed what she said, it sounded muted.

"I'm sorry...I didn't get that. I'm hard of hearing, I need to see your face to lip-read."

She looked up at me. "Oh! I didn't know! You speak so well!"

"That's okay. I'm used to it," I said nonchalantly.

Dani glanced at me, picking various things out of her suitcase. "Were you born like that?"

I shook my head. "No, I lost my hearing when I was five. It's funny though...I can't remember what it was like to be able to hear."

"Oh wow, I can't even imagine that," Dani said. "You do have a neat accent though."

"I do? I have had people ask me if spoke French...guess I sound French to them."

She giggled. "I would've pegged you as more Russian than French."

"Cute," I replied. "How very James Bond of you."

"You watch James Bond?" asked Maggie as she pulled out another drawer.

"My dad, he loves them. I think he secretly wishes he could be a suave and charming spy like him."

"What does he do?" asked Maggie while she folded her clothes carefully into the empty drawer. She made sure she turned to look at me as she spoke.

"He's a university professor."

"Heh, my dad's a high school teacher. He's hoping that I'll follow in his footsteps. He loves it."

I rested my chin on my hand as I leaned on my knee.

"How about you? Have you decided what to do once you graduate?" asked Maggie.

"Um, I don't know. I'm still trying to figure that one out."

"I know what you mean. I was like that throughout my senior year," chirped Dani as she pulled her clothes from her suitcase and placed them on top of the bed.

"Really? I feel so lost. It seems like everyone else is so sure of what they want to do."

"A lot of my classmates said exactly the same thing Jessie. It wasn't until I went to University that it finally clicked in terms of what I liked doing."

"What did you end up taking?" I asked.

"Psychology, believe it or not. Don't let the pool chick title fool you. I'm a lot smarter than most people give me credit for." She held up her fingers in a quote as she said, "Pool chick."

"Same here, some people assume I'm stupid because I can't follow them." I replied, nodding in understanding. "So, how did you decide on psychology?" I was surprised. I'd never pegged her for a shrink.

"Camp. This place, the kids. They really opened my eyes and made me realize how much I wanted to work with them and help them."

"A lot of us changed our minds when we came here. Some discovered the hard way that it wasn't for them." Maggie and Dani exchanged knowing glances when she said that.

Curious, I asked both of them, "How old are you guys?"

Maggie raised her hand and said, "I'm twenty-five."

"Twenty-three," Dani said. "This is my second year here."

"Most of the staff are in their twenties, some are required to work with kids as part of their studies for school."

"Ah," I said, nodding.

"How about you? You're what? Nineteen?" queried Maggie with a wave of her hand.

"I'm seventeen. I'll be eighteen in the fall. I'm actually older than my classmates at school since I missed part of a year when I got sick and had to repeat a grade."

"Hmm, interesting," replied Maggie.

"What?" I asked as my eyes darted back and forth between them.

"You seem mature for your age. What's the word I'm looking for? Focused."

"I do? Is that a good thing or bad thing?"

"Is that a good thing or bad thing?" Dani gestured at me and said to Maggie, laughing. "Isn't she cute?"

Maggie chuckled. "It's a good thing, Jessie. It means you have a good head on your shoulders."

"Oh thanks. It must be from hanging out at the dojo with Ethan so much."

"How long have you been with Ethan?" asked Dani.

I thought about it for a moment and said, "This will be our second year together."

"That's impressive. Ethan must really be smitten with you," said Maggie.

"Why do you say that?"

Maggie tucked more clothes into the drawer. "You're the first one he's brought to camp. He never brings anyone here."

"That says a lot," Dani remarked as she turned around from placing items on the shelf above her bed.

I was speechless.

It was at that point I heard a metallic bong coming from outside.

A broad smile spread across Dani's features, lighting up her eyes. "The bell! I missed that sound!"

Maggie nodded her head. "Isn't that funny how it brings back so many memories?"

Dani reached out and grabbed my hand, pulling me off the bed and out the door. "Come on, Jessie, it's lunch time!"

As we charged down the steps and onto the pathway, there were more people walking toward the Dining Hall. Others were heading to their cabins carrying their stuff. I could hear some of them calling out to each other as they spotted someone they knew.

Maggie couldn't contain her excitement as she stepped through the doors and spotted Luc. She hurried over to give him a hug. "Jean Luc! Bonjour!"

"Bonjour, Maggie! And Dani, too! Aw, it's good to see you guys again," he said as they all hugged.

"Group hug!" yelled a tall guy wearing a red football jersey, black track pants, and running shoes. He came out of the kitchen, put his plate down on the table with a clatter, and ran over to hug all of them.

"Uh oh!" said Luc.

A couple more guys peered through the kitchen doors then ran over to them. It was a giant hug-a-thon.

"Hello? I can't breathe."

The group dispersed.

"Ah, merci! Please, go and get something to eat."

Some began to sit down, others proceeded to the kitchen.

"Ethan!" someone yelled out as they looked up from eating and gazed over my shoulder, waving.

I turned around and saw Ethan stride toward me, wearing an easy smile.

"Hey Mike! Good to see you man! Rick!" He waved crazily at them and they waved back.

Ethan walked over to me, putting his hands on my shoulders and ushered me to the kitchen.

I looked at him and said, "Holy cow, this place is hopping."

"This is not exactly what I call hopping, not yet anyway," he said beaming at me.

I raised my eyebrows at him.

"You'll see," he said with a sly grin as he grabbed two plates and handed one to me.

We made our way through the kitchen, our plates brimming with hot food, and sat down. The noise level in the room crept higher as more people came in. Their excited chatter mixed with the scraping of chairs on the floors and made it difficult for me to hear anything clearly.

I stared at the plates and utensils, as I realized that they were not exactly standard fare. I picked up my faded yellow mug and waved it in Ethan's direction. "Why is everything made out of this yellow plastic?"

"It's not hugely obvious yet but this is really not the place where you want to have real plates and cups that could become potential weapons."

I tilted my head to the side and stared at him. "What do you mean?"

"Let's just say that there are some kids that wouldn't hesitate to chuck a plate or two at us."

I stifled laughter as I had a vision of forks being embedded into the logs on the wall of the hall.

"And not to scare you," he continued, "some of them also have a habit of standing on the chairs and tables, literally."

My eyes nearly bugged out of my head. I was unsure whether I should believe him. "You're joking right?"

He shook his head as he took a sip from his cup.

Looking around the room, I saw Dani and Maggie watching us, smiling as they ate.

CHAPTER 17

Emerge

E than took me on a tour, showing me where all of the activities would take place. Some of the staff members were inside, sorting through the boxes of equipment, cleaning, or getting everything ready.

We both pitched in to help some of them carry their stuff into their cabins, and he introduced me to many of them, the majority of them leaping into his arms, bouncing up and down with glee.

I met two more of my cabin mates, Natasha and Jill. Natasha had straight brown hair, cut into a simple bob which framed her small face, showing off her dimples. She wore jeans, blue Converse sneakers, and a simple indigo-blue T-shirt with an orange and white striped scarf draped around her neck. Jillian, who preferred to be called Jill, had curly hair like mine, long chestnut waves that cascaded down to her shoulders. She had on a soft green plaid shirt and beige khaki shorts with white running shoes. Both said a polite hello to me and went back to unpacking.

After watching the campground turn into a whirlwind of activity throughout the afternoon with the arrivals of more staff members, it was a welcome respite when the bell rang in the evening. By then, I had already forgotten some of their names, there were so many of them. We all strode along the path in the direction of the dining hall, like a row of ants. Overall, there were twenty-five staff members, not including Luc and the kitchen crew, all obediently lining up to be served in the kitchen.

On our way out of the kitchen, several baskets were laid out on the table along the wall, filled with bread and crackers. Ethan and I leaned in and each snatched up a slice of bread to add to our plates.

The noise in the dining hall rose to a loud din once everyone sat down and began to eat their meals.

Luc stood up and raised his hand in the air, waiting for the room to fall silent. Everyone looked up at him. "I just wanted to say how wonderful it is to see all of you here. My heart swells with so much pride and happiness that so many of you have returned this year." He placed his hand on top of his chest, his voice booming. "Everyone, please raise your cups so that we may have a toast." He waited for a moment and then spoke again, holding his cup high. "May we be blessed with good times and happy memories this summer. Cheers!"

"Cheers!" Everyone chorused, raising their drinks in unison and tapping their neighbor's cups and mugs with a dull clunk.

Midway through the meal, something caught my attention from the corner of my eye. Along the wall, on the table by the bread and crackers, there was flicker of movement. My hand froze in midair, my fork hovering in front of my mouth as I stared in that direction, wondering if it was a figment of my imagination.

"Is something wrong?" said Ethan as he cocked his head to the side, eyebrows raised inquiringly.

"You know...I could've sworn I saw something over there," I said, jabbing my fork at the table, squinting my eyes at the baskets.

"Huh? Are you sure you're okay? Did you get too much sun today?" he said in mock concern.

I playfully stuck my tongue out at him and went back to eating.

Then it was Ethan's turn to freeze as he gazed at the table. "You know, I think you may be right."

Suddenly, a furry, little head popped up from behind the bread basket and darted toward the crackers. I gasped as I realized it was a chipmunk.

I watched in amusement as it deftly snapped up a cracker with its teeth and dragged it out of the basket and onto the table.

"Alfred!" Rick's voice burst through the chatter, causing me to drop my fork. Everyone went silent.

"Wha...He has a name?" I leaned forward to see what was going on. "What is this, the Batcave?"

"Alfred! Ya little munchkin!"

The startled chipmunk dropped the cracker as Rick stood up and yelled at him.

Several people gasped and pointed at him. Some were delighted at seeing the sneaky chipmunk, others were simply curious.

"Get outta there!"

Alfred quickly snatched up his cracker and hid behind one of the baskets.

Hearing the commotion, Jamie burst through the kitchen doors, carrying a spatula in his hand, high above his head. He marched over to the table and spotted Alfred madly zipping across the surface with the cracker held firmly in his teeth. "Oooh, I'm going to get you!"

Just then Alfred scrambled down the table leg and made a mad dash across the floor, running between the chairs and over our feet. Jamie lunged at him, diving under the table. "Come here you little troublemaker." There was a loud bang from underneath which shook the plates and cups. He stood up, rubbing his head, "Son of a—" He caught Luc's glare. "—chipmunk."

I snorted back laughter. Ethan was smirking, clearly amused by the events unfolding in front of us. Several people were looking around the room and under the tables, wondering where Alfred had gone.

As we dispersed after supper, everyone went back to unpacking and organizing their cabins, catching up on the latest news and gossip.

Later in the evening, Ethan met me beside my cabin on the way back from the shower. He grasped my hand and tugged me off to the side, into the darkness. The outside light from the cabin cast a soft glow on to his features, allowing me to read his lips. He caressed the sides of my neck with his fingers. He leaned in, giving me gentle kisses along my lower lip as I wrapped my arms around his torso, feeling his warmth beneath my hands. I grasped his shirt as he grew more passionate, not wanting him to stop. After a minute or two...or three, it took all of my strength to pull away.

"Ethan," I gasped, breathless from his kisses. "Someone will see us!"

"Yeah? So?" he said, running his hands down my arms, intertwining our fingers, and leaning his forehead against mine.

"We could get into trouble for this!"

"As long as we're discreet, we should be fine," he said as he nuzzled his lips against mine, pulling me in again.

I moaned, savoring the touch of his lips against mine. My mind said no, my heart said yes, yes, yes!

Suddenly he broke contact, snapping me out of the languid spell he'd put me under. He looked out into the darkness, placing a finger against my lips and said, "Someone's coming."

I smacked him on the arm, "See? I told you!"

"Crap." He pulled away but gave me one last quick kiss before sneaking behind my cabin and making a mad dash to his.

I sighed, missing him already. I walked up the steps into my cabin. Everyone turned around as I closed the door and made my way across the floor to my bed.

Maggie studied me. She wore yellow flannel pajamas, featuring monkeys, and held a towel and toothbrush in her hand. She squinted her eyes as she said, "You okay Jessie? You look a bit flushed."

I reached up and touched my skin, which felt hot to the touch. So much for being discreet. "Uh, yeah I'm fine. I'm still warm from my hot shower," I said earnestly, hoping that she wouldn't see through my lie.

She did. "Uh-huh, and I suppose Ethan didn't have anything to do with your, uh, glow?" she asked as she slipped on her flip flops and started walking toward the door.

I felt my face flush hotter, feeling caught off guard. My eyes darted at the windows and I had the distinct feeling that they overhead everything.

I saw Dani look at me and then at Maggie, smiling mischievously.

"We said good night, that's all."

Dani snickered. "Uh-huh." She sat on her bed, writing in her journal, no doubt about me and Ethan. She wore pink pajamas covered with cute little owls on them, her toes sported bright cotton-candy pink nail polish.

Natasha was hidden beneath her covers, seemingly sound asleep or at least trying to sleep, while Jill was reading a novel by the little light that peeked over the shelf. I sat down on my bed, tucked my sandals underneath, took off my hearing aids, and placed them on the shelf. I wriggled into my sleeping bag and grabbed a magazine to read for a few minutes. I felt comfortable and right at home, surrounded by their presence.

In the middle of the night, I rolled over and had the foresight not to repeat last night's fiasco by gripping the edge of the bed. My heart thumped wildly from the near miss. Heaving a sigh of relief, I snuggled deeper into my pillow and gradually fell asleep again.

I woke with a shock due to the vibrating pillow, still not used to the Sonic Alarm. It worked well, I thought as I turned it off. Maggie was already awake, pulling on a sweatshirt. She waved at me as I pulled my feet out of the sleeping bag. I shivered from the cool morning air in the cabin. I got up and reached for my pullover, T-shirt, socks, underwear, and black sweatpants. I sat back on the bed and quickly put my clothes on. It was disconcerting to completely undress in front of someone else. Maggie was too busy tying up her shoelaces to even notice and everyone else was still asleep or just waking up, stretching.

I put my hearing aids on as I walked out the door with Maggie who was yawning and squinting at the bright morning sun. The sky was already a clear blue as we strolled across the campground to the washrooms. I looked over at the other cabins. There were a few more people walking in our direction, zipping up their hoodies or stretching. It was utterly quiet except for the occasional chirp of a nearby bird. I didn't see Ethan anywhere and wondered if he was still asleep.

He didn't show up until after I sat down and began to eat breakfast. His hair was ruffled and he looked tired. He sat across the table from me. We both did a little finger wave at each other.

After everyone finished eating, Luc stood up for a moment and raised his hand, waiting for us to listen. "Today we will have two sessions, discussing camp rules and common issues with the kids, and a visit from a psychologist. If you need to get a cup of coffee or go to the washroom, now is the time to do it. It's going to be a long day, folks."

I met up with Ethan as he stood up to get another cup of tea, heading through the kitchen to the pot of hot water. As he plunked down a tea bag and began to pour in the water, he looked at me with tired eyes, barely smiling. He didn't seem like his usual self. "Morning, Jessie."

"Good morning to you, Mr. Grumpy-pants," I said jokingly. I tilted my head to the side and asked, "You okay?"

He shook his head as he picked up his mug, cradling it in his hands, and sighed. "Didn't get much sleep," he said as he looked around the room, checking to make sure no one overheard him. "Someone in my cabin snores, loudly."

"Seriously? Anything you can do about that?"

He sighed again. "Aside from strangling him? Unfortunately not much," he said as he rolled his neck.

"Want a hug?"

A small smile grew on his lips as he nodded. "Yes, please."

I reached out to him and pulled him into a tight, loving, bear hug.

"Hey! Where's my hug?" yelled Rick as he emerged from behind the kitchen doors.

I giggled, releasing Ethan. "I'm so sorry, did you want one too?"

"Of course!" He stretched out his arms, wearing a silly grin. I walked over to him and gave him a hug as well. He rocked me back and forth playfully. "Aw, thanks, Jessie."

I walked back to Ethan, who was now smiling, and grasped his hand as we went back into the dining hall and sat side by side at the table.

Luc walked up to a small wooden podium by the fireplace and began rifling through sheets of paper clipped to a binder, the fire crackling behind him. All eyes were on him, waiting for him to begin the session.

"All right, good morning, everyone," he said cheerily as he looked out at us, wearing a broad grin. "Now, as I said before, we will be discussing rules, which are a supremely cheerful topic," he said. He scanned the list in front of him. "For everyone's safety and well-being, we do not condone drinking, smoking, swearing, nor public displays of affections, including—" He raised a finger "—kissing."

"Aw nuts," Ryan said sarcastically.

"If I may continue Ryan," Luc said as he stared at him, "and obviously, sex at any time." He glowered at us, his eyes stopping at me and Ethan which made me wonder if it was deliberate.

Dani raised her hand. "What about hugs?"

"Ah! Excellent question Dani. Yes, we do permit hugs and, in fact, we encourage them. Some of these children need them. However, it's best to ask their permission or simply allow them to give you a hug first.

"Consider this a warning. If you are spotted drinking, acting inebriated, or have any alcohol in your possession, you will be fired immediately." He looked up from his list. "No second chances here, folks. We have had incidents in the past that have forced this ban to come into effect. I'm sorry but we need to set a good example for these kids and focus on providing a healthy, joyful, and nurturing environment.

"This camp is for children with learning disabilities, such as ADD, OCD, and Tourette's. Some may have one or two of these disorders, others may have a very specific type of disorder such as difficulty following instructions, doing what they are told, problems writing, or understanding how to do a particular task."

Luc looked up from reading his list, hands holding on to the sides of the podium. "Some of these children have been treated horribly, not only by their parents, but also by their classmates at school and by the people they should have been able to trust. Some have been physically abused."

There was a collective gasp throughout the room as he said this.

"Others bear the emotional scars of being bullied or taunted, every single day. Many of them feel rejected by society because of their disability. They are often misunderstood on a daily basis by others around them. The majority of these kids are very smart and are simply wonderful, wonderful people. We need to give them a chance to be themselves in an environment where they will not be judged, but will be embraced for how special they are."

I nodded, agreeing with him and remembering my own experiences at school.

"Since some of them come from difficult backgrounds, they are often plagued by unimaginable stress. Some are very poor or have a single parent raising them. Others come from a negative upbringing and lack manners or discipline."

Mike stood up and ran to the table where a large stack of folders sat on top. He quickly rifled through them and plucked out one of them, flipping it open. "If I may, Luc?" He gestured with the file.

"*Oui.*" Luc nodded. "For those of you not familiar with Mike, he is the Assistant Director for this year."

Cheers and applause rang throughout the dining hall.

"Ah, thank you. This is an excellent example of what Luc is talking about. We did a surprise home inspection earlier this year to view the situation of a child coming to camp." He looked down at the page, his finger scrolling downward until it came to a stop and said, "It was one of the worst conditions we have ever witnessed in a child's home. The curtains were badly torn. The floor was littered with toys and crap. Rotting food still sat on plates scattered everywhere. I couldn't walk very far without stepping on something. The living conditions were atrocious. Everything was filthy as if it had never being cleaned. The child's bedroom was squalid. There was simply a mattress on the floor with a thin sheet and blanket on top. Clothes were strewn everywhere. It's a miracle that this child has made it this far."

Mike closed the file, put it back on the pile and sat down.

Luc looked at him. "Thank you, Mike. Yes, a perfect example of some of the kids you will see this summer. For the most part, their faith in adults has been beaten down, and it's up to us to regain that lost trust."

He paused for a moment as if collecting his thoughts. "Now, since some of these children come from such difficult homes, it's up to us to keep our eyes and ears open for any signs of abuse, physical, mental, and emotional. Physical abuse can be hidden. Watch for kids that tend to wear long sleeved shirts or pants. They often try to cover bruises on their arms or legs.

"If you see any signs of physical abuse, such as bruises, on their arrival at camp, you report it to me or Mike immediately. This is a very serious matter and the proper authorities will be contacted to deal with the situation.

"When it comes to mental or emotional abuse, the clues are often found in the way they react to situations. They may become silent and cringe if they feel they are being treated negatively. Others may have reached their limit of being pushed around and will lash out verbally."

Luc paused for a moment before speaking again.

"Every child is different and we have to treat each and every one of them with compassion. Be forewarned, some are physically aggressive and will throw things at you or try to hit you. Under no circumstances are you allowed to strike back. We will show you how to subdue a violent child later this week by a professional who deals with these types of situations." Luc looked up at us, his features set in a serious cast.

"Some will suddenly snap and mouth off at you. Just because they mouth off at you doesn't mean that it's okay for you to mouth off back at them. That's the button that they are trying to find in you. They will taunt you and drive you crazy, trying to figure out how to make you react to their behavior. They can and will do it on purpose. Let them scream. It's okay. The only things they will scare around here are the animals."

"Talk to them in a neutral voice. Help them figure out what's wrong. Maybe it was something someone said that hurt their feelings. Perhaps they felt left out of an activity, or they feel homesick. There always a reason. We are here to help."

This was a lot for me to take in. I felt overwhelmed just listening to him. After what seemed like hours, Luc finally gave us a break. I was happy to get up and go outside. Many of us took a bathroom break and went for a stroll, others laid out on top of the picnic tables, relaxing in the sun. It wasn't hot but it wasn't cold either. Just a warm, lazy day. It felt too much like school, being stuck indoors and listening to lectures.

Ethan sat down beside me on the wooden bench, draping his arm across my shoulders, placing his hand at the back of my neck. I could feel his chest rumble as he spoke. "It's a bit much, isn't it?"

I nodded. "Yep. I was thinking that it was a lot like school."

A smile tugged at the corner of his lips. "I know what you mean. That's life."

I blew out a frustrated sigh, feeling a bit bored. I was not expecting camp to be like this.

He turned and gazed at me. "Don't worry, it will all make sense when the kids arrive. Everything that we learn today will stay in the back of our minds, so it's there when we need it. Trust me. Most of us needed to use that information last time. It helped us, a lot." He emphasized that last word which made me wonder just how bad it was going to get.

"If most of you have already learned it, why is he going over it again?" I asked as I shoved a strand of hair out of my eyes.

"It's a good review and he sometimes adds new rules, plus we get a different psychologist every year. They tend to give us fresh insights or better techniques to use."

"Ah, I didn't know that. Should I be scared? Because right now I don't know if I'll remember all of this stuff."

He laid his head back onto the table as if, savoring the sunlight. "Don't worry about it. The counselors are the ones who are with the kids all the time."

Luc walked over to the bell tower and pulled the rope, making it chime. He bellowed at us, "Okay! Break's over! Come on back in!"

"Boy, he's punctual and loud." I chuckled. "You know, he reminds me of a drill sergeant."

He sat up, smiling and said, "Funny you should say that—he was a drill sergeant."

We both stood up and started walking toward the doors to the dining hall. "Noo, seriously? You're pulling my leg!"

He nodded. "Scout's honor."

Holy schamoley, I thought as we marched in.

At the podium stood a lady about the same age as my mom. Her straight red hair was cut in a simple bob that ended just above her shoulders. She had cute freckles that dotted across her nose and cheek bones. She wore simple black trousers, gray sandals, and a light gray, V-neck shirt with a dark-cherry-red shawl around her shoulders. She smiled eagerly at us as we all sat down, our chairs scraping loudly on the wooden floor.

Luc stood beside her and introduced her, gesturing with his hand in her direction. "Everyone, this is Doctor Amanda Patterson. She will be our psychologist for this summer."

"Thank you, Luc," she said. She nodded at him and then turned her gaze upon us. "You can call me Mandy or Dr.

Patterson, whatever you feel comfortable with." She took a deep breath. "Before we start, how many of you have been to this camp as a counselor or instructor prior to this year? Please raise your hands so I can see."

Most of the staff raised their hands, including Ethan. There were only four or five of us that did not raise their hands.

"Oh! Wow, that's a lot of you for this year. Impressive. How many of you have been a staff member at another camp last year?"

Only two raised their hands this time.

"Okay, interesting. As most of you already know, this camp is quite different than others, primarily because it's for children with learning disabilities. They do not function at the same level as other children. They often behave in a different manner which requires us to think more outside of the box. They have a tendency to be very smart and intuitive. They love the challenge of trying to push your buttons, simply to get a reaction out of you."

She paused for a moment as her eyes roamed around the room. "Children with heightened emotions will often be sensitive to their surroundings. They can trigger a reaction in you that you may not have been aware of, perhaps some unresolved issue, or pent up anger. The best way to handle these types of situations is to remain as neutral as possible. Don't let them figure out what bugs you, do not react to anything they say or do. That's just adding fuel to the fire for them." She looked up from her sheet on the podium and waved her hand at us. "Does anyone have any previous experiences that they would like to share with us?"

A muscular guy with short, black, spiky hair and dark-blue tank top, sprouting a silver ring from his right eyebrow, raised his hand. He was one of Ethan's cabin mates. His name was Eric. "Yeah, we had this one kid who just snapped one day. It was completely out of the blue. He went after several of us, hitting and screaming hysterically.

He was totally out of control and we had no idea what set him off. Afterward, we felt as if we had failed him. We felt so powerless that we couldn't help him."

"So, how did you feel at that point?" asked Mandy as she watched him carefully.

Eric looked up at her, his fingers playing with the cup on the table in front of him. He squinted his eyes as he recalled the experience. "Um, incredibly sad. It was a dark day, very intense. It was as if I had the weight of the world on my shoulders. It was like a crushing sensation."

Mandy gestured at him. "Obviously that was a traumatic experience for you if you can still feel that pain and describe it so accurately."

He nodded, his eyes cast downward. "Yeah, it bugged me because I felt like I let him down. We all did."

"So were you aware of where it had the most impact on your body?" Mandy asked.

"Oh yeah, it was like a huge hole in my heart and a sucker punch to my gut."

She nodded. "That says a lot and also indicates that you are very aware of your body and your feelings. Thank you for sharing that." Mandy looked around the room. "Has anyone else experienced anything with their body or physically reacted to a situation?"

Everyone suddenly looked down, sneaking peeks at each other out of the corners of their eyes or staring intently at the pad of paper in front of them. Some grabbed their pens and began scribbling to look busy.

"Perhaps it was a clue that your body was trying to tell you something? You know...a feeling or sensation?" Mandy casually moved her hand up and down in front of her body, trying to emphasize her point.

Something pinged in the back of my mind, something that Serena, well...in her spirit guide form, had said to me. Feeling curious, I slowly raised my hand.

"Yes, um, what is your name?" She pointed at me with her pen.

"I'm, Jessie."

"Jessie, okay, what would you like to say?"

"Um, I've had these intense cravings for yellow. It's weird but I've been wanting to wear bright and colorful things like a yellow scarf. I usually prefer pink or green."

"Ooh, see now, that's interesting and really quite fun! I'm sure all of you have felt the desire to wear a particular color at some point in your lives. It could be when you wake up in the morning and desperately want to wear a yellow shirt, or maybe green or red shoes. It's an instinctive and strong feeling, which is your body sending you a message."

"Now in Jessie's case, it could likely be related to one of her Chakra's. Did you know that there are seven major Chakra's in your body?"

She looked at me and asked, "Where in your body did you feel this intense craving? Where did it come from?"

I thought about it for a minute. "Mmm, I would say probably in my solar plexus."

"Aha!" she said, her finger pointing up the sky as if she had a sudden epiphany. I heard a pen clatter to the floor and I presumed that someone was startled by her response. "That's because there is a chakra associated with the color yellow in that exact spot. Well done, Jessie!" She beamed as she looked in my direction.

"Yellow is associated with the third chakra which is a sign of change or growth. It's leading you in a new direction."

Now that is cool, I thought as I listened to her.

"This is fabulous! You guys are so in tune with your emotions!" She smiled broadly. "Now, this is a perfect time to focus on your chakras and get more in touch with yourselves."

I heard someone snicker and sputter nearby. Ethan had been sipping his cup of tea when his hand stopped short of reaching his lips. He gazed at me with one raised eyebrow over the brim of his cup. I had to look over his shoulder to stop myself from laughing out loud which didn't exactly help since I saw Ryan gleefully clapped his hands together with mock enthusiasm.

"Let me guess...yoga is next on the agenda?" he asked, smiling mischievously.

Luc casually leaned back in his chair and smacked the back of Ryan's head with a pad of paper, sending his hair flying over his face.

I had to clamp my hand over my mouth to stop myself from giggling.

"*Mon dieu*! Where are your manners, boy? Have you lost your mind?" Luc said, his French accent sounding thicker as some anger seeped through.

To my surprise, Mandy smirked. "By the way, congratulations."

Ryan looked at her quizzically. "For what?"

Mandy's grin grew wider. "You just volunteered to be my assistant."

Ryan's face fell as he realized the consequences of his snarky behavior. "Aw, son of a..."

"Ahem!" Luc glared at him with a warning look that spoke volumes.

"Fabulous! Come on up here and stand next to me please."

Ryan got up and dragged his feet across the floor like a petulant child dreading his punishment. Once he reached Mandy's side, he turned around wearing a sour look on his face.

Not to be undeterred by his grumpiness, Mandy continued. "Perfect. Now, I'm going to give you these stickers and you are going to place them on your body."

His eyes darted frantically from her to us as if silently pleading for help. Luc had his arms crossed over his chest, smiling broadly.

"As I was saying before, there are seven chakras in our bodies. They start at the top and go down throughout the body. The one of the top of your head is known as the seventh Chakra and is associated with the color purple and the meaning of wisdom." She gave him a large purple sticker.

He held it gingerly with his fingers.

I stared at him, waiting for his reaction. Laughter threatened to bubble up and escape. I clapped my other hand on top of my mouth to stop it.

"Now..." Mandy's grin grew even wider, revealing her white teeth. "Could you please place the sticker on top of your head?"

Ethan snorted his tea down his shirt as I began to giggle loudly. Luc howled with laughter and Mike pounded his fist on the table. I had tears forming in my eyes from laughing so hard.

"Perfect," said Mandy which brought on more laughter. Ryan's face turned beet red.

"The sixth chakra is associated with the color of indigo. Some of you may be familiar with the phrase, 'The all seeing eye.' This is the spot that the reference comes from." She flicked over a dark-blue sticker. "Could you place this on your forehead please?"

Ryan sighed forlornly as he slapped it on his face. It stood out brightly like a bull's eye target smack dab in the middle of his forehead.

More laughter erupted around the room.

"That's great, Ryan. You're doing a good job," Mandy said as she reached for another sticker. "Next is the fifth chakra, which is associated with a lighter shade of blue and, represents speaking the truth." She gave him the sticker. "This one is located in the throat area."

Ryan grimly took the large round dot, clearing his throat dramatically, and managed to get it to stay put.

"There we go...isn't that lovely?" Mandy remarked, smiling like the cat that swallowed the canary.

"The forth chakra is typically featured as being the color green and represents love." She turned around and peeled off a green sticker from her a sheet of colorful dots and handed it to Ryan. "It's usually located near your heart," she said and then turned to face Ryan. "Am I correct to presume that you know where your heart is?"

Ryan gave her a wicked smile and slapped it onto his chest.

"Now, as we previously discussed with Jessie, the third chakra is the power of transformation, or more commonly known as direction, and is represented as being yellow. It is located in the area of the solar plexus."

She held out a bright yellow orb to Ryan and stared at him mischievously, raising her eyebrows at him. "Do you need assistance with this one, Ryan?"

He snatched it out of her hand and stuck it onto his shirt. Looking down, he smiled. At this point, he was starting to resemble a clown with colorful pompoms.

Various chuckles and twitters ran through the room.

"Moving on...the second chakra is typically associated with the color orange and represents creativity. It can be found just below the belly button."

Mandy held the orange dot on her finger and waved it at him. "Orange you going to put it on?"

He jokingly smiled and said, "I'll take that, thanks." He slapped it on top of his belt buckle.

"And last but not least is the first chakra which is featured as the color red. It is a powerful color that represents grounding, which is located near the tail bone."

The room went silent. Ryan's eyes narrowed at her while she spoke, the wheels of his mind spinning mischievously. She held out the red sticker for him.

"Gimmee that!" he said as he quickly reached out for it and plucked it off her fingers. He spun around, slapped it onto his butt and proudly wriggled it.

At that, all hell broke loose and everyone broke down laughing uproariously.

"Let's give Ryan a round of applause for being such a good sport."

Ryan bowed profusely to us. Mike and Eric stood up and yelled, "Encore. Bravo!"

As Ryan started to walk back to his chair, he gave Mandy a big hug. In doing so, he stuck a green sticker on the back of her shoulder, and placed a finger on his lips as he looked at us.

He made his way to his spot and started pulling off the stickers, sticking them on Jean Luc and everyone else around him.

"Obviously the point of this exercise was to show you how our bodies react to what's around us. Have you noticed how much lighter the room feels now? We feel silly and happy because everyone around us is in a good mood. We are very sensitive to our surroundings. Children are even more vulnerable to this and can react very strongly, perhaps becoming more hyper than usual or lashing out in anger."

She paused for a moment, flipped a page over, and continued. "Have you ever walked into a room full of people and reacted badly to it? Maybe you got the strange feeling that something was wrong or it simply didn't feel right. There was probably someone in that room who was full of anger or sadness. We can often pick up on those emotions at a subconscious level."

She looked up at us. "My point is that the kids you will be working with are very sensitive to their surroundings. They can react very quickly and negatively if something is not right. If you're upset or having issues, they can sense that which can make the whole situation even worse."

She grabbed a tall, wooden stool by the table and sat down on it. "You will need to be calm, focused and patient with them. Some of them will be supremely good at finding out what buttons to push to make you snap. They can be relentless and enjoy doing it. Here, we won't give them that opportunity."

She paused for a moment, "All right, I want everyone to close their eyes for a moment and listen to my voice."

A shock of alarm rushed through my body at the prospect of not being able to hear her. I quickly yanked my arm up. "Mandy? I won't be able to hear you if I close my eyes. I need to be able to lip-read."

"Oh! I'm sorry! You can keep them open if you wish. That goes for anyone else who may be uncomfortable with having their eyes closed."

Feeling relieved, I sank back into my chair. Ethan rubbed my back as we traded glances. He nodded his head at me as if to say, "Way to go!"

"Okay, take a deep breath and slowly let it out." Mandy waited a moment before speaking again. "Pay attention to your body, think about how it feels right now."

The room was eerily quiet except for the snap and crackle of the fire.

"Now...imagine how it would feel if something or someone you love was suddenly taken away from you. Really concentrate on that sensation."

I thought about Parker and Serena and imagined how I would feel if I couldn't see them anymore. My chest grew unbearably tight. I couldn't stand the thought of losing them.

"Good...and open your eyes."

Nearly everyone blinked in the light, their eyes filled with serious and somber expressions. The atmosphere of the room felt different now.

"Does the room seem different now? What do you think? Any thoughts?"

Luc raised his hand. "Aside from it being much quieter, it feels like there is a heaviness in the air, like a pall over us."

"That's right. Everyone's mood changed, thus altering the overall essence of the room. That's because we were feeling sad or upset. Not only did you feel it in your body, it also affected everyone around you. We are sensitive beings and very aware of each other. Children are much more susceptible to this.

"Keep this in the back of your mind if you find yourself in a chaotic situation or dealing with a particularly difficult child. Take a moment to calm down and remain calm around them. It will make a world of difference for both of you."

Mandy looked at her watch and then asked Luc, "Did you want to take a break for a few minutes?"

"Ah, *oui*. All right everyone, go grab a cup of tea or coffee, have a pee, stretch, just be back here in 10 minutes."

Chairs scraped loudly on the floor as everyone stood up, stretched, and left the room like ants scattering at a picnic.

Ethan and I strolled outside in the sun in silence, holding hands. After a few minutes, I said, "Wow, that was intense."

Ethan sighed loudly and nodded. "Yeah, she's good. We didn't have her last time. Wish we had though, it could've helped."

I glanced up at him, seeing a faraway look in his eyes. "What do you mean?"

He looked away for a moment, his eyes scanning the landscape, and then back at me, "Remember the kid Eric was talking about, the one who snapped one day?"

He sighed again. His shoulders seemed to bear a heavy burden. "His name was Josh, and he was no more than nine years old. We had him at the beginning of camp. He was really bright, loved being outdoors. His parents warned us that he could difficult, even exceptionally violent and that we were to keep a very close eye on him at all times."

He looked over my shoulder for a moment then back at me again. "Jessie, you would've cried if you had been there with us. It was awful." He swallowed loudly and took another deep breath.

"At first he was doing fine. We were able to tolerate his moodiness and occasional outbursts. Then after a few days of being here, he got worse. Much worse. He became mean to everyone. He was deliberately cruel. If we were lining up to get food, he would suddenly turn around and kick someone because he felt like hurting them. Then one day, he just lost it. He snapped big time. He shoved a little boy into the water for no apparent reason. It took four of us to subdue him. He kicked, punched, screamed, and bit us. He became so enraged that we had no choice but to send him home."

His voice wavered as he uttered the last few words and he hung his head for a moment, rubbing his eyes. "I'll never forget that day...we had such high hopes for him."

I pulled him into a hug. "Aw Ethan, I'm sorry," I said as I wrapped my arms around him tighter.

He embraced me, holding on. "Thanks, Jessie, I needed that."

We touched our foreheads together, not wanting to let go. We took a few minutes to walk through the woods along the pathway, inhaling the sweet scent of pine and enjoying the play of sunlight through the trees.

Ethan spoke up after a few minutes. "You know...Mandy is right about how our emotions affect others. That day left a dark mark on all of us. You can still see it in Eric. He was his counselor and he took it really hard. It took several days for our spirits to rise once again."

I pondered on that for a moment as we made our way to the dining hall. "So, will he be coming back this year?"

"Who? Josh? No." Ethan shook his head somberly. "We found out from his parents later that summer that he'd become even more violent."

I gasped. "At that age?"

He nodded. "Luc really wanted to give him a chance to be himself, to grow up into a good person. He cried when he had to send Josh home. We all did."

CHAPTER 18

Affinity

We spent several days sitting through more sessions and getting to know each other through a variety of challenges, games, and brainstorming sessions, all designed to form a tighter bond between us. Luc explained to us that it was geared to help us to become comfortable with each other. It worked. I began to remember the names of most of the other staff by the end of the last session. I clicked with many of them although I was still a bit leery and shy around some of the guys. Trust was a big factor for me which became apparent halfway through.

Guys like Rick, who was a walking teddy bear, made it easy for me to like them. Eric was more quiet and looked menacing. His tall and muscular physique made me feel intimidated. It wasn't until Ethan told me that he was just shy and really a good person that I began to relax around him.

Kevin, the ecology instructor and Pete, the teacher for archery were both easygoing. They loved to laugh and played the guitar around the campfire. Kevin had short brown hair, a down-to-earth personality and was in the habit of wearing plaid shirts and vests. Pete also had short brown hair but he was more on the scruffy side, wearing hooded sweatshirts and torn jeans. He was a very laid back kind of guy. I immediately liked Samantha, who preferred to be called Sam. She had a bubbly and contagious personality, her blue eyes twinkled, and she always wore a smile. She reminded me of a Barbie Doll with her long blond hair and slim features. She had a tendency to wear bright colors like yellow, light blue, and green. She was the arts and crafts instructor and very popular, particularly with the guys. Emma, the camp nurse, tended to be more on the quiet side, very polite and reserved. She wore her long auburn hair up in a clip and wore a simple silver necklace with the emblem of a winged cross and snake, the icon for nursing. She was older than most of us although younger than my mom, and I liked her soft-spoken nature.

Today was the first official day of camp, when the kids would arrive. They were due to show up later today, sometime after lunch. We were all sitting down at our tables eating breakfast when Ethan and Pete finally showed up, their hair sticking up in all directions, looking exhausted. I took one look at them and figured that they didn't get much sleep last night. They made a beeline to the kitchen and came out carrying cereal bowls filled to the brim with fruit loops, and hot cups of coffee. Ethan placed his bowl and cup down on the table beside me and walked over to the table that had baskets of muffins. He picked up a basket and was holding it midair, absentmindedly, as he stood there talking to Mike who was also at the table.

I saw a furry little head pop up from the basket he was holding on to. I waved at Ethan trying to get his attention. "Um, Ethan?"

He was so engrossed in his discussion with Mike that he didn't notice me. I waved again. "Ethan!"

They both stopped and stared at me. Ethan said, "What!?"

"Look in the basket!" I said as I frantically gestured at it.

Both of them gave me a dumbfounded look and raised their palms up, shrugging their shoulders, not understanding why I was concerned.

Exasperated, I rolled my eyes. "It's Alfred!"

They suddenly locked gazes and then looked down at the muffins. Alfred chose that exact moment to peek at them, twitching his whiskers. He stood up on his hind legs, front paws raised in the air, and stared at Ethan defiantly.

"GAH!" yelled Ethan, flinging the basket into the air. Alfred jumped out and leaped onto Ethan's head, bouncing off him, and flew toward my table. He skidded past plates, cups, and bowls and disappeared off the edge.

Everyone was stunned, their forks suspended in midair as they watched the whole thing unfold in front of them. We all started laughing, pointing at Ethan and then at Alfred, howling until our cheeks were wet with tears.

"Alfred, the Ninja chipmunk!" gasped Mike in between burst of wheezing laughter.

After breakfast, Luc spent a few minutes sharing some inspirational poems with us and handed us our schedules. Afterward, he went around the room giving us our camp T-shirts, dark-hunter-green with a golden oval in the center in the shape of branches. Inside the circle was a simple outline of an owl and pine needles, running along the outside of the logo were the words "Camp Balsam." The T-shirt was adorable and I loved it! Everyone promptly took off their hoodies or went back to their cabins to put them on, we couldn't wait to wear them.

I was sitting down on the steps to my cabin when Ethan stopped by and sat beside me. I was flipping through the schedule for this week's session, gaping at it. I raised my eyebrows. "Is this for real?" I asked, flapping the sheets of paper at him.

He nodded and said in a languid drawl, "Yep. Heh, wait until you see day eight."

I narrowed my eyes at him, scanned the dates, held my finger frozen in that particular slot, and gasped, "What!? Are you crazy? Five classes in one day?"

"Mmm-hmm. Sometimes six if the campers request another session in the evening."

I felt dazed. I couldn't even fathom doing that many classes in a single day, let alone for the entire week. I counted the classes, the pitch of my voice rising higher as I spoke. "That's like twenty classes for the first session! And there's what? Four sessions this summer!"

He nodded, smiling and casually leaning back on the steps with his elbows propped against them. "Yep. Don't worry, you'll get used to it. We all do. Think about it. Some of us are out in the hot sun longer than others, like Dani, Rick, and Maggie."

I visualized Dani, our only official lifeguard, sitting by herself at the pool, watching the kids and felt my heart break. I should've been more grateful since I had Ethan as my partner. Rick and Maggie worked as a team. They worked side by side giving each other support. Pete and Kevin worked in the same area by the lake.

I looked down at my shirt, smiling. "I love this shirt, why didn't Luc give it to us sooner?"

"He usually waits for a week to see what happens with us, not everyone stays here."

I cocked my head at him. "What do you mean?"

"They sometimes quit," he said.

I gawked at him. "Seriously?"

"Yep, that happened last time."

Just then Dani came out of the cabin and leaned on the railing behind us, wearing her new shirt, her sunglasses on top of her head. "What happened last time?"

"Remember Olivia? She didn't last more than a couple of weeks."

"Oh yeah! I thought she was cool, too bad she didn't stay," she mused.

Aghast, I asked, "I don't get it. Why would they quit? That's not fair to Luc."

Ethan nodded. "I know. They just discover that it's too hard, especially with the kids."

Dani chimed in, "You know, Ethan's right. Camp is not for everybody, especially this one."

"Oh, because of their disabilities?"

Both Ethan and Dani bobbed their heads. "Should be an interesting week," said Dani.

"Ha! No kidding." said Ethan, chuckling quietly.

The children started trickling in around one thirty in the afternoon. By three o'clock they poured in, one after another, like clowns coming out of a small car at the circus. After they dumped their backpacks and sleeping bags in their cabins, they ran around outside, playing basketball, kicking around a soccer ball or playing Frisbee with their cabin mates. Some ran around screaming merrily across the campground.

"AHHhhhhhhHHHH!" said one boy with messy red hair as he ran in circles around us and then took off in another direction.

"Whahoo!" shouted another boy with a buzz cut as he darted past us, wearing black shorts, white t-shirt and running shoes, he was holding a toy doll in his hand, chucking it into the air, and catching it.

I pointed in their direction. "Um, Ethan, is this normal?"

He stood there, grinning, with his hands in his pockets, rocking back and forth on his feet. "Yep, welcome to Camp Crazy."

A girl stood not far from us, arms outstretched, twirling around and around. Her face was turned up at the sun and she wore a broad smile. Her curly blond hair bounced and swayed as she rotated at a dizzy speed. When she stopped, she fell to the ground with a thud, laughing.

I felt as if I had walked into the middle of an insane asylum, a wild and weird adventure. The energy of the camp rose to a feverish pitch as the day went on. It was simply nuts. I felt like I was slowly going nuts, too.

"Oh wow. This is..." I gestured at them, trying to come up with the right word. "Um, how should I say this?"

Ethan pitched in, "Crazy? Lively? Insane?"

"Yeah, you could say that."

"You know, it helps to be a little unique, too. Some of us are like them."

I gaped at him, waving my hands toward the kids. "You? You were like this?"

He nodded. "Still am sometimes. So were Rick, Mike, Ryan and Kevin," he said, his eyes twinkling in the sunlight. "It seems to affect boys more than girls for some reason."

"Geez, now it all makes sense. Especially with Ryan, he's like a kid sometimes."

"And you know what? The campers love him because of that."

"Sensei Ethan!" yelled a tall boy, who looked to be about eleven years old. He ran over to him and grabbed him around the waist, giving him a big hug.

"Oh no! It's Alex!" said Ethan sarcastically. He looked down at him, smiling, and ruffled his brown hair with his hand. "Hey man, it's great to see you! You know what?"

Alex looked up at Ethan. "What?"

"You have a new instructor this year. This is Sempai Jessie. She's helping me out this summer."

"Oh cool!" he said. He promptly let go of Ethan and clamped his arms around me.

"Uh, Ethan? I seem to have an octopus stuck on me," I said as I looked down at Alex.

Alex giggled, stepped back, bowed to us, spun around, and took off for the basketball court.

I arched my eyebrows. "Wow, does he ever take karate seriously."

Ethan beamed. "Yeah, he's an amazing kid, and wickedly smart. He's one of my favorite campers here." He tipped his head at Alex. "He calls this place home."

By six, Luc rang the large bell, its metallic bongs reaching every corner of camp. Kids came running out of their cabins to line up at the closed doors to the dining hall. After a few minutes, Mike burst through the doors and held them open. The kids poured in with the counselors, picked up their plates, and streamed through the kitchen to be served by Jamie. The noise rose to a loud roar. The campers chattered loudly, utensils and plates clattered onto the tables, and chairs scraped across the floor. It was a hive of constant activity. It was the loudest room I'd ever been in my life. Not even the cafeteria at school matched this level of intense sound. I had to turn my hearing aids down to soften the impact, but even then I could still feel the sonorous thrum pounding into my ears like a thousand heartbeats.

"Holy cow, is this ever loud!" I said as I sat down beside Ethan, Rick, and Maggie.

"What?! I can't hear you!" yelled Maggie, smirking.

I narrowed my eyes at her, picking up on her sarcasm, and pointed at my hearing aids. "Funny. Wanna borrow these?"

"Cute," she said then told Ethan, "I like her sense of humor!"

Rick leaned in toward me, "Wait until after supper—then ask me if this still sounds loud."

"Why?" I asked feeling suspicious of what was yet to come.

He raised his eyebrows, shaking his head and smiling. "Oh, you'll see."

Dani and Pete joined us a few minutes later and dug in, munching on the garlic bread.

I stared at them as they all exchanged knowing glances and grinned broadly.

Once we finished eating and put away our plates, Luc strode up to the podium with a guitar, placing the strap over his head and onto his shoulder.

"Quiet!" he bellowed and the room fell silent. "Welcome to Camp Balsam everyone!" Luc said wearing a wide grin, his cheeks rosy red.

Cheers rang across the room as everyone applauded.

"It's great to see so many of you here tonight! Most of you were here last summer. Now we do have some new staff members this year. Please stand up when I call out your name."

He went around the room, naming each counselor, saving the instructors for last. "And for climbing, we have Rick and Maggie, whom many of you already know from last year." A loud cheer rose up as they stood up and waved. "For karate, we have Sensei Ethan and Sempai Jessie." I stood up and smiled, feeling nervous. Again, everyone cheered loudly, clapping their hands enthusiastically.

"Now, just to let you know, Sempai Jessie is hard of hearing and wears hearing aids. You'll need to remember to speak clearly with her." I saw some of them point at my hearing aids, and I heard one kid near me exclaim, "That's so cool!"

Luc laughed upon hearing that. "Okay. Is everyone ready for some songs?" he asked as he plucked the strings on his guitar. His fingers began to pick up the pace.

"Almost heaven, West Virginia...Blue Ridge Mountains..."

The kids began to pound their hands on the tables with the beat. Some stood up, clapping their hands in rhythm.

"Country Roads, take me home...to the place I belong...West Virginia..."

I gasped as I recognized the song, bringing tears to my eyes. Ethan looked at me and, seeing my reaction, placed his hand on my shoulder. I nodded at him, letting him know I was okay.

On the chorus, everyone made large gestures with their hands, mimicking driving a car, "Country Roads..." For "Take me home..." they drew a house in the air with their fingers. "West Virginia..." they thumbed over their shoulders as if hitchhiking.

The more they sang it, the louder it got. I watched in shock as many of them stood on their chairs, singing so loudly that it was deafening. The tables shook violently as they pounded on them more enthusiastically. It went on like this for another twenty minutes with several more songs.

Luc's face was flushed, glowing a bright red from exertion, by the time he finished singing. "What a great way to start this session. You guys are amazing! Okay, we will have a quick break and begin our next activity outside at seven thirty. Off you go!"

We all piled out of the dining hall and began to make our way to the washrooms and cabins. Some of the kids made a beeline to the basketball court or started playing on their own.

It was a welcome relief to stand outside in the cool evening breeze. I stood on the porch sipping my mint hot chocolate while watching everyone disperse. Ethan came to stand beside me, also carrying a cup of hot chocolate. Hmm, we seem to be on the same wavelength, I thought.

"Hey, Jessie, I wanted to ask you something." He motioned at me with his mug. "You had this strange look on your face when Luc started playing 'Country Roads.' Any particular reason for that?"

"Hmm? Oh! Mom used to sing that song to me in sign language when I was maybe six years old. It just brought back a lot of memories that I'd forgotten a long time ago."

"Really? That's kinda cool." He did a double take, then stammered, "I—I mean the—fact that she did it in sign language. I would have loved to have seen that."

"So, what are we doing next?" I inquired as I turned around and looked up at him, cradling my warm mug.

He scrunched up his nose, thinking about it. "Um, I think Mike wants to do the 'capture the flag' game with them."

I groaned. I truly hated that game. I never really understood the rules or the concept behind it. I always seemed to be one of the first ones tagged.

"What? You don't like that game?"

"Nope, hate it in fact."

A look of surprise flashed across his face as his mouth opened in astonishment. "Seriously?"

I sighed rather dramatically. "Yes, I suck at it."

He gaped at me, shaking his head and raising his eyebrows in disbelief.

"Ethan!" yelled Mike from across the compound. "Wanna give me a hand?"

"Yeah. Give me a sec!" he bellowed back, waving at him.

"Hey, why don't you come and help out?" He nodded his head toward Mike, who was carrying a large batch of supplies in his arms.

"Sure," I said. "Want me to take your cup back to the kitchen?"

"Yeah, that would be great. Thanks, Jessie," he said. He passed it over to me and dashed down the steps and across the field.

I placed the mugs in the bin filled with soapy water and strolled over to where Mike and Ethan were plunking down pylons. A long rope was strung out on the ground, forming a distinct line. It was crooked part way down, so I bent over, grasped the end, and pulled it taut. Just then Ryan strode into my line of vision. He looked down at the rope and then back at me, a wide, wicked grin slowly spreading across his face. "Hey, Jessie, you thinking what I'm thinking?" he asked, pointing his finger down at the rope then miming circles with his hand.

Skipping? Is that what he has in mind? I wondered as I held the end of the rope in my hand.

By then, several more counselors and kids had formed a group beside us, waiting for the activities to begin.

"Sure! Ready?" I began to heave the rope around in a giant loop, which was harder than it looked.

Gasps of delight and giggles broke through the crowd and they began to leap in, jumping up and down. More and more of them came pouncing over for a chance to skip rope. Some came running over, yelling, "Wait for me!"

There were over fifteen people skipping all at once. I watched in amazement as I spun the rope around. It had to be a record. Everyone was thrilled to participate in the giant skip-a-thon. It was the highlight of the evening.

On my way back from the shower later, I came across Ethan who was standing near my cabin. He leaned in and gave me a generous hug. He was about to bend down and give me a kiss when I placed my hand on his chest. "Ethan! The rules!"

He sighed loudly, rolling his eyes. Just then, a piercing cry made me jump. The hair at the back of my neck stood on end. Ethan lunged through the door to my cabin, the screen door squeaking loudly.

I followed in behind him and saw Jill standing at the foot of her bed, pointing at her pillow with a shaking finger. "There's something moving in my bed! It was cold and wet!"

Looking puzzled, Ethan slowly walked over to her bed, lifted the corner of her sleeping bag, and peeked in. His eyes grew wide as he spotted what it was. He dove frantically at her pillow with both hands, trying to follow its desperate path. Then he fell onto the bed as his hands leapt around in the air, trying to grasp it.

"Aha!" he said, satisfied with his catch. "Here ya go...it's just a little tree frog," he said smugly, letting the frog climb across his fingers like a ladder.

Jill was not impressed. "Out!" She pushed on Ethan's back, shoving him out the door.

He turned around, holding it in front of her. "Aw, come on. He's harmless. See?"

She scowled at him, shoving him a little further. "Shoo."

"Night, Ethan," I said as he went outside.

Jill slammed the screen door shut with a bang.

"Night, Jessie. Love you," he called back as went down the steps, still holding onto the tree frog.

"You too."

"Shhh," Natasha hushed at me.

I giggled at Jill, replaying the whole scenario in my head.

"That was so cute," I told Jill.

She scowled at me then yanked her sleeping bag off the bed and hung it upside, shaking it. Satisfied that it was empty, she flung it back on top of the bed and sat down with an exasperated sigh. "Hmph!" She then pulled out a book from the shelf and began to read.

Dani and exchanged glances and giggled.

Whomp! A pillow landed in my face. I grasped it and looked around the room, wondering who threw it. It was Natasha, her bed clearly pillow-less.

Dani snatched up her pillow and tossed it across the room at Natasha's head. It landed in her lap. She began to giggle, too.

I threw the pillow back at Natasha. It landed across her shoulder, her hair flying up. She blew out a breath to clear her eyes then stared at us, determined to get back at us. Hefting both pillows in her hands, she stood up and chucked them at us, laughing. We all turned around and stared at Jill, whose book was frozen midair. A wicked smile spread across my face as I giggled louder. All three of us exchanged a quick glance at each other, then at Jill. All three pillows flew through the air at her. She screamed, letting the book fly as she ducked. We piled on top of her bed, gleefully smacking each other with our pillows.

CHAPTER 19

Glee

I woke up to a warm morning, a nice change from the frigid evenings. It looked like summer was officially starting. I pulled on my uniform, tugging the obi tight around my waist. Ethan and I had our first class right after breakfast, which should be interesting—well, for me any-way. Ethan was already looking forward to it. Me? I was a nervous wreck. The butterflies in my stomach threatened to declare a strike on breakfast.

The dining hall was already buzzing with everyone lining up to get their food. Today's menu featured pancakes, sau-sages, and as usual, muffins. I smiled as my gaze landed on the muffin baskets, remembering Alfred's antics.

When the bell rang at nine-thirty, everyone gathered around the dojo, eager to start this morning's session. Ethan had me demonstrate to the crowd how to bow at the "door," the opening between the two trees. He introduced me as Sempai Jessie which prompted a thin girl wearing denim jeans studded with glittering rhinestones, a pink shirt, and two long pony tails, to jerk her arm up in the air, waving it at Ethan.

"Yes, Miss Sparkly Pants, do you have a question?" Ethan said cheekily.

She giggled as she dragged her toe shyly through the dirt. She tucked her hands into her jean pockets and shrugged her shoulders. "Why is Jessie called Sempai instead of Sensei like you?"

"Ah. Good question. Sensei means teacher." He turned in my direction, gesturing at my belt. "Jessie is not a black belt yet. She is an assistant which is why she is called Sempai."

"Oh. Cool!" she said. Her body swayed side to side impatiently, full of energy.

"Any other questions?" He scanned the group standing in front of us. "No? Going once...going twice...oh! Time's up! Okay, let's get this class started."

We spent the morning teaching them what our uniforms and belts were called, the meaning of the word dojo, and how to count and say "thank you" in Japanese. We had them form a circle and work on their *kiais*, yelling as loud as possible, which they enjoyed. They learned how to do basic punches and kicks, adding a *kiai* at the end of each strike. We did this again for another class at ten-thirty, repeating the same drill to new faces, equally as eager.

By the time the lunch bell rang, I was feeling very warm from wearing my full uniform all morning in the sun. I darted back to my cabin and stripped off everything, putting on shorts and a green tank top, and felt much cooler. Our next class wasn't until four in the afternoon which meant that we had a nice, long break.

It was utter chaos when I walked into the dining hall. The noise from the kids rose to a deafening roar. Their chatter filled the hall with excited laughter. They were full of enormous energy, literally bursting at the seams, far too much for such a small space. Some of the staff members were sipping their cups of coffee as their eyes darted back and forth at the activity all around them, gripping their mugs as if they were their lifelines to sanity.

One in particular stood out from the rest of the group. He was a tall guy with messy black hair, a perpetually perky fellow who was well loved by the kids. They followed him everywhere. His name was Chris, one of Ethan's cabin mates. He walked past me wearing a superman cape pinned to his red shirt, pretending to flex his muscles or he would go into a flying pose, sending the kids into gales of laughter, some falling off their chairs, giggling madly. Chris grinned broadly, clearly pleased with the results. I clapped my hand over my mouth, laughter bubbling up as he walked over to another table doing the same thing. The irony was that he fit right in.

Ethan sat down beside me, plunking down his plate and cup of juice. Maggie and Samantha sat on either side of us and began to dig in. The wheels of my mind were spinning. Chris had given me an idea.

Curious, I looked up at Sam and asked, "Sam? What kind of stuff do you use for your classes?"

She thought about it for a moment, then replied, "You know, the usual: colored paper, sparkles, glue, string, beads for making bracelets...." She tilted her head to the side quizzically. "Why do you ask?"

"Just an idea...Would you by any chance have any balloons?"

She nodded. "Yes, I just opened a big package of them the other day. I gave some to Pete for his archery class. Did you want some too?"

A smile slowly spread across my features. "Can I? That would be awesome! I would love to use them for class this afternoon."

"Hmm, should be interesting to see what you come up with!" she said grinning.

"Uh, Jessie? Hello?" Ethan said, waving a fork in my direction, watching the conversation between me and Sam. "Were you going to clue me in eventually or were you planning on running the class by yourself?"

"Chris gave me an idea. I wonder if the kids would like to hit balloons as a fun target practice."

A broad smile grew across his features as he thought about it. "Oh yeah. They would love that. Great idea, Jessie!"

"Thanks. Well, actually the credit really goes to Chris," I said and pointed in his direction. His cape flowed across the back of the chair as he sat down.

"Uh-huh, yeah, he's a funny guy." Ethan said.

"You know, I just realized something. That's going to be a lot of balloons to blow up," I said to Ethan.

Maggie leaned in toward me. "Why don't you get the kids to blow them up themselves? Although, you may want to keep an eye on them. I have a sneaking suspicion that they may get the bright idea to turn them into water balloons."

"Ooh, good point. Thanks for the tip."

I took a moment to sip my juice, thinking up more ideas. "Ethan? You know how we talk about respect and courtesy with the kids?"

"Yeah?"

"Do you think it would be a good idea to show them how to do a handshake? You know, good firm grip, looking at the person in the eye, that kind of thing?"

His eyes wandered for a moment as he considered it. "Yep, I can totally see them doing that. It should be interesting though. Some are really shy and have never done it before," he said as he jabbed his fork into a pile of leafy greens.

"So, it's a good thing to teach them that?"

"Yeah, why don't we do that one for tomorrow's class?"

"Okay."

Someone dropped a plate on the floor off to my left. It landed with a hollow clunk and the food went flying, including an errant bun that rolled past my foot. Now I knew why they were plastic, I thought as I watched one of the counselors leap out of her chair to help clean it up. No one else batted an eye and the noise level continued to be a loud buzz all around me. That was apparently just the way it was around here.

After lunch I found Ethan at the swimming pool, sitting beside Dani and watching the campers frolic in the water. They were bobbing up and down, splashing around like crazy and screaming with delight. Many of them hung onto the colorful pool noodles that were sprinkled liberally throughout the water. I grabbed a chair from the side of the storage shed and plunked it down beside Ethan.

I spotted Natasha in the water, playing with one of the kids. I waved at her. She waved back, smiling.

"Hey, Jessie! Why don't you come on in? The water's nice," she called out to me.

I wasn't sure if we were allowed to do that since it was Dani's class. "Uh, is that okay, Ethan?"

"Oh, yeah. Go get your bathing suit."

I practically skipped to the cabin and quickly got changed into my bathing suit. On my way out, I grabbed my towel, a small plastic container with a lid, and put on my flip flops, making a beeline back to the pool.

Dani looked up at me from her chair, raising her hand to her brow to shade her eyes. "Do you want to play Marco Polo with us?"

I shrugged my shoulders and shook off my flip flops, tossing them by the chair. "I've never played that. How does it work?"

Her eyes practically bugged out as she looked at me in surprise. "Really? Well, one person in the water is Marco who has to find the rest of the swimmers who are calling out the word Polo. The only trick is that the Marcos have to keep their eyes closed, listen to the Polos, and try to tag them."

My heart sank like a heavy stone. There was no way I could play since I wouldn't be able to hear.

"Oh. I can't play Dani. I don't wear my hearing aids in the water." I said, feeling miserable.

Her hand flew to her mouth, then she smacked her forehead with the palm of her hand. "I'm so sorry, Jessie! I didn't know! So that's why you didn't know about the game. I feel so stupid!"

"It's okay. I'll just swim around. Can I use one of those pool noodles?"

A big grin spread across Dani's features as she exchanged a glance with Natasha. "You sure can!"

As soon as she said that, there was an avalanche of pool noodles in my direction. Apparently everyone had tossed one at me, culminating into a giant pile at my feet. I looked down and plucked out a bright neon green one.

"Thanks, guys," I draped my towel across the chair, took off my hearing aids, and tucked them into the plastic bowl, sealing the lid tightly. The noise level went from a loud combination of squeals, chatter, and splashes to absolute silence. My attention shifted to what was around me, from the warmth of the sun on my skin to the gentle touches of the breeze in my hair. It was a dramatic shift and I suddenly felt very exposed, unaware if someone was trying to talk to me or even if anyone was behind me. It always unnerved me to take off my hearing aids in public.

"Dani, where can I put my hearing aids so they won't get lost?"

She pointed at the shed, near the radio. Ah, a good spot which was dry, obviously electricity and water didn't mix.

I gestured at the mountain of pool noodles. "Did you guys want these back?"

I saw everyone's head nod at me. Grinning, I scampered over to them, bent down, and picked them up. I walked to the edge of the pool and heaved the noodles. It was a pretty cool sight as the bright tubes rained down on them. The kids laughed as they reached up to snatch one.

I jumped in, feeling the smooth water wash over me. I could see everyone's feet bobbing all around me, the ripples from the sunlight making them seem like tentacles. I swam around, feeling like a dolphin, so free. I could see the blue sky above as I rose up to the surface. It shifted and danced like a disco ball, sparkling brightly.

I came face to face with Ethan as I broke through the surface, nearly scaring me to death.

"Ethan! You rascal! Where did you come from?"

He laughed and pointed at the bouncing board. Of course, he dived. I came to the realization that the shorts he'd had on earlier were also for swimming. Lucky guy.

A little boy hung onto his neck, peeking out over his shoulder, smiling broadly as Ethan swam around.

We spent the rest of our free time playing with the pool noodles, doing handstands underwater, and jumping off the diving board. It wasn't until Ethan tapped me on the shoulder that I realized how long it had been and reluctantly dragged myself out of the water. As I reached for my towel, inspiration struck me. I dried off my hair and quickly snatched up my hearing aids, tucking them back into my ears.

"Dani, I have a question for you." I bent down and picked up a pink pool noodle and waved it at her. "Do you have lots of these?"

Ethan stood beside me, his forehead crinkling as he listened.

She looked up. "Yeah, why?"

"Can I have a couple?"

"Sure, what are you going to use them for?"

"Teaching karate!"

"Wha...How?" asked Ethan.

I shot him a smug smile, put on my flip flops, and marched to my cabin, carrying the bright noodles over my shoulders. "You'll see."

He groaned. "Oh geez, not another idea."

After we got changed and met our next group of kids in the dojo, Ethan proceeded to teach them basic skills such as doing proper kicks and punches, punctuated with loud "*Kiais*" which they seemed to love doing. Once he was satisfied that they'd learned enough, he had me demonstrate my latest idea featuring the balloons.

"Okay, I want everyone to quickly grab a partner," I said as I pulled out a bag of bright balloons. I watched the kids scramble together, their eyes growing wide at the sight of the balloons in my hands.

"Does everyone have a partner?" I asked. Most of them nodded, standing beside their chosen buddy. All except one. I looked down and saw a small girl with cute, curly, blonde hair, wearing a simple blue T-shirt, shorts, and pink sneakers. She hung her head down, sniffling.

"Aw, you don't have a partner?"

She shook her head forlornly which made me wonder if she was really shy. It seemed odd that no one had paired up with her. It was a painful reminder of what it was like for me to be left out like that.

"That's okay! I'm sure Jill would love to be your partner!"

I motioned for Jill to join us. Smiling, she came over and knelt beside the girl.

"Yes. How about it? Wanna be my partner?" she asked kindly. Her manner toward the girl was very gentle, as if she walking on eggshells.

The little girl nodded her head. She glanced up at me then back to Jill.

I picked a bright pink balloon and gave it to her. She smiled

"And whadda ya know?" I exclaimed, pointing at her feet and grinning "It matches your pink shoes." Her smile grew wider.

Jill beamed. "Thanks, Jessie."

"No problem," I replied. "All right, everyone, I want all of you to start blowing up your balloons. Your task is to punch it so that it floats over to your partner. Then your partner tries to do the same thing. However, there is one rule...you can't let it touch the ground."

"Oooh," said Ethan. "That makes it more challenging. I like it." He wet his finger and held it up in the air. "And...I think there is a slight breeze, too."

"Your counselors can give you a hand blowing them up," I told them. "Don't be afraid to ask them for help. Okay, go for it!"

Eric and Jill gave them a wave and nodded their heads in affirmation.

Ethan and I went around tying knots on the ends of the filled balloons as the kids huffed with all of their strength to puff them up. Their faces were turning beet red with the exertion. They were giving their lungs a serious work out. Some of them managed to blow up their balloon as big as their heads.

"Cool!" they said, giggling.

"Okay. Everyone ready? Spread out so there's lots of room...and begin."

They squealed with delight as they frantically tried to punch their target without letting it hit the ground. It proved to be a fun exercise for them.

After several minutes of laughter and mayhem, I stopped them to give them further instructions.

"This time, you are going to kick the balloon across to your partner, same rule, no touching the ground. Ready? On your mark, get set...go!"

They dashed after the floating orbs, their faces set in concentration and intense determination. They made wild lunges, trying in vain to keep with the ever changing path of the bobbing globes.

As the bell rang, everyone bowed out of the dojo, screaming merrily across the campgrounds, carrying their balloons with them. We handed out a few extra balloons to those who didn't get one.

Ethan and I packed up our equipment and started walking back to our cabins.

"You know, that was nice of Eric to help the kids with their balloons," I remarked, recalling his enthusiasm toward them.

"Yeah, he's great with the kids."

My eyes grew wide in surprise. "Really?"

"Well, he's really patient with them. He has a gentle nature, but he does come across as being shy sometimes."

"Eric?" I exclaimed in shock. "But he seems so, so Goth. You know—dark clothes, spiky hair, eyebrow ring. He's intense."

He shrugged his shoulders. "Looks aren't everything. It's like the saying, you can't judge a book by its cover."

"Ha! Yeah, no kidding. He's proved that to me," I said wondering why he dressed like that. Was it a ruse to hide his lack of self-esteem or to simply appear tougher? I considered the possibilities as I walked up the steps into my cabin.

After supper, as I was getting ready for bed, I asked Jill about the shy girl, wondering what she was like.

"Who?" she asked as she looked over her shoulder while she rifled through the drawers. Then she snapped her fingers when she realized who I was thinking of. "Oh. You mean Olivia."

Dani looked up from writing in her journal. "Holy mother of God, that is one wicked kid,"

"Yeah, no kidding, she's the Devil child," interjected Natasha.

Astounded, I stared at them, my head bobbing back and forth like a tennis ball as I watched them offer their opinions on Olivia. "We are talking about the same kid, right? Cute, blond curls, shy, about yay big?" I raised my hand up to her approximate height.

"Oh, she's anything but shy. She's stubborn," remarked Natasha as she lathered lotion on to her hands.

"Stubborn as a cranky, old mule," replied Dani.

"And, as unmovable as a telephone pole," Maggie chimed in.

"You want to know what she did today? Let me tell ya...I swear that I came that close to strangling her tiny neck," Jill said, pinching her thumb and forefinger nearly together. "She refused, refused, to do anything we asked her to do. She just stood there, in front of everybody, griping, with her arms across her chest."

"Like this," Dani said. She stood up, mimicking the pose, pouting her lips. "Even when everybody else was in the pool, she refused to get changed into her bathing suit."

"And, she refuses to be friends with anyone," Maggie said, throwing up her hands in frustration. "She's always grumpy. Then she complains when no one wants to play with her!"

I was utterly confused. "This can't be the same girl I had in my class today. She seemed so shy."

"Ha! She's anything but shy. She's got the Devil inside of her," griped Maggie, shaking her finger, like a preacher on the podium driving the final point across.

I sat down on my bed with a resolute thump. I'd had no idea that her attitude went deeper than simple shyness. Although, there was something strangely familiar about her. I couldn't put my finger on it, and I made a mental note to watch her more closely.

"You're joking." I looked up at them. "You have got to be joking. Did Ethan put you up to this?" I sat there shaking my head feeling so stupefied. "Wow! I mean—" I said stammering. "Wow!"

That revelation was a doozy. It left me flabbergasted for the next couple of days.

"Ethan? When are we going to teach the kids how to do a handshake?" I asked him at breakfast, biting into a blueberry muffin.

"I was thinking about doing that today." He looked up from his clipboard sitting beside his plate. It held a list of his lessons and the camp schedule for this week. He flipped through the sheets, running his fingers down the page. "Why? Did you have something else in mind?"

"No, no that's perfect. It's just that Dani, Maggie, and Jill all said the same thing about one of the campers."

"Ah, you must be talking about Olivia." He raised his fingers and mimed air quotations. "The devil child."

I threw up my hands in exasperation. "Oh, come on! Not you, too!"

"I've had her in previous years. She's not exactly what I'd call easy."

"Uh-huh." I nodded, but there was still something bugging me about her.

"What?" You've got that look."

"What look?" I asked as I narrowed my eyes at him.

"The 'I'm thinking' look. I could swear that there was smoke coming out of your ears."

I glared at him. "Is that a dumb blonde joke? It's not exactly funny you know."

"I was just kidding," he said and reached for my shoulder.

I shrugged it off, feeling the hot steam of rage bubble inside of me. I was getting tired of so many clues about some of the kids like Olivia. It was bad enough that I had trouble keeping up with their dialogue in a such a noisy environment, but being "the new instructor" meant that I was in the dark about the kids personalities that everyone else already knew about. I felt really dimwitted compared to the other staff members who had more experience with them.

I shoved my chair back, its feet scraping loudly across the floor, put the plate away, and walked over to the dojo. I worked on some of my stretches, watching the sunlight stream through the morning mist in the trees. The scent of wet pine wafted around me. I inhaled it deeply, loving the smell. It reminded me of Christmas.

I saw Luc walk over to the bell tower and pull on the rope, sending loud metallic chimes across the campground. Ethan was coming toward me, carrying his clipboard, when our group of campers poured in, bowing at the door.

Sure enough, there was Olivia amongst them, wearing her infamous perpetual scowl. Charming, I thought dryly.

We went through the usual drills, practicing some of the blocks. Once they'd mastered the basic movements and positioning, Ethan stopped the class and had everyone sit down.

"What does respect mean?" he asked, his eyes roaming over the group, gauging their reactions.

A lanky boy with wavy brown hair and freckles shot up his hand. "To be nice to others?"

"Yes!" Ethan nodded eagerly. "That's exactly what it means. Very good! How can we do that? What kinds of things can we do that show respect?"

Everyone thought about it for a minute, their brows burrowing in concentration. One girl was drawing random squiggles in the sand, not really paying attention. I sighed inwardly. It was Olivia. No big surprise there, eh?

After another minute of silence, I decided to step in and offer a suggestion. "May I?" I looked at Ethan as I gestured at the group. He nodded, curious as to what I had in mind.

"Okay, how about this?"

I took a step toward Olivia and said, "Hi!" I smiled and pointed at her pink shirt. "I love your shirt!"

Surprised, she jerked her head up then glanced down at her shirt self-consciously. "Oh! Thanks," she replied in a shy and quiet voice.

For a moment there, I didn't think she would respond at all.

"It's so pretty when it sparkles in the sun like that."

Her smile grew wider as she touched her shirt lovingly, admiring the sparkly affect.

I glanced back at the group and asked them. "Was that respectful?"

Pretty much everyone nodded their heads.

"What else can we do or say?' I asked as I watched them think about it.

"Um." One of the taller girls sitting at the back with her long brown hair in two braids raised her hand. "Maybe help carry something? Like groceries for our parents or sports equipment for our coaches?"

"Yes! Next time you see someone, maybe at school, ask them if they need help. If you saw someone in a wheelchair, what would you do?"

The girl with the braids shot up her hand again. "Oh! Hold the door open for them?"

"Yep, or perhaps carry their books for them, or even grab something off a shelf that's too high for them."

I paused for a moment, to see if anyone else offered a suggestion. "Should we be mean to people or animals?"

A chorus of heads shook side to side.

"Why not?"

"Because they can be mean to us?" said one of the boys in the front, wearing a striped shirt and blue shorts.

"That's right! Respect is a two way street. If you're nice to someone, they'll be nice to you. Today, I'm going to give all of you a mission. Your mission is to say something nice to someone. It can be something such as 'I like your smile' or 'I like your shoes.' Okay? Can you do that?"

They all nodded in unison, grinning.

"Sensei Ethan is going to show you how to do a hand shake. How many of you have done that before?" I looked out across a sea of glazed looks. "Oooh, tough crowd," I said to Ethan.

He smirked. "When you do a handshake, grasp their hand firmly, pump it eagerly as if you're happy to see them, look them in the eye, and give them a smile. Watch how I greet Sempai Jessie," he said as he turned around to face me and held out his hand.

I grasped it and said, "Hi! I'm Jessie."

"Lovely to meet you, Jessie, my name is Ethan!" He greeted me in a polite manner, like the perfect gentleman. "Now...watch this," he said and started over again, taking a step back, and then extending his hand toward me. He approached me with a limp hand and averted his eyes, looking elsewhere. I grasped it, but it was like holding a dead fish. He mumbled a greeting which I didn't understand. "What did I do wrong?" he asked as he faced the group.

Several hands shot up in the air as they shouted out their answers.

"You didn't look at her," said one girl, wearing two ponytails.

"That was a bad handshake," added a boy with scruffy hair.

"I couldn't hear you," said another girl with braces.

"That's right. Everyone come on up here and join us. I want all of the counselors to line up with Jessie and me. The rest of you will form a line starting in front of me."

He organized everyone in two groups, lining up the grownups in a single line with the kids at one end, ready to go. He faced the kids and explained their task to them. "Each of you are going to give us a good handshake and greet us in a polite manner. Okay? You go first and shake my hand, then do same thing with the next person line," he said to the boy standing at the beginning of the line, who looked a little nervous.

They all gave us a hearty handshake, saying their names or a simple hello. Some were rather shy and giggled, others loved doing it, eager to grip our hands as hard as they could.

Later that evening, at supper time, Olivia walked past me and said to me, beaming "Hi! I like you!"

I quickly stammered back a reply "Thank you. That's very nice of you."

I was stunned at the sudden change in her. I watched her skip joyfully over to her table carrying a bread basket. I heard someone drop a fork beside me and glanced to my side. Ethan stared at her, slack jawed, as he picked up his fork from the plate. Maggie and Rick exchanged curious looks.

Dani looked over her shoulder at Olivia then back at us. "Was that Olivia?"

"Holy cow, what did you guys do to her?" Maggie exclaimed.

"We taught them how to show respect to others. They were supposed to go around saying something nice to people today," Ethan replied. "Guess it worked," he said chuckling as he gave me a high five.

I held up my hand and slapped his palm. "Yay!"

Maggie shook her head, looking completely dumbfounded. "Amazing!"

CHAPTER 20

Glimmer

It wasn't until I looked into the mirror while brushing my teeth that I realized what was nagging me. I turned around and barked a laugh. *Olivia! She's a mini me!*

One of the counselors snapped her head sideways, staring at me with a puzzled expression. I did a fake punch to her shoulder, laughing. "I did it! I finally figured it out!"

She watched me in consternation as I spun around and scooted out the door, merrily running down the steps. I walked briskly back to my cabin with a bounce in my step.

I wanted to do a mental head slap. No wonder she was so familiar. It was like looking in the mirror. I was exactly like that at her age, right down to the curly blond hair and snarky attitude.

As I sat down on my bed with a whomp, I asked Jill why Olivia was at camp. She didn't seem super hyper or out of control like the other kids.

"You're thinking of ADHD. She has ADD," she replied.

Ah, yes, I see the difference...not. I thought as I stared at her, gesturing with my hand for her to embellish.

She caught the hint. "In her case, it means that she has a very short attention span. She really struggles in school. She has a lot of trouble with her reading and writing skills. You don't notice it here because we're not in a classroom." Jill sat on her bed with her legs crossed, resting her elbows on her knees. "She seems younger than most kids her age, so they tend to treat her as if she's mentally slow."

Something pinged in the back of my mind as she spoke. I felt a twinge of familiarity about that. They treated her like an outcast, like they did with me. Like a *freak*.

No wonder she was in a perpetually bad mood. She felt shunned, as if she didn't fit in anywhere.

"Jessie?"

"Hmm? What?"

"What are you thinking?"

"Oh, that Olivia is so much like me. I was exactly like her at that age. It was something you said that brought back some memories," I said, feeling very far away.

"Good memories or bad?" she inquired.

"Horrible. It was one of the worst periods of my life. Because of my hearing aids, most kids at school treated me like an outcast. They refused to play with me. Even the teachers were awful. I could feel them pushing me away. As a result, I was always angry. I guess you could say I felt un-loved."

Jill nodded her head like a professional shrink, listening to my thoughts as I poured out the old emotions that had been buried a long time ago. "You don't suppose that Olivia feels that way, too?"

"I think that's exactly how she feels. Anger. Rejection. And I'll bet you that she has trouble trusting anyone."

"Oh my! It would explain so much."

"I saw a glimmer of hope today when I said something nice about her and she did the same thing back to me. I was honest with her, you know, kind. Maybe that's what she needs to hear more often, more compliments right from the heart," I said, remembering her smile.

"I like that idea, Jessie. I agree. I think it would do her a world of good if we kept saying nice things to her. You know, I'll try to do that more often, too. Who knows? Maybe she'll end up like you," she said, her eyes twinkling mischievously.

I narrowed my own eyes suspiciously. "Is that a good thing or bad thing?"

"Ha," she said, which didn't exactly provide me with any clues.

Maggie came bursting through the door, slamming it shut with a loud bang, causing us to jump.

"Grrrr," she growled as she stormed in, wearing an angry scowl that outmatched Olivia's grumpiness.

Jill and I both stared at her, wondering what was going on. "Uh? Maggie? Problem?" asked Jill.

"Oh you betcha. I could strangle him!" she said as she held out her hands in midair as if she was choking someone.

"Who?" I asked.

"Ryan! He drives me up the wall! You know what he did to me today?"

Before I could even get a word in, she kept barreling on.

"Heh. He had the nerve to do nothing but watch me pack up my equipment after the last session. I asked him, politely, if he could give me a hand. You know what he said?"

I raised my finger and was about to respond when she went ahead and finished it for me.

"He said, 'Bite me,' and walked away." Maggie picked up her fluffy, white, stuffed bunny and tossed it into the wall.

This prompted an idea into my head. "You know, Maggie, I think I have an idea that you'll love..." I looked around the room, peeking under my bed. "Do you have an empty box or bag?"

"Why?" asked Jill.

"Because we'll need it to play a successful prank on Ryan. You reminded me of a movie that I once saw, and this would be the perfect pay back."

Maggie spun around and checked under her bed. She stretched out onto the floor and began tugging at something, dragging it out with a final grunt. It was a clear plastic storage bin.

"Oh yeah, that's perfect! You want to know how to drive him crazy? Fill his bed, shelf, anything that belongs to him with girly stuff. Anything pink, fluffy, cute, even lipstick, make up, and feminine products. Our goal is to make him blush. Especially in front of the guys when they show up in the cabin."

"HA! I love it! All righty, let's fill this up!" Her face beamed as she set the bin on top of her bed and began filling it with her stuffed toys, hairbrush, mirror, and various other items. I contributed to the pile with my own items that were sure to make him blush. Jill came over and added her stuff to the growing mountain of cute, adorable, and totally girly products.

Jill turned around to face me, hands on her hips. "Why, Jessie! I didn't know you had this in you! You're so wicked!"

We all gave each other high fives, giggling.

"Hee, hee! I'm going to go look for Natasha and Dani and ask them to contribute to this prank. This is so much fun!" Maggie said, squealing as she practically skipped out of the cabin carrying the plastic bin, determined to complete her goal.

By morning, the bin was completely packed with lots of very girly stuff, including a heart shaped pillow and vibrant red feather boa. Maggie woke up in a buoyant mood, sharing her plans with us to sneak out to his cabin during breakfast. Dani volunteered to be on the lookout in case any of the guys tried to make their way back to their cabin. Both Jill and Natasha offered to follow Ryan around all day to watch his reaction and if they were lucky, get some good shots with their cameras. Apparently, Emma also pitched in to help by keeping tabs on him when Jill and Natasha were busy with the kids. It was going to take a bit of team effort but it would be well worth it if we could pull it off.

"It feels like Christmas," squealed Natasha. "I can't wait to see his face!"

During breakfast, we struggled to keep straight faces once Ryan walked into the Dining Hall. So far he was completely oblivious to what was going on behind the scenes. Out of the corner of my eye, I could see Dani munching on an apple as she hung out on the porch, constantly on patrol. A few minutes later, both Dani and Maggie casually strolled in, giving me a thumbs-up as they sat down, wearing mischievous grins.

For the morning session, I approached Ethan carrying two pink pool noodles and asked him if he was planning on having the kids work on their blocking techniques.

He did a double take as his eyes landed on the vibrantly colored tubes in my hands. "Um...yeah. Dare I ask why?"

"You know how we use those big foam blockers to test their reflexes at the dojo?"

He nodded his head, squinting suspiciously at me. "Yes?"

"Well, I thought since we don't have any of them here, that maybe we can use these instead?" I bonked the noodle on his head to drive the point home.

A grin slowly widened on his features as he saw where I was going with this idea. "Oh yeah." He reached out and grabbed one. "Geez, Jessie, where are you getting these ideas?"

For a moment I stammered, totally at lost for a suitable explanation, "I—I—guess it runs in the family. My brother, Ken, did similar things at camp, too."

Once the session started, Ethan had them form a circle around us. We would dash from one camper to another, trying to whack them over the head with the pink noodle as they tried to block us. They screamed with laughter as we tried to catch them off guard. Then we had them try to jump over the noodles as we swept the vibrant tubes under their feet. It was a challenge. They loved it when we suddenly changed directions and they giggled as they waited for their turn to leap up.

Mike just happened to be strolling by our class as we were doing this particular exercise, and he suddenly dashed over wearing an impish grin. He quickly bowed in, calmly walked over to Ethan, tapped him on the shoulder, and gestured at the pink noodle. "Can I borrow that for a moment?"

"Sure," Ethan said.

"Aha! Now I'm gonna get my revenge!" Mike cackled, holding the pink noodle high above his head, as he stared down at the kids around him.

He leapt forward and starting chasing the kids around the dojo, smacking them over the head with it, laughing deliriously. They taunted him, daring him to catch them as they zigzagged all over the place. Eric came over to me and plucked the other noodle out of my hand. He did the same thing as Mike, waving it with glee, trying to tap them over their heads, too. The scene looked like one of those whack-a-gopher games as they bobbed up and down, trying to outwit Mike and Eric. By the time the bell rang, both them had worked up a bit of a sweat. They gave the kids high fives as they left the dojo, moving on to their next session, all wearing happy grins.

"Okay, that was hysterical! We gotta do that more often," Ethan said as he draped his arm around my shoulders, chuckling. He looked down at me, his eyes crinkling around the corners as he smiled. "Got any more ideas floating around in that brilliant mind of yours?"

I embraced him, thrilled that it worked. "Guess we'll find out soon enough, eh?"

At lunch time, Natasha sat down beside me and showed me the interior of Ryan's cabin on her camera. I had to cover my mouth with my hand to stop myself from laughing out loud. The scene she showed me was absolutely hilarious. Ryan's bed was overflowing with stuffed animals and pillows in all shapes and sizes. Sitting on top of his pillow were fashion magazines. The shelf over his bed was filled with every girlish product imaginable. It sent a clear message to him that we were not to be messed with.

Ethan raised his eyebrows at us, his fork hovering in midair as he watched us browse over the images. He gestured with his hand for us to show him, but we shook our heads, giggling.

"Oh no, this is a surprise and we don't want to spoil it," Natasha said, holding the camera close to her chest and wagging her finger at him. "You'll find out later tonight."

Bemused, he stared at us, obviously wondering what we were up to this time.

I waited anxiously for the rest of the day to see a reaction from Ryan. He showed no signs that he had been in his cabin yet. Either he hid it from us very well or he had an ace up his sleeve.

Sure enough, as we sat down to eat our supper, he burst through the dining hall doors wearing a bright red feather boa around his neck, a pair of pink sunglasses, a sparkly purse on his shoulder, and carrying a pink stuffed kitty in his hand, waving it at us.

There were hoots and whistles as he pranced around the room in a ladylike manner, moving past our table like a model on the catwalk, blowing kisses our way.

Everyone laughed and cheered, clapping their hands for his impromptu performance.

I looked across the table where Maggie and Dani sat, clearly dejected that their stunt backfired. Maggie tightened her hands into fists while Dani plunked her chin into the palm of her hand and sat with her elbow on the table, completely disgusted.

I felt bad when I saw the look on her face. "Aw, crap. I had such high hopes that it would work. I'm so sorry, Maggie."

Maggie nodded and sat there fuming. "That's okay, Jessie, at least we had fun doing this."

Dani drummed her fingers on her cheek bone, obviously plotting another prank against him. "Yeah, it doesn't end here."

A few days later, we came up with another plan, one that was sure to work this time. They waited until the afternoon, when everyone was too busy to notice their actions. After the bell rang, signaling the last session of the day, everyone streamed out on to the campground and stood stock still, laughing and pointing their fingers at Ryan's cabin. Just in front of the cabin sat his bed complete with mattress, pillow, and sleeping bag. Beside it was his little table with a lamp on top. His clothes, towel, paddle, and lifejacket were all heaped into one big pile on top of the bed.

Dani, Maggie, and I anxiously watched his reaction from the side of the pool.

Ryan went by whistling, staring at everyone, obviously wondering what was going on. He stopped mid-tune, walked backward, and stood there dumbstruck as he realized what had happened. He slapped his palm on his forehead and dragged it down his face. He shook his head side to side, seemingly deflated.

"Yes!" I said as I pumped my hand in the air, euphoric that it worked!

"Whoo hoo!" Maggie exclaimed, jumping up and down, laughing. She gave both of us a hug, clearly elated.

On the last day of camp with these kids, we held a special dinner for everyone. The staff, namely the instructors, acted as waiters and waitresses for the evening. Ethan and I joined Dani, Maggie, Rick, Sam, Kevin, and Pete and stood by the kitchen, doling out the food to the campers and counselors. The kids got a huge kick out of seeing us dressed to the nines and serving them food.

Afterward, we went out to the special fire-pit, the large one by the lake, near the watchtower. As we walked along the path, our feet treaded softly on the pine needles. The sun sank deeper behind the woodland, sending a cascade of golden beams through the tall, majestic trees and onto the forest floor. I could smell the rich scent of the smoke as we got closer to our destination. In front of us loomed two totem poles, one on each side of the path like a door, signifying the entrance to the campfire area. The fire was already lit. The flames roared several feet high, sending sparks swirling into the sky. All around it were long wooden logs, sitting lengthwise on the ground. I couldn't help but feel chills as I entered this sacred spot. My eyes wandered around, taking in the sights. It felt very tribal, like a scene right out of an episode of Survivor.

Everyone sat down, whispering in hushed tones as we waited in anticipation for the evening's ceremonies to start. A drum began to beat all around us. A steady and constant rhythm. I twisted around, looking over my shoulder, searching for the source of the sound. It grew closer and closer. There! The leaves started to rustle as something or someone moved toward us. The beat grew more intense, louder and louder. Suddenly, the leaves parted. Emerging from the forest was an "Indian Chief," pounding on a drum. He wore an enormous headdress, green and gold feathers spanning across the width of his head like a peacock's fan. His face was painted with green and gold tribal streaks across his cheeks, forehead, and chin. I stared at his face intently. I knew that face. It was Jean Luc!

He came to a stop in front of the fire. "Welcome." He bowed his head lavishly and waved elaborately with his hand, a sweeping gesture to include all of us.

His voice boomed as he spoke, full of power and strength. "Tonight is the last night for many of you. We have gathered here to give our thanks, share our thoughts and stories, and sing songs to celebrate our time together!"

Everyone applauded and cheered. He waited for a moment until it died down.

Placing his hand solemnly over his heart, he said, "Tonight we will share a powerful bond that unites us all." He paused theatrically and smiled. "It's an old tradition that goes back many generations—" He clapped his hands together, and then his fingers rose up toward the sky. "—let us give thanks to our ancestors for providing us with this wonderful, wonderful, ceremony. It's time to roast marshmallows!"

I snorted back laughter.

He put down his drum and started to hand out marshmallow roasters to the staff, then he passed around a bag of marshmallows. All of the counselors and instructors leaned in toward the fire and began to brown the marshmallows, letting them puff up and sizzle in the heat of the flames.

As the campers bit into the goopy marshmallows, Rick pulled out his guitar and started playing. Mike, Ryan, and Maggie started singing and nodded at the others to join in. We all swayed side to side on the logs, feeling the rhythm of the song. Afterward, Luc told stories, the feathers on his headdress bouncing comically as he spoke. The deep golden light from the fire glowed on his face, providing a dramatic backdrop to his tales. Once he was finished, one person from each cabin stepped forward, holding a long and thin stick. At the end of it was a small strip of paper, rolled up tightly. Written on the inside of the paper were wishes from everyone.

Luc stood up, raising his arms up at the black velvet sky, now sparkling with glittering stars. "As we place these wish sticks into the flames, we ask the spirits to receive our messages, helping them come true."

We all watched the orange and red flames consume our wishes, sending wisps of hope up into the night sky as they spiraled along the path of glittering sparks.

Luc went around the campfire, giving each of us a small white candle, just a few inches tall.

"As we begin to say goodnight and give our thanks, we light these candles to preserve our memories of all the good times we've had here at Camp Balsam. Whenever you want to remember your friends here at camp, all you have to do is light your candle and you will recall this night of magic."

I had goose bumps all along my arms. He went around and lit the candles, their small white flames glowing softly on our faces. As I looked at the campers and staff, the flames started to grow, like magical fairies fluttering around us, blessing us with special memories of our time together.

Once we were finished and blew out the candles, we all made the solemn trek back to the dining hall where we were treated to a slideshow of this week's session, featuring candid shots of our campers and staff members as we munched on popcorn. It was the perfect ending to a perfect evening.

CHAPTER 21

Respite

We all stood in the lane, waving at the last camper as the car drove past the lake. The air was eerily quiet, once all of the kids left.

We walked across the campground to Luc's cabin. Piling into the living room, we all sprawled out over every chair, sofa, cushion, and pillow. It was a tight squeeze but we did it. It was cozy and at this point, we all felt like family. A really, really big family.

We listened to Luc as he went over any issues or concerns we'd had from this session and discussed solutions and ideas for the next one. Our official day off didn't start until this afternoon and most of us were looking forward to it, our minds already long gone from exhaustion. Once he was finished, he handed us green hooded sweatshirts featuring the camp logo.

"Oh wow! This is awesome," I said as I pulled it on, trying it out for size. It fit perfectly. "Thanks Luc!"

"You're welcome, Jessie." He nodded his head and smiled, his cheeks rosy like Santa's.

Everyone else chimed in, saying thanks as they tugged the sweatshirts over their heads.

By the time we finished the meeting with Luc, it was already noon. We marched over to the dining hall and stood there in the kitchen scratching our heads. It was the chef's day off so we had to make do with whatever was left over. Every time we reached for something on the shelf, there was a label on it, written by Jamie, warning us not to touch it. Some had been marked for "Session Two" or "Session Three". We stood inside the walk in refrigerator that was nearly as big as my bedroom and rummaged through the paltry cheese and meat rack looking for something suitable for making sandwiches. I pulled out a plate of cheese and looked at it gingerly. I could see specks of mold growing along one edge. Ew.

"Hey! There's a loaf of bread here," yelled Ethan who was rifling through cupboards filled with cereal boxes and crackers. He held it up in the air for us to see. We cheered, thrilled that we could make a decent meal. Well, sort of...

We sliced the meat, cheese, and bread and put them on our plates. Then we sat down and took a bite. The sandwich tasted stale, the bread a day or two past its expiration date. But we were starving and didn't exactly want to eat cereal, again.

"Has anyone decided what to do for their day off yet?" asked Mike as he took another bite out of his sandwich.

"Sleep!" replied Ryan.

"Read!" said Maggie which didn't come as a surprise to me. She had an entire shelf full of books back at the cabin. It sounded like she was itching to read a couple of them.

"Get a vasectomy," deadpanned Chris.

We all stopped eating and stared at him.

"Is he serious?" I asked Ethan.

He shrugged. "Uh, guess we'll find out."

I rolled my eyes and sighed.

"Hey, you know what we need?" asked Mike.

"No, what?" replied Rick.

"I feel the need—" Mike started.

"—for speed!" Rick said, finishing Mike's sentence.

They reached out and touched each other's fists, knuckle to knuckle.

I blinked, perplexed. "*What?*"

"It's from one of the best movies of all time." Mike raised his eyebrows, expecting me to get the hint.

Rick waved his hand as if trying to jog my memory. "You know—Maverick?"

"Goose?" Mike hinted.

Ethan chimed in, "It's the one I watch all the time."

I narrowed my eyes, trying to recall the details. "You mean the one with Tom Cruise and the fighter jets?"

Mike banged his hand on the table enthusiastically. "Yep! That's the one!"

"But...that's an eighties flick," I said.

Rick smirked as he playfully punched Mike in the arm. "Dude, I don't think she knows how old we are."

"Ha! Jessie, we grew up in the eighties. We lived through the eighties. That was our era," Mike said laughing. "You know, *The Breakfast Club*, *Ferris Bueller?*"

"Yeah, I miss those days of skipping school," Mike said as if he was daydreaming. "Oh wait, that wasn't me. That was Bueller. Ha!"

Aghast, I stared at them, my jaw nearly dropping to my chest. "Seriously? You guys seem so much younger!"

Mike put his hand to his chest as if deeply flattered. "Why thank you very much."

Rick shrugged his shoulders. "I guess being around these kids keeps us young. It's a great excuse to act like a kid every single day!"

I could totally see that, especially the child within them. Their personalities seemed to defy their real age.

Mike grinned. "Oh hey! She just gave me an awesome idea!"

"Why don't we have a movie night and show *Top Gun*?"

"Oh yeah, as a matter of fact, we're showing it tonight," replied Rick, his face suffused with glee, raising his finger in the air, driving the point home.

"Bring on the popcorn baby," Mike said eagerly.

We spent the rest of the day hanging out by the pool, swimming, and sitting on the edge reading magazines and books as we dangled our feet in the water. Early in the evening we took the canoes out to the lake and paddled around on the calm water, searching for beavers and moose. To our delight we saw three tiny, baby beavers swimming along the edge of the shoreline, happily munching on twigs. By supper time we were famished.

We all stood in the kitchen scratching our heads again, wondering what to make. It was absolutely pitiful to walk around the refrigerator and not be able to eat some of the food since the chef had declared it off limits. Finally, Mike had an epiphany and suggested that we have a cookout. We grabbed hot dogs, marshmallows, bags of chips, and anything else we could find that was edible, and strode over to the campfire. Rick was already piling on the pieces of wood and lighting it up. Within a few minutes the wood was engulfed in roaring flames that stretched high into the sky. Ethan and I sat side by side on the long wooden logs as we cooked our hot dogs, enjoying the ambience and the silly chatter all around us.

Afterward, we marched into the dining hall, threw down thick padded gym mats in front of the flickering fireplace, and sat down. All around the fireplace mantel was a strand of Christmas lights, the glowing colorful bulbs providing an air of holiday cheer throughout the room. I smiled as soon as I saw them. Apparently Luc had already started the fire for us and was currently making popcorn in the kitchen. Mike plugged in the TV, turned it on, and loaded the DVD in the player. Luc breezed in, carrying several small bowls of popcorn, handed them out to us, and sat down beside us. I leaned against Ethan, grasped his hand, and wove our fingers together as the movie began to play.

Session two came too soon for us. We reluctantly dragged ourselves out of bed and stood on the steps of the cabin yawning and stretching. The sun was just rising over the trees and several kids were already playing soccer and Frisbee. The dining hall was once again filled with the loud din of enthusiastic campers as everyone marched in and helped themselves to breakfast. As I sat down and munched on the bacon and eggs, I casually scanned the room, watching the animated discussions between the counselors and new campers. It was fifteen minutes later when I realized that one of the instructors was notably absent.

I jabbed Ethan's ribs with my elbow. "Ethan, where's Pete?"

He glanced up and looked around the room then asked, "Rick! You seen Pete yet?"

Rick shook his head "Think he slept in again?"

Pete was notorious for being grumpy first thing in the morning and absolutely hated getting up, especially really early like today.

Ethan groaned. "Yep." He paused for a moment then said, "So, who's going to volunteer to wake him up?"

"Heh, no way. Don't look at me," replied Rick, holding his hand up like a stop sign.

Everyone else was apparently too busy eating, staring at their plates, and digging their forks into the eggs.

I had an idea. "Mike?"

He glanced over at me. "Yeah?"

"You know that air horn that Luc uses for starting races?"

A slow smile began to spread across his face. "You thinking what I'm thinking?"

I nodded.

Several people at the table watched us with keen interest, suddenly getting the idea.

Sam gasped as she got the picture. "Oh hell yeah! I'll do it! I'll go wake him up!"

She dashed over to Luc and told him her plan. He looked over at our table and gave us two thumbs up and a big smile.

As she burst out the door, running over to Luc's cabin. All of us at the staff table went outside and stood on the porch to watch.

It took her a minute or two to find it and then she suddenly ran out of Luc's cabin holding the air horn high in the air, skipping with glee toward Pete's cabin. She hid beneath his open window, raised her arm, and pressed the button. There was a long and loud honk. Within seconds, Pete burst out of the door, hopping on one foot and grasping his toe. His hair looked completely disheveled, sticking out all angles like a porcupine's. He wore plaid, red and black pajama bottoms, and a green tank top. He raised his fist and yelled incoherently at Sam who was already making a beeline back to us, wearing a huge grin.

She came to stand beside on the porch with her hands on her hips and sucked in a gasping breath. "Whoo! That was awesome! HA!"

We all gave each other high fives, turned around, and waved at Pete who was watching us from the doorway of his cabin.

A few minutes later Pete stormed into the dining hall looking quite peeved. He marched into the kitchen to grab whatever was left over. Luc threw him a stony glare as he walked past him, obviously not amused by his tardiness. Pete sat down at our table with a huff, wearing an angry scowl and grumbling to himself. We all watched with him amusement.

"And good morning to you too, Pete," Maggie said sarcastically.

Dani chimed in, "It is a lovely day isn't it? The sun is shining and the birds are chirping."

"Who would want to sleep in on a gorgeous day like this, eh?" I pitched in, being as jovial as possible. Beside me, Ethan snickered as Pete glanced up, wearing a dark look, and sighed dramatically.

Today was all about getting acquainted with the new campers. Remembering their names proved to be a challenge since there were so many of them coming and going. It was like a revolving door of jubilant kids.

I was watching them stroll into the dojo when I turned around and came face to face with a tall girl with straight blond hair in a pixie cut, vivid blue eyes, and a buoyant smile. She was bouncing up and down on her feet.

"Hi! I'm Natalie!" she said, giggling, and pulled me into a hug.

"Oh, thank you, Natalie," I replied as she joined the group.

Facing Ethan, I gestured in her direction feeling a bit bewildered. "What was that?"

"Isn't she sweet?" asked Ethan beaming.

I watched her as she hung out with the other kids. Her behavior seemed odd, compared to the rest of them.

Tilting my head quizzically at Ethan, I asked, "Something's not right...how old is she?"

"She's ten but has the mental capacity of an eight old year."

I stood there, stunned. "Eight? Isn't this session for the older kids?"

"Yeah, but can you imagine her with the younger ones? She would tower over them. Luc thought it would be better to have her with the older group this time."

"Well, true, but's still, she's so tall."

"She's growing too fast that's why."

I felt a pang of pity. She's in for a rough ride, I thought. "Geez, at that rate, she'll be a giant by the time she's actually thirteen."

Ethan nodded and said, "Luc said that the doctors are trying to find a way to slow down her growth rate but aren't having much luck yet."

"Wow," I said breathlessly, shaking my head from side to side.

"Her parents wanted her to have a good time and just 'be a kid' this summer. Apparently she's had a tough time at school," Ethan said somberly.

"Heh, she came to the right place."

The next few days went fairly smoothly. We were all holding our breaths, anxiously waiting for something to go wrong. Sure enough, on the fifth day, one of the staff members snapped. It was Josie who lost her temper, which took us all by surprise.

"That's it Simon! Out of the pool! Now!" she yelled. Her fist were clenched, her face red and flooded with anger.

Dani stood up and walked over to Josie. "I'm sorry, Simon. You are going to have to leave the pool. We will not tolerate that behavior."

Simon was a scrawny kid with raven black hair and dark eyes. He gave Josie the finger and screamed at them, "No! You can't tell me what to do!"

Ethan shot out of his chair, stormed over to the edge of the pool, and yelled at Simon, "Don't you make me come in there and physically take you out of water!"

"I hate you!" he yelled back at Ethan.

Ethan turned to Eric and said, "Eric, go get Luc. Quickly!"

Eric ran out of the pool enclosure, through the gate, and over to Luc's cabin.

Rick walked briskly to the other side of the pool closer to Simon. He gave Simon one last warning, sat down, and slid his legs into the water, ready to dive in as Ethan reached out, trying to grab Simon by the arm.

Simon was having none of it. He was splashing angrily at Ethan and making a huge scene.

"All right! That's it! Everyone out of the pool! You have five seconds to get out." bellowed Dani as she blasted on her whistle, sending a loud and piercing noise over us.

The kids promptly started pulling themselves up onto the edge of the pool and moving to the shallow end toward the stairs. All except Simon. He was the only one left in the water.

Rick and Ethan jumped in with Dani and began trying to grab Simon. He flailed his arms wildly, making it more difficult to get a hold of him. Eventually, Ethan was able to snatch him and herd him toward the stairs. As Simon got to the top step, he yelled at Josie, pointing his finger at her, swearing nonstop.

Josie stared back at him and said, "Same to you!"

Simon stood there, stunned.

Then after a moment of silence, he replied, "You can't say that to me!"

"Sure I can!" responded Josie.

There were guffaws and snickers from several staff members.

Luc arrived at the gate and surveyed the scene. Rick, Ethan, Dani, and Simon all stood in front of him dripping wet. Simon continued to struggle in Ethan's grip. Luc nodded at Ethan who escorted Simon out of the pool area. The two of them then dragged him to Luc's cabin, a place to give kids like Simon a timeout until they calmed down. Simon kicked and screamed the entire way.

Dani blew on her whistle again. "Okay. You can go back in the pool."

Everyone gleefully jumped into the water.

"Whoo! Way to go, Josie." Dani gave Josie a high five. Rick came over to Josie and gave her a hug, leaving a giant wet imprint on her shirt, making her smile.

"Thanks," she said quietly, still a bit shook up from her encounter with Simon. "He really knows how to push my buttons. I swear, I just want to strangle him at times."

After a few minutes, Ethan came back in and sat down in the chair. He was very tense and angry. I walked up to him and gave him a hug from behind. "You okay?" I asked.

He sighed. "No," he said as he shook his head. He reached up and brushed his fingers through his hair. His hands shook badly. I grasped them and held on.

"Sensei Ethan, watch this," yelled out a tall boy with spiky blond hair. He stood on top of the diving board, bouncing up and down.

We watched him. He leapt up in the air, did a front kick, and yelled, "*Hiyah!*"

"That's awesome! Way to go," said Ethan, giving him two thumbs up.

Several other campers got the clue and lined up on the diving board to do the same thing. One after another, they all leapt off the board shouting out loud "*Kiais*" in midair.

Ping! A light bulb just went off in my head. "Ethan? Have you done Karate in the pool yet?"

He looked at me curiously. "What do you mean?"

"Like that." I waved my hand at the kids diving off the board, doing kicks. "We can have them practice their kicks, blocks, and punches under water in the shallow end. And do kicks and punches with *kiais* as they dive off the board."

He looked at me, then looked at the kids, and back at me. A slow smile grew on his face. "Holy cow, Jessie, that's a great idea."

"We should do that for tomorrow's class," I said eagerly.

It proved to be the most popular class at camp.

CHAPTER 22

Heat Wave

Session three hit us with a double whammy. Not only were we exhausted, but we were also dealing with an unusual heat wave. The temperature soared to nearly forty degrees Celsius. Standing in the sun in full uniform made it feel much hotter. I felt as if I was in a blistering sauna. The air hit me like a soggy warm blanket and it was immensely uncomfortable.

By the time I reached the dojo, I was already sweating. I licked my parched lips and blew the wet hair out of my eyes as we began the class. It took a lot of effort to keep going despite the balmy heat. My mind kept wandering over to the pool, dreaming of feeling the cool water on my skin. Today was a busy one. We had four classes, two back-to-back this morning and then again after lunch.

Finally the bell rang, ending the class. Everyone poured out of the dojo and marched over to their next station. I was soaking wet and my legs felt like lead. I had no energy left. I bent down to pick up a pool noodle that we used for blocking and my vision suddenly went black. I wavered for a moment as I struggled to stand back up. I felt Ethan's hand on my arm. Looking up, I saw him staring at me, his features wrinkled in concern.

"Jessie, are you okay?"

I stammered, taking deep breaths, "I—I think so. I felt weird for a second."

He had placed both hands on my arms and scrutinized me. "Weird? How?"

"For a moment, I couldn't see anything. Everything went black." I gulped, feeling unsteady, and leaned into him as I spoke.

He placed his hand against my cheek. Alarm raced across his face. "You are awfully hot, Jessie. You need to cool down. Come on over here." He steered me to the steps at the nurse's station and sat me down. He placed his hands on top of my knees as he knelt down in front of me.

Feeling woozy, I closed my eyes, taking some more deep breaths. Bad idea. That made my head spin even more. I felt him touch my face with his hands. "Jessie, look me at me please." I looked down at him as he gazed up. "Do you feel nauseated?" he asked.

I nodded.

He sighed and brushed his hand over my bangs, rubbing his fingers on my brow. "Did you want to lie down in the nurse's office?"

I shook my head. "No, it's okay. Just give me minute."

"Jessie, I want you to take a cool shower right away. You're overheating. Take off your top." He reached out and undid my obi, helping me shrug out of my white jacket. I began to feel a little better. "Can you stand up?"

"Yeah, I think so."

I stood on shaky legs. He grasped my hand as we started moving across to the washrooms. "Um, I don't have a towel."

"Don't worry, I'll get one for you."

"Can you hold onto my hearing aids for me while I take a shower? I don't want to lose them."

"Yeah, sure," he said.

We reached the top steps to the washrooms. I took out my hearing aids and placed them in his hands.

Heading straight for the showers, I turned on the tap with shaking hands. I quickly stripped down, feeling tension build in the back of my neck. My head was beginning to pound, making me more nauseous. I hung my uniform on the hook and stepped into the stall. The cool water fell across my shoulders and back. I began to feel a little better as I turned around, letting the water fall gently on my face. Once I was sufficiently cooled off, I turned off the water and pulled back the curtains. There was a blue towel on the hook on top of my uniform. It was Ethan's. I had seen him carry it with him on several occasions. I reached out for it as I wondered how it ended up in here. I briskly rubbed my skin dry and pulled my damp uniform back on, wishing I had something else to wear. I stumbled as I reached the doorway.

Ethan caught my arm when I stepped outside. He held up my hearing aids.

"Thanks," I said, putting them back on, hearing the loud hum of activity once again all around me.

I handed him his towel. "Um, dare I ask how this ended up in the shower?"

He smiled briefly "Emma put it there for me."

"Ah."

"Come on, I think you should lie down," he said as held onto my hand and led me back to my cabin.

I sat down on the bed. Ethan helped me take off my shoes.

"Thanks," I said quietly as my head began to pound harder.

He looked up at me in alarm. "Jessie, you're as white as a sheet."

I closed my eyes, placing my head in the palms of my hands, mumbling, "Bad headache...it's coming from my neck."

He climbed on top of the bed and sat behind me, massaging my neck. After a minute I was able to sit up a little. He rubbed my back in soothing circles.

There was a knock at the door.

It was Emma, holding a bottle of pills and glass of water in her hands. "Hi Jessie, Ethan told me that you were not feeling well."

I nodded.

Ethan spoke up. "Bad headache."

She knelt down in front of me and gave me a white pill. "This is ibuprofen. It should help with the pain and fever." She handed the glass to me and I swallowed the water, gratefully sipping the cool refreshment.

"Thanks Emma," Ethan said kindly.

She looked at me with concerned eyes. "Is there anything else you need?"

I shook my head, not wanting to talk much. She patted my knee and left.

Ethan touched my shoulder. "Jessie? Did you want to lie down?"

I nodded again, feeling quite fatigued, and slid down onto the bed, closing my eyes. He continued to massage my neck and back, making me feel more relaxed. Waves of exhaustion rolled over me.

I woke up with a start to an empty room. I could hear faint screams of delighted kids coming from the direction of the pool. I looked at my watch. It was already afternoon and I had missed both classes. My headache was mostly gone and I felt better.

Crap, I thought as I stood up. The room swayed and I promptly sat down again, cursing myself for moving too fast.

Maggie came walking in through the door, with sunglasses on top of her head, carrying a beach towel. "Hi, Jessie! Feeling better?"

"Yeah, a little...wait, how did you know?"

"Everyone at camp knows. It's a small world here."

I rolled my eyes. "Of course they do."

I could hear the bell ringing in the background.

"Supper time," Maggie said. "Did you want anything to eat?"

"I'm not sure. Maybe something simple like crackers or a cup of tea?"

"Not a problem. One cup of tea coming right up." Maggie dashed out the door and bounced gleefully down the steps.

I looked down at my uniform and decided to get changed. I swapped the long pants for blue shorts and was just pulling on a green tank top when there was a knock on the door.

Odd. Why would Maggie knock on the door? I wondered.

A voice bellowed from the other side of the door, "Room service!" Ethan peeked in, carrying a mug and a plate filled with crackers and a cookie.

"Aw! Thanks, Ethan. I thought Maggie was coming back?" I said as he sat down beside me and handed me the cup. He placed the plate on the bed between us.

"She was until I intercepted her. I wanted to see how you were doing and this was the perfect excuse to stop by." He reached out and touched my cheek with the back of his hand, "How are you doing? You feel a little bit cooler."

I snatched up a piece of cracker. "A little better, still a bit dizzy when I stand up too fast."

He glanced down at the plate and pointed at the cookie. "Jamie saved a cookie for you."

"Tell him thanks, that was nice of him. I'm sorry for missing this afternoon's classes Ethan. I feel kinda bad about that."

He placed his hand on the back of my neck. "Since it was so hot today, I decided to have karate in the pool instead. It worked like a charm and kept everyone cool."

I felt a tear roll down my cheek.

He reached out with his hand and gently wiped it away with his thumb. "Jessie, it's all right." He grabbed the cup and placed it on the floor, moved the plate aside, and pulled me into an embrace. He kissed my forehead while rubbing my back in slow circles.

"You're just tired. I mean we all are. This is your first year and it's a lot to take in. Luc has always said that session three is the hardest one to get through."

I could feel his chest rumbling as he spoke which comforted me.

"The same thing happened to me the first time I taught here. I was with Dad when I almost passed out one day. Me and three other staff members got really sick for a couple of days. It has happened to almost everyone that has worked here before."

That took me by surprise. "Really?"

"Yeah, sometimes the campers bring a cold or flu from home."

"How come the heat didn't affect you today?"

"Probably because I'm used to it. You know, it's okay to wear a T-shirt instead of the full uniform."

I grabbed another cracker and munched on it. "Are you sure?"

"Tell you what, for the rest of the summer, we both can wear T-shirts okay?" he said as he plucked a cracker from my plate and nibbled on it.

I nodded in assent.

He picked up my cup of tea and handed it back to me. He gave me a quick kiss and stood up. "I'm going to go have supper. I may stop by later," he said with a wink and strolled out the door.

It felt very strange to sit in the cabin by myself during dinner. There was silence all around me and I suddenly felt very alone. I slowly got up and ventured outside, bringing my cup of tea and cookie with me and sat down on the steps. Out here I felt a little better.

After supper, the campers and staff filed out of the dining hall and onto the main campground. The level of chatter rose as everyone began their outdoor activities. Tonight it looked as if they were playing capture the flag. Various people waved at me as they walked by me, shouting out greetings. As promised, Ethan stopped later in the evening on his way back from brushing his teeth. He grabbed my hand, tugged me off to the side of the cabin where we were hidden from the campers, and pulled me into an embrace. I wrapped my arms around his ribs, feeling comforted by his presence.

"Thought I stop by and say good night," he said in a husky voice as he grasped the sides of my face with his hands, leaned in, and gave me a tender kiss.

We broke apart after a few minutes. "Thanks, Ethan, I needed that."

"So did I," he said as we touched foreheads for a moment.

Wearing a T-shirt instead of my long, full uniform, and taking showers during our breaks made a big difference for the rest of the heat wave. Several of the other instructors did the same thing on the insanely hot days, jumping in the pool to cool down. The compelling heat was taking a toll on everyone, making tempers flare easily. Temper tantrums spread like wildfire amongst the campers, which in turn tested our patience more than usual. Luc asked us to watch our moods since they were affecting the kids. He'd noticed that they were picking up on our negative vibes and lashing out. As a result, Luc insisted on more pool breaks instead of the regular activities in between classes to keep everyone happy. It worked like a charm. The overall mood of the camp shifted dramatically toward a much more jovial atmosphere.

I was sitting at the table with Mike, Rick, Maggie, Dani, Ethan, and Emma during lunch one day as session three was nearing the end. Exhaustion had settled over us like a heavy cloud. We could barely keep our eyes open. No one said a word, and we all simply stared blank-faced as we held on to our cups of tea and coffee. The consumption of coffee was on the rise as we all struggled to keep our wits about us. It felt as if we were hanging on to the last thread of sanity.

I took a sip of my tea, a sweet concoction with extra sugar in it. My body was craving the extra boost of energy. I desperately needed something to get me through the next few days. I nearly ended up snorting the tea out my nose when Sam breezed in through the door. Strapped to her back were large translucent, glittery butterfly wings. She wore a bright pink, fluffy tutu around her waist. In her hand, she held a silver wand with a pink star on top, completely covered in sparkling rhinestones. On top of her head was a shiny silver tiara with pink ribbons cascading down from it. She was a vision of shimmering pink and silver. Even her lipstick was a bright cheery pink.

I clapped my hand over my mouth, trying not to spill the tea all over the table. I was giggling manically as I stared at her.

Ethan's eyes opened wide in alarm. I jabbed my finger at Sam, past Ethan's shoulder.

"HA! What are you up to now Sam?" I asked her once I finished gulping down the tea.

Her eyes twinkled merrily. "Ah. Glad you asked. I'm the Happy Fairy."

"The Happy Fairy?" I repeated. I couldn't help but smile as I admired her outfit.

"Yep. My job is to wipe those mopey looks off everyone's faces today." She looked at Ethan, tapped her wand on top his head and said, "Ding!"

Everyone at my table burst out laughing at Ethan's expression. He looked at her then back at us, wearing an exasperated look, and then rolled his eyes. He was trying to be as serious as possible which made us laugh harder.

"See? I told you it would work," she remarked as she merrily flounced over to the next table and said, "Hi, I'm the Happy Fairy." She tapped Natasha on the head saying, "Ding!" The kids at her table giggled and squealed with delight.

She pranced around the room, her ribbons flying in the air, putting smiles on everyone's faces. She stopped at one table full of petulant boys and stood with her hands on her hips. "And who is this Gloomy Gus?" she asked in a grumpy voice as she pouted her lips. She reached over and tapped Eric on the head with her sparkly wand. "Ding!"

Eric suddenly smiled, exaggerating his features like a silly clown and said, "Thanks, Happy Fairy," prompting the boys into gales of laughter. One of them even fell off his chair.

Midway through session four, we were feeling the effects of a long summer. At this point it felt as if we were losing our minds. We were practically giddy with exhaustion. Many of us wore the same glazed look in our eyes, an expression featuring the "far–away-stare." Hungry for a snack, we gathered in the kitchen late at night, rummaging around for something to eat. The supplies were starting to dwindle and the food was running dangerously low. Everything was rationed. Jamie was supremely organized. He had labeled everything and grouped them accordingly for each day. Many items featured tape with the words "Don't Touch!" Some had dates written on them, which were for this week.

On the counter in the middle of the kitchen sat a large basket of fruit. We all lunged for it, grabbing an apple or orange. Ethan came out of the giant walk-in refrigerator carrying a jug of pink juice. He closed the door with the back of his foot as he kept an eye on the juice, trying not to spill it. He poured himself a drink, gave one to me, and then placed the pitcher down on to the table for everyone else to help themselves.

Mike suddenly turned around, yanked open a drawer, and pulled out a metal fork. "Jessie, toss that apple to me. I'm going to catch it with this fork." He gestured with his chin toward my hand then glanced back at his fork, holding it out in front of him.

I stared at him incredulously, thinking that he had truly gone mad from being outside in the sun for too long.

He nodded encouragingly at me and waved with his free hand for me to go ahead.

I took a deep breath. "Okay, you asked for it. I think you're crazy to even try it."

I lobbed it gently in the air toward him. Everyone held their breath as they watched it fly across the room.

He deftly moved his hand beneath the apple as it fell. It landed perfectly on the fork with a soft thunk. Unbelievable!

Maggie and Rick howled with laughter while Pete comically clapped his hands to his face in stunned silence. Ethan and I burst out laughing, too. I slid down to the floor, grip-

ping my sides as tears ran down my face. Ethan pounded
the table with his hand as he guffawed. We looked as if we
were punch drunk, bent over laughing and snickering. Several of us sat on the floor, giggling and wiping tears from
our eyes. It was just the release that we needed.

There was a loud bang behind us as someone burst
through the back door. It was Jamie. He came to a stop in
front of us with his hands on his hips. "What is the meaning of this?" he ranted as he waved his hands at us, clearly
dismayed at the scene in front of him. "I have to be up at
five in the morning! You do want to eat breakfast don't
you?" He reached over and slapped the back of Mike's
head. "I could hear you guys from my cabin!" he com-
plained as he stood there watching us slowly stand up again.
"And what in the world are you guys doing?"

Mike held up his fork with the apple on top and took a
bite out of it.

I clapped my hand over my mouth, feeling the giggles
rise again.

"Stealing the food?" Jamie demanded. "Out! You know
the rules! *Out!*" He pointed his fingers at the door.

His gestures and tirade made us all start laughing again.

"I want to see those tushies going out the door now!"
He grabbed a nearby towel and started herding us in the
general direction of the door, flapping the towel at us as if
we were wayward geese.

Rick laughed. "Hey Mike! Did you hear that? He said to
move your tushy!"

"No, he was talking about yours!" replied Mike, grinning
sardonically.

"*Out!*" bellowed Jamie as he continued to flap the towel
at us.

"Sir, yes, sir," Mike said as he saluted him then took another bite out of the apple.

"Gimme that!" Jamie said as he reached for the fork
Mike was holding. Mike ducked out of his reach and

pranced across the room. "I expect to see that fork back here by tomorrow morning! Excuse me, where do you think you're going with that?" He deftly plucked the pitcher out of Pete's hand as he tried to sneak out the door past him. "Thank you, now scoot! Or you'll be stuck with cold cereal in the morning!"

"Ooh, cold cereal. How exciting," Pete exclaimed as he strolled out the door, smirking.

Jamie turned around and stormed back into the kitchen muttering, "Oh yeah, that's real nice of you guys, just leave out everything for me to clean up."

CHAPTER 23

Believe

I awoke to a clear blue sky. The temperature had dropped dramatically this past week, and the nights were getting cooler once again. I shivered and quickly changed out of my pajamas, pulling on a thick fleece jacket and jeans. Everyone else was still sound asleep as I tugged on my shoes and donned my hearing aids. I clumped down the steps and hurried across the campground over to the dining hall where the chimney puffed out clouds of smoke, a sign that a warm fire awaited us. Suddenly the loudspeakers came to life. I jumped and looked around as the theme song to *Top Gun* blared through them. I listened to it, letting the rising sun fall on my face, warming my cool skin. It finally dawned on me why they liked the movie so much, aside from the obvious. It was about seizing the moment and taking control of your life.

As I thought about it, I continued walking to the dining hall. I realized that something in me had changed. I felt different. The song was a perfect reflection on how I felt today. As I was just about to step onto the porch, I saw Mike strolling across the campground. He saw me watching him and waved. He began to do a champion's dance, pumping his arms in the air, in slow exaggerated movements as if reaching the final moment of the race.

I laughed, did a little wave, and walked into the kitchen to grab a cup of hot chocolate. It was absolutely silent. Most of the tables were folded up and leaning against the wall. Only a few remained in the center of the room. I stood in front of the crackling fire for a few minutes, absorbing the wonderful smell and warming my hands.

By the time I went back outside, Rick and Maggie were sitting on the steps chatting with Mike. I sat down beside them and watched them talk.

Luc clomped up the steps, uttered, "Bonjour!" to all of us and briskly headed for the kitchen, no doubt to get a cup of coffee.

Dani came over to join us. "Good morning, everyone," she said. "Mmm. That smells delicious, Jessie. I think I'll get some, too."

Sam, Pete, and Ethan climbed up the steps, weaving around us. Ethan sat down behind me, rubbing my back in slow circles with his hands. He leaned down and gave me a hug.

"Aw, thanks, Ethan," I said as he placed his chin on my shoulder.

"Ooh, can I have some of that?" he said, grabbing the mug of hot chocolate and took a sip.

Within a few minutes, everyone was either standing on the porch or sitting on the steps, simply relaxing. It was our first quiet morning in a long time. I leaned back into Ethan as he embraced me and watched the breeze ruffle the branches on the trees across the campground. Some of them were already changing colors, their tips dappled with bright orange and red. In the stillness of the camp, I could hear the leaves shake as the wind blew through them. It was similar to the sound of a rain-stick. They seemed to shimmer in the early morning sunlight.

Luc stepped out onto the porch behind us, sipping loudly on his coffee.

I glanced up at him. "Luc?"

He nodded. "*Oui?*"

"What kind of tree is that?" I pointed at a tall majestic tree featuring a long white trunk with mint green leaves shaped liked spades.

He flicked his eyes toward the forest. "Ah. That would be a Quaking Aspen because of the way the leaves shake like that."

"Oh cool. They look like hands clapping together and it sounds like faint applause to me."

He took a moment to listen and watch the leaves shake and shimmer in the breeze. He gasped. "You're right, Jessie. I've never noticed that before."

Everyone turned to watch the leaves ripple in the gentle wind as the weight of the world seemed to fade away. It was at that moment that Alfred made his reappearance. He popped his head up from beneath the bottom step, looked at us, tilting his head side to side, and then scampered into the dining hall. Within minutes, there was a loud crash and shouts from Jamie. "Alfred!" exclaimed Jamie as he ran around the room, chasing after him with a spatula in his hand. We all turned our heads to watch the two of them run around, laughing at their antics.

We spent the rest of the day cleaning up the cabins and putting the equipment away. Then we started packing. It was somber time as we all realized that it was finally over, and we would soon be going our separate ways. That night we built a huge bonfire and sat around it roasting marshmallows, sharing stories, and singing. As everyone around me chattered, I watched the glowing sparks spiral up into the sky as they joined the stars high above.

A flicker of movement caught my eye. I turned my face away from the fire and stared at the velvet sky. There! I saw it again.

I grabbed Ethan's hand and tugged at it. "Ethan, look up. Is that what I think it is?"

He followed my line of sight. I waited for a moment until his eyes adjusted to the changed in light. He cupped his other hand over the side of his face to block the glow from the fire. "Oh wow! It's the Northern Lights! Hey, everybody, look up!"

The chatter ceased as they all turned their faces up at the night sky.

A curtain of bright mint green and rosy red shimmered and wavered across the stars over our heads. Its ever changing path danced in front of us. The powerful ripples glowed brightly against a twinkling backdrop. It was a magical moment that sent chills down my spine.

I leaned against Ethan and we held hands while we watched the flickering lights. He took a deep sigh and gripped my hand tighter.

"It's perfect," he said. "It couldn't get more perfect than this...our last night together here at camp." His chest rumbled, a familiar feeling that was comforting to me. He turned to look at me. The glimmer of the campfire projected a golden glow onto his face. I was grateful for the light. It lit up his features and made it easier for me to read his lips. "So, what do you think?" he asked. "Was it worth it?"

"What? Camp?" I thought about it for a moment then nodded. "Yeah, it was. It's been amazing. I honestly have to say that I have never met so many nice people who treated me like a real friend."

He smiled. "Do you feel any different?"

"Heh, aside from wanting to sleep for three weeks straight? Yeah, I do. It's hard to explain, you know? If I had to put it in words, I would have to say that I feel stronger, more sure of myself." I paused for a moment as I collected my thoughts. "Before, it was like my mind was splintered and my soul was shattered. It felt as if I was struggling to put the pieces together." My voice began to waver as a lone tear ran down my cheek. "I felt so lost."

Ethan reached out with his hand and gently wiped it away with his fingers. "And now?" he asked as he looked into my eyes.

"Now, I feel empowered." I took a moment to take a deep breath and watch the Northern Lights, letting the cool breeze dry my face. "Is this what it's going to feel like when I get my black belt?" I asked, suddenly curious.

"What do you mean when? How do you even know you'll get it in the first place?" he replied with mock sincerity.

I playfully punched him on the arm. "Ethan!"

"All right! Just kidding!" After considering it for a moment, he said, "Um yeah, it's kinda like that. It's a monumental victory after working so hard for so long and finally getting what you want." He took a deep breath and grasped my hands. "It's a huge relief and a triumph at the same time. It's an amazing feeling. You feel so strong and unbreakable. You begin to see the world through different eyes. It changes you, Jessie."

I was speechless. I couldn't wait to get my black belt. Maybe by next summer I'd be wearing one. I looked up at the stars and sent a silent wish. All I needed to do was believe.

TURN THE PAGE TO READ THE

BONUS

SHORT STORY

Awake

I was surrounded with an immense feeling of warmth, joy, and boundless love. Golden, glittering facets of light fell all around me. I smiled, feeling giddy from all of the happiness. I wanted to spin around and around with my arms spread out like a young child, laughing with delight. I could feel my chest glow with warmth as I watched the shimmering light shower down all around me. My heart seemed to grow bigger, filling up with bliss. I tried to reach out and touch it.

My fingers grasped at nothing.

I jerked awake in a room filled with flickering light. I looked around in panic. My fingers gripped the edges of a smooth table. The walls of the room seemed to move strangely as the light and shadows danced over them. I peered more closely at the surface of the walls. They seemed to glitter like sand as it caught the light. Tiny sparkles glinted everywhere I looked. Curious, I turned my head, searching for the source of the illumination.

Just off to my left was a smooth alcove with a high archway, almost as large as fireplace. It was filled with long, angular prisms that resembled quartz crystals. I stood up and moved slowly toward them. They glowed brightly, glimmering as if a flame was caught in the center of each one. Some were larger than others and glowed more brightly. Others seemed to struggle to glow, dimming then growing brighter again. The flickering lights didn't give off any heat. Instead, they seemed to be more like grains of glittering sand, floating around and sparkling like rainbows. I gasped, stunned by what I saw.

Out of the corner of my eye, I caught some movement. I spun around and was startled to find a tall, robed figure standing in the arched doorway. His features were chiseled and athletic. He gave off an essence of smooth confidence and grace. The golden robe he wore shimmered in the light. It draped elegantly over his body and appeared to be made of some unusual material that seemed to glimmer. I looked at his face again. His skin seemed to have a golden sheen to it. Everything glowed in here. It simply radiated all around me.

"Ah, you are awake" He seemed to have spoken to me, yet his voice boomed all around me as if he was inside my head. I jerked around to see if anyone else was in the room with me. As I glanced back at him, he chuckled lightly and smiled, making the lines around his eyes crinkle. He clasped his hands together and bowed slightly to me.

"Please do not be afraid. I am your guide. Welcome." He waved his arm toward the door and beckoned me to follow him. I looked at him then back at the room, pointing toward the crystals. "Wait! Um, what are those?"

"Ah, those would be the life force crystals." He gestured at them with a graceful sweep of his hand. "See how some are brighter than others?" He pointed toward a large one that glowed so strongly the light reflected onto me like a disco ball. "Those contain hope and remain strong and vibrant."

He moved to a dimmer crystal. The flickering light inside struggled to glow. "This one no longer has faith and is becoming weaker." His eyes seemed sad as he leaned in to gaze at it, the soft light barely illuminating his face. It sputtered from time to time, trying desperately to expand, but seemed to be out of energy.

"Is there anything that we can do to help?" I asked quietly as I watched them in awe. It was such a transcendent moment that I didn't want to break away.

"Unfortunately, no. It's not up to us. They need to find the strength from within to grow resolute again," he replied softly. "Come, there is more to see." His voice echoed in my mind. He strolled down the hallway with such grace that I could swear that he was floating.

The ceiling rose up like a grand cathedral. The walls seemed to be made out of smooth, polished white marble. Tiny, glittering facets could be seen in the surface as we strode past various rooms. I quickly glanced in one of the rooms. It looked like a smaller version of the majestic dome. Above each archway was a name elegantly sculpted into the surface. From a distance, they looked like runes, and as I approached them, they changed into English right before my eyes. One said "Hall of Muse," another declared "Hall of Hope," and past it was the "Hall of Healing." We entered the one that revealed the words "Hall of Knowledge."

As we went inside, the room seemed to expand. All around us were small pillars that reached my waist. They appeared to have been carved out of the same smooth quartz as the room, as if they grew up from the floor. On top of each one was a flat tablet, positioned on a slight incline. Several robed figures stood at some of the tablets. They looked different from each other. Their glittering robes featured a variety of colors. The tall figure at the back was wearing an orange robe. Another wore a pale green. The one on my right was in a soft plum purple.

My guide gestured to them with a graceful sweep of his arm. "As you can see, we observe and learn in this room."

As I watched them, one of them waved their hands over the tablet as if to flip the page in a book. I craned my head to the side to get a glimpse of what was on it.

I looked back at my guide and was just about to ask if we could see it when he nodded at me as if to say, "Yes, you may."

As we approached the new figure, he looked up and smiled. He wore an indigo blue robe that shimmered as he moved.

When we came to a stop in front of him, my guide bowed his head at the blue-robed figure. The man in blue repeated the same gesture with a soft nod to us. Then turned back to the tablet and waved his hand over it again. The tablet flickered, sending a cascade of blue light over him. A series of transparent letters, symbols, and images suddenly appeared in front of him, constantly changing, moving in rapid succession. His eyes darted back and forth as he scanned it.

I moved closer to him, trying to see what he was viewing. There were live images of people, then natural disasters, animals in distress, children crying, all switching back and forth from everywhere at once. It was a constant stream of data, overlaid on top of each other. He abruptly brought his hand to the lower right section of the tablet and flicked his wrist, bringing the image to the center. The screen stopped, expanded, and continued on.

A trembling, helpless child sat on top of a car as a huge surge of water began to flood around him. As the force of the water swept over him, he fell off, gripping the side mirror, barely hanging on. He was screaming in terror.

The blue robed figure shimmered for a moment, disappeared, then reappeared. He stood and watched the scenario. Within a minute, rescue personnel approached the child in a bright orange boat. They fought hard against the force of the current as they reached out, nearly missing him, and then pulled him to safety. They wrapped the shivering child in a red blanket.

Stunned, I gaped at him. "Was that you? Did you do that?"

"It was a collective effort," he said with a subtle shrug of his shoulders. "I summoned one of our younger angels to send a muse to the rescue team. This way, we do not directly interfere with their lives. We simply help spark an idea and try to send them on the right path. The choice is left up to them."

"Wow. That's impressive." I said breathlessly as I watched him and the others scan their tablets, their eyes rapidly absorbing the material as it played out in front of them.

"Shall we continue on?" asked my guide.

I nodded and followed him down a long hallway. Each room featured an array of angels, wearing robes in all colors of the rainbow. Some appeared to be teachers or guides, who seemed to be overseeing the rest of the group like in a classroom. They walked around, watching, and consulting with the others.

We came to a stop in front of the room entitled, "Hall of Reflection." As we strode in, it was immediately obvious that it was set up differently. Instead of pillars, there were curved benches, following the shape of the wall. In the middle sat a large, elegant, circular well. Inside it, the surface rippled like water. Curious, I moved closer. I could see my reflection in it as it swirled around, twinkling. It quickly dawned on me that it wasn't water. It was more like millions and millions of glittering facets, like tiny grains of shiny sand. Its effect was magical and mesmerizing.

I turned my head toward my guide and asked, "What is this?"

He smiled, his eyes crinkling at the corners. "This is the Pool of Reflection. A time to ponder the true meaning of your path."

I leaned in and stared at it in wonder. Suddenly, flashes of images appeared before me, one on top of another, flickering in and out. I gasped out loud. They featured me, at various ages: as a young child, playing and laughing; then as a teenager; and into an adult. Some images were bright and vibrant, full of happiness, love, and warmth. Then it changed into dark and somber depictions that I didn't recognize: a lone soul, crying, who seemed lost. The visions started changing, bouncing back and forth between the light and dark scenes. I could hear sounds of voices, giggling, then screams and cries that echoed all around me.

It didn't make any sense. Confused, I glanced at him and asked, "I'm confused. Is this supposed to be my life?"

He nodded. "Yes, my dear."

"But they keep changing!" I growled, flustered. "And why are some of them so dark?"

He moved to stand beside me as if to offer support. "Your path will always be transforming itself, depending on the decision you make. An event can alter your direction. Your sense of courage can waver from time to time."

It felt like my world was suddenly tipped upside down, and I was falling rapidly. I was stricken with a sudden sense of gloom. "That can't be me, can it? I mean, how can I stray so far off the path?"

He reached out and touched my shoulder as he spoke in a soft and gentle voice. "It's up to you to remain resolute and find a way to rise up out of the ashes of darkness."

I could feel a sense of warmth spreading from his hand, a tingling sensation that surged along my arm. Sparkling white light flowed throughout my body as I continued to observe the flickering images in the well. The shimmering facets started to float and swirl up, twinkling. The room seemed to glow and glisten all around me. Then I was infused with an incredible sense of hope. I lifted up my arms, laughing as the glittering sparkles danced in the air.

I suddenly woke up in my bed at home, the glittering light a faint echo in my mind. Beside me, my brown tabby raised his head at me and blinked his eyes. I reached out and stroked his soft fur, feeling his rumbling purr beneath my fingers. I stared at him, momentarily dumbstruck, as I realized that there was something deeply familiar about him. For a moment there, I could've sworn that I saw a golden sheen glimmer within the fur.

I tilted my head to side and stared at him, wondering, then shook my head. "No, it's not possible. Or is it?"

About the Author

Growing up surrounded by a seemingly never ending supply of books provided an ample playground for Jennifer Gibson's imagination. A voracious reader at a young age, she delved into the rich worlds created by talented writers like Madeleine L'Engle, *A Wrinkle in Time,* which planted the seed of her passion for unique adventures. Encouraged by her creative writing teachers, her love for books blossomed into a full grown talent when she became inspired to create an original series based on her life as hard of hearing teenager.

CPSIA information can be obtained at www.ICGtesting.com
Printed in the USA
LVOW04s1238240315

431803LV00001B/79/P

9 781937 329907